Chrystle Fiedler seamlessly blends spine-tingling suspense and a passion for alternative health in her acclaimed Natural Remedies mysteries!

SCENT TO KILL

"A well-crafted mystery. . . . Devotees of natural medicine and aromatherapy will enjoy the tips that appear at the beginning of each chapter." —*Publishers Weekly*

DEATH DROPS
A DearReader.com Mystery Book Club pick

"An engaging investigative thriller . . . an enjoyable whodunit." —*The Mystery Gazette*

"Fiedler has a knack for detailing aspects of acupuncture, massage, yoga, and homeopathy . . . fertile ground for further adventures of an unconventional but eminently likeable doctor." —*Mystery Scene*

"As engaging as it is educational about natural remedies and full-body health." —*Herb Companion*

"Entertaining, informative. . . . *Death Drops* is a gem!" —Gayle Trent, author of *Killer Sweet Tooth*

"Absorbing and entertaining." —Linda Bloodworth-Thomason, writer/producer of *Designing Women*

Also by Chrystle Fiedler

Garden of Death
Scent to Kill
Death Drops

Dandelion Dead

• A Natural Remedies Mystery •

CHRYSTLE FIEDLER

Pocket Books

New York   London   Toronto   Sydney   New Delhi

DISCLAIMER

This publication contains the opinions and ideas of its author. It is intended to provide helpful and informative material on the subjects addressed in the publication. It is sold with the understanding that the author and publisher are not engaged in rendering medical, health, or any other kind of personal professional services in the book. The reader should consult his or her medical, health, or other competent professional before adopting any of the suggestions in this book or drawing inferences from it.

The author and publisher specifically disclaim all responsibility for any liability, loss, or risk, personal or otherwise, which is incurred as a consequence, directly or indirectly, of the use and application of any of the contents of this book.

Pocket Books
A Division of Simon & Schuster, Inc.
1230 Avenue of the Americas
New York, NY 10020

This book is a work of fiction. Any references to historical events, real people, or real places are used fictitiously. Other names, characters, places, and events are products of the author's imagination, and any resemblance to actual events or places or persons, living or dead, is entirely coincidental.

First Pocket Books paperback edition October 2016

POCKET and colophon are registered trademarks of Simon & Schuster, Inc.

For information about special discounts for bulk purchases, please contact Simon & Schuster Special Sales at 1-866-506-1949 or business@simonandschuster.com.

The Simon & Schuster Speakers Bureau can bring authors to your live event. For more information or to book an event, contact the Simon & Schuster Speakers Bureau at 1-866-248-3049 or visit our website at www.simonspeakers.com.

Manufactured in the United States of America

10 9 8 7 6 5 4 3 2 1

ISBN 978-1-4767-4893-1
ISBN 978-1-4767-4894-8 (ebook)

To Holmes, this girl's best friend.
Always loved. Forever missed.

What is a weed?
A plant whose virtues have not yet been discovered.

—Ralph Waldo Emerson

Dandelion Dead

the humble dandelion

The next time you see a dandelion in your yard, put away the weed killer and stop and take a closer look. Inside the leaves of this unassuming herb is a power-house of nutrients, including iron, beta-carotene, and potassium, that can contribute to better health and wellness, and it's free! Best of all, nearly every part of the dandelion plant is edible.

You'll often find me in the kitchen at Nature's Way Market & Café, my health food store on the East End of Long Island, experimenting with recipes that include this unsung hero of culinary excellence. My favorite thing to do is to sauté well-scrubbed dandelion roots in a little toasted sesame oil and tamari. Yum!

Herbalists have long prescribed dandelion-root tea as a natural remedy to relieve acne and eczema as well as to enhance liver function. You'll learn more about the dandy dandelion and other edible plants in the pages of this book and the resources section in the back. I've even included recipes for you to try! Enjoy!

Yours naturally,
Willow McQuade, ND

chapter one

I absolutely love edible plants, many of which are also my favorite natural remedies. But I don't mean fruits and vegetables. I mean weeds that are usually perceived as a nuisance and something to be "rid of," but are, in fact, packed with nutrients and have amazing healing powers. Take the much-maligned dandelion, for example. Believe it or not, it's actually chock-full of good-for-you vitamins and minerals, including magnesium, vitamins C and E, iron, potassium, and calcium, and can be used to make everything from smoothies to salads.

I'd been fascinated by edible plants ever since my late aunt Claire Hagen handed me her dog-eared copy of naturalist Euell Gibbons's book *Stalking the Wild Asparagus* when I was fifteen years old. An instant hit when it was first published in 1962, it provided a blueprint that anyone could follow to find, gather, and prepare wild foods.

After giving me the book, Claire encouraged me to go along with her as she foraged for wild edibles in the fields and woods of the North Fork, on the East End of Long

Island, New York. I was born out here, in Greenport, and Claire moved here after living in London for many years, where she worked as an editor for British *Vogue*. My passion for edible plants and natural remedies came from her, and seventeen years later, I was just as fascinated.

For this reason I was out in the fields teaching a class in edible plants one early Sunday morning in October, a week before Halloween. Fall was one of my favorite seasons and a prime time to be out in nature, identifying and foraging to my heart's content. Fall was also the North Fork's best-kept secret. Not only were the summer tourists gone and the beaches and the woods empty, the weather was cool, with just a little nip of cold, signaling that winter was on its way, but not here just yet.

My latest project, a medicinal herb garden dedicated to Claire, opened last year and had turned out to be a smashing success. This despite my finding a dead body near the digitalis plants, on the opening day of the annual Maritime Festival. Fortunately, with the help of my boyfriend and ex-cop, Jackson Spade, and my ex-boyfriend, television writer-producer Simon Lewis, we brought the killer to justice. The garden became a popular place to visit, and I kept busy leading tours several times a day along with running the health food store I'd inherited from Claire, Nature's Way Market & Café on Front Street.

Now, with the cooler weather, the garden had turned dormant, rejuvenating and regenerating itself for spring. So, in the off-season, I'd turned my attention to my workshops in Nature's Way on how to benefit from edible plants, and other natural remedies, for health and wellness.

This morning we were foraging in the fields behind Jackson's house and animal sanctuary, far from the road, and away from exhaust fumes and nasty chemicals that could contaminate any plants we picked. Each class participant had a copy of one of Claire's most popular books, *The Edible Planet*, which featured twenty-five commonly used plants complete with color photographs.

The first rule of foraging was to be absolutely certain in plant identification, and the photos helped ensure this. While most plants were safe and helpful, poisonous plants also existed, and we wanted to avoid these. I led the group, which was made up of ten women of various ages, some local, some from New York, and a few from a day trip from Connecticut across the Sound. Lily Bryan, twenty-five, my new assistant at Nature's Way, was also here.

Lily had graduated from the New York Culinary Institute in June and hoped to open her own restaurant on the East End one day. Lily was intelligent, motivated, and a hard worker—much like her uncle, Wallace Bryan, my manager—and an enthusiastic student. I was glad to have her along today.

We continued to head east across the fields as the early-morning sunshine slanted through the trees at the north edge of Jackson's property, and birds wheeled and chattered overhead. A few feet later, I spotted a cluster of yarrow, a plant with firm, compact lacy white flower clusters on top of long, elegant green leafy stems.

"This is a good start," I said as I got on my knees and examined it, and the group gathered around me. "Yarrow is one of my favorite herbs, especially in the fall. You can make a lovely cup of tea with its leaves if you have a cold, and it's also relaxing and a mild pain reliever. This was also one of my aunt's favorite edibles, and there's a section on it in the back of your book that will tell you more about it." I paused as everyone found the section.

"There's plenty of it here, but we never take more than we need," I said. "But since we'll be using the leaves, flowers, and stem, I'll take this plant whole." I used my spade to gently dig it up and handed it to Lily, who put it in the big blue bucket that she always carried when foraging. "Now, at our next class, on Monday morning, I'll show you how to use these to make tea and a yarrow, calendula, and oatmeal facial. So we need to find calendula next. Let's turn to that page in your book and start looking for it."

The group eagerly began to search for calendula plants, which sported bright yellow and orange flowers. "Some people say that calendula glows like the sun," I continued. "It's a member of the daisy family, also known as English marigold. It's one of my favorite edibles. We can use it in the facial, but it also adds taste and color to salads and other dishes."

As we continued to head in an easterly direction, we moved beyond Jackson's property to the parcel next door, and the Pure vineyard. I had permission to forage here as well, since the property belonged to Simon. Simon had purchased the winery a year ago, as an investment, with David Farmer, a talented winemaker who came from one of the first families of winemaking on the East End. Together they had turned the vineyard into an organic, sustainable winery using biodynamic methods and native yeast, powered only by wind and sun.

Today was important for Pure and all the vineyards on the East End—the first day of North Fork UnCorked!, a weeklong affair that featured wine tours, tastings, and events from Riverhead to Orient, sponsored by the Long Island Wine Council and *Wine Lovers* magazine.

Pure and other wineries were competing for the title of best North Fork vintage, and a cash prize of $200,000. The judging of individual wines produced by the vineyards would take place throughout the week, and the winner would be announced a week from today, at a gala ball at historic Southwold Hall.

Simon's winery was the clear front-runner in the competition. Not only was his vineyard the first on the East End to grow and make organic wine, but his vineyard had already nabbed several top awards this year and had received a ton of positive press. Of course, the rival vineyards were jealous. But facts are facts, and David Farmer was now widely regarded as one of the up-and-coming winemakers out here and in the United States.

This afternoon, Simon was hosting a cocktail party and tasting for the editor of *Wine Lovers* magazine at Pure and had asked Nature's Way to cater it for him. So, along with teaching my class this morning, both Lily and I were on the lookout for tasty edible plants to add to the menu.

An hour later we'd discovered not only calendula but chamomile and mint, and Lily had added a few handfuls of dandelion greens for garnish. While she led the class back to Greenport and Nature's Way, I headed over to see Simon in his office at Pure to discuss last-minute preparations for the party.

As I walked past Pure's sunflowers and corn maze on the way to the winery, I realized that today I felt good about everything. Not only was my business doing well, along with the medicinal garden and my classes, but my relationship with Jackson was stronger than ever since we'd met four years ago. Although we'd talked about marriage—I was thirty-two and Jackson was thirty-four—for right now we were happy with the way things were. We also lived on the North Fork, one of the most beautiful places in the world. So, yes, I *was* lucky. We both were.

But I was startled out of the musings about my good fortune by a shouting match from just inside the corn maze. It sounded like David and his wife, Ivy.

"You never listen to me!"

"That's a laugh, you're a control freak. Ivy, you micromanage everything and everyone here."

"That's what we're here for."

This was true because Simon had been busy producing his new show, *Visions*, in L.A. and was in pre-production on his new movie about Captain Kidd, based on his screenplay. He'd left the day-to-day running of the winery to David. Ivy Lord was the tasting-room manager, while her twin sister, Amy, ran the bed-and-breakfast at the vineyard.

"But you take it too far. This morning you tried to tell me how to craft our latest vintage! That's my job!"

"David, please, you wouldn't even be here if it wasn't for me. It's my money that enabled you to invest with Simon. You've never even supported yourself, not once since you've been married to me."

This, too, was true. David had been able to buy the winery thanks to Ivy Lord, and a quirk of fate. When the twins were just five years old, their parents died in an auto accident on the Long Island Expressway. Because of this tragedy, their grandfather Walter Lord, a wealthy hedge-fund manager, and his wife, Emily, agreed to bring up the girls and act as their guardians. When Walter died at the ripe old age of ninety-five in 2012, Ivy inherited a vast fortune because she was the oldest twin by twenty-two minutes. She was also put in charge of Amy's trust fund. From what I'd heard, Amy, like David, wasn't happy about Ivy's being in charge. Although, Ivy had given Amy a quarter stake in Pure as a consolation prize.

"You know, when you say things like that, I feel like you're killing a piece of my soul."

"Oh, David, don't be so dramatic."

"No, really, you make me feel like nothing. Like I'm nothing at all. Do you know what it feels like to be a man and know that your wife is supporting you?"

"Get over it. You knew what you were signing up for."

"I can't listen to this anymore. I've got to go."

Quickly I moved on, but as I walked past the east entrance to the maze, David stormed out and ran right into me. I stumbled backward, but he grabbed my arm and kept me from falling. "I'm so sorry, Willow, are you okay?"

"Fine, David, thanks."

David, in his early thirties, could have been a TV or a movie star. His best features were his chocolate-brown eyes, a thick thatch of dark brown hair, that unshaven look, and a dazzling white smile. A smile that obviously hid some unhappiness.

"What are you doing out here?"

I pointed to the winery, which was about twenty yards away. It looked like a classic French château, with weathered slate-blue paint, tall pitched roofs, and mustard shutters, covered in ivy and in every way completely charming.

"I just finished giving a class on wild edible plants and now I'm off to see Simon to make sure everything is on track for this afternoon's party."

"I'm glad to see that you are doing your job," Ivy said as she walked out of the maze and over to us. While David sported a casual look with jeans, a faded Coldplay T-shirt, and a brown corduroy jacket, Ivy wore a beige Chanel suit with four-inch heels, her auburn hair tucked behind her ears.

I nodded and smiled, ignoring her sharp tone. "Of course. I always check on the venue before any event, and I'll return with my crew shortly."

"Just so you know, we're nearly ready on our end." Ivy tapped her expensive-looking black-and-gold Apple watch.

I glanced over her shoulder and read a text message that had popped up: You bitch! You'll pay for this!

But Ivy didn't react. Instead, she turned to us. "In fact, the tables were just delivered and my staff is setting them up now."

"And the tasting for Nora Evans, the editor at *Wine Lovers* magazine?" David said, sounding anxious. "That's the most important part."

"I know that, David. And we're ready, of course we are. But I do need to check with Amy to make sure the accommodations for the guests are in order." Without saying good-bye, Ivy left us and headed inside.

David seemed embarrassed. "You'll have to forgive her, Willow. We've got a lot riding on this."

"Don't give it a second thought." I suddenly felt sorry for David. Ivy was a lot of work; that was for sure.

Inside, I found Simon in his well-appointed loft office with an expensive sofa, bookcase, and desk that overlooked the bar and lounge area. Its enormous picture window had a view of the vineyard, the sunflowers, and the corn maze, and beyond that the trees, with peekaboo views of a pond and, farther north, the Long Island Sound.

Simon, thirty-five, wasn't conventionally goodlooking. He was slender and bookish, but something about him, his charm, made him absolute catnip to women. Dressed in khakis and a black dress shirt with the sleeves rolled up, and white Jack Purcell sneakers, he sat on the edge of the desk, talking into his headset while his adorable dachshund, Zeke, chewed a bone at his feet. Zeke spotted me, left the bone, and scampered over to say hi, tail wagging.

"Cassie, I told you that you should have taken him with you," Simon said into the phone, and rolled his eyes dramatically. "I just don't have time to give him the attention he needs. I'm very busy right now."

Cassie, his now ex-girlfriend, was a documentary

filmmaker on location in London. Simon blew out a sigh, took his wire-rim glasses off, rubbed his eyes, and put his glasses back on. "But you said that you wanted him there once you got settled, remember? He was going to stay in your trailer while you were working, and your assistant would walk him and play with him. Now you say you both don't have time for him?"

I scratched the dog under the chin and put two and two together. Now that their relationship had ended, neither of them wanted the dog they'd acquired as a puppy six months ago.

This made me angry, first of all because Cassie had bought the dog at an NYC pet store that was known for selling animals from abusive puppy mills, and second because of their sudden change of heart once they broke up.

I'd seen this happen all too often at Jackson's animal refuge. People were super-excited about getting a pet, but when they realized that it would require time, energy, attention, and effort, they wanted out.

"Fine, I'll deal with it," Simon said, hanging up and giving me a beseeching look.

I knew what that meant. "Let me guess, you want me to take the dog." I picked up Zeke and gave him a kiss on the nose. Zeke was what is known as a red dachshund, with big brown eyes and a sweet disposition. He licked my face in return.

Simon nodded. "Would you? Cassie is too busy and so am I."

"I told you to think it through before you got him, but you didn't listen. Having a dog, a puppy especially, is a lot of work. It's worth it, but you have to put the time and effort in to care for him, walk him, and play with him. You said you would, Simon."

Simon shrugged. "I know I did. I meant to, but . . ."

What I wanted to say was *But you're selfish and only think of yourself.* Still, we were friends now, not boyfriend and girlfriend, and I needed to act like a friend. So I tempered my reaction. "I know that you've got a lot on your plate, especially right now. It's okay, we'll take him."

He arched an eyebrow. "Jackson won't mind?"

I shook my head. "We've already talked about it. We both knew it was coming."

"You are good friends. Better than I deserve."

Instead of focusing on Simon's flaws, I thought about all the times over the past few years that he'd been there for Jackson and me, with the murder investigations and incarcerations, and his help with lawyers and support. "It's fine, Simon, really. I'm going over to Jackson's now, so I can take him with me."

Simon blew out a breath. "Good, thanks, Willow. That's a relief."

I put Zeke down on the area rug and pushed his bone toward him. He grabbed it and began to happily chew, his tail wagging. "So are we all set for this afternoon?"

Simon nodded. "Ivy has the tasting-room setup handled, and the dining room, while Amy's managing the B and B." The bed-and-breakfast, behind the tasting room, was a quaint clapboard house painted seafoam green with bright white shutters, containing four bedroom suites.

The B and B had been up and running when Simon

and David had taken over the vineyard and was a good moneymaker, especially after a complete interior and exterior renovation. Wine lovers enjoyed staying on-site, with the wine, the walks, and being in nature.

I told Simon about running into David and Ivy outside. "She's a real piece of work, isn't she? David seems miserable."

"They're always like that. The whole family has been fighting for years. He argues with her and his family, and Ivy fights with him and Amy." Simon pushed off the desk and came over to me. "Don't worry, Willow, no one is going to kill anyone."

"What are you talking about?"

He put his arm around me. Simon had always been demonstrative, and fortunately Jackson didn't mind. "C'mon, friend, it's been over a year since your last case. You haven't been able to play detective since that murder in your medicinal herb garden. Are you sure that you don't want something to investigate?"

I shook my head. "You are *nuts*. I was just reporting what happened."

He smirked at me. "Whatever you say."

"If that's all, I'm going to go home and get ready."

"Don't forget your new little buddy." Simon picked up Zeke and his bone, patted his little head, and handed him to me. "I put all his stuff in that bag by the door—his dog bed, his blanket, his special puppy food and treats, bones and toys, you know, the works."

The duffel bag was big and heavy, but I managed to hold Zeke and his bone and put it over my shoulder.

Simon waved to us as we went out the door. "Have fun, you two."

• • •

I decided to stop by to see Jackson and introduce him to Zeke before I headed back to Nature's Way. Less than five minutes later we arrived at his two-hundred-year-old house, on a generous two-and-a-half-acre lot, seven minutes east of Greenport.

I found him out back repairing the paddock for the horses, while volunteers buzzed around him, tending to rescued animals in the paddock and in the adjacent barn, including donkeys, goats, pigs, birds, opossums, raccoons, and two turkeys.

Rescue dogs and cats were placed in temporary foster homes with volunteers until they were adopted. Jackson put photos and bios of available animals on a website, and potential pet parents had to fill out an extensive application with information about themselves, their vet, and personal references. If the applicant looked promising, Jackson or one of his volunteers conducted a phone interview and a home visit before any adoption.

Unfortunately, animals had often been injured, abused, or abandoned, and when necessary, Jackson worked with the local vets to treat them and raised money from the community to care for them. Recently, he'd received a New York State grant that would fund his refuge through the end of next year and enable improvements to the paddock and the barn and the addition of more fencing out in the field for the larger animals.

I'd also been able to contribute quite a bit, and regularly, thanks to my profits from Aunt Claire's Fresh

Face herbal antiaging cream. The money took the pressure off Jackson, but fund-raising was a fact of life. Tomorrow night, we were hosting a dinner at Nature's Way where dishes would be paired with Simon's wines to benefit the sanctuary.

Healthwise, Jackson was feeling good. The back injury he'd sustained on the job from a slip on black ice, which resulted in his retirement, was no longer an issue, and he credited me with his recovery. Really, it was a combination of my natural cures and therapies such as massage and acupuncture from my in-store practitioners and good friends, Allie and Hector.

One problem for Jackson, though, was Simon's new vineyard next door and the resulting noise from tour buses, limos, and visitors. Jackson also didn't like Simon's frequent pop-ins. While Jackson tolerated and even liked Simon, he could only take him in small doses. Simon could be charming and helpful but also selfish and self-centered. Often, he was oblivious of the effect his actions had on others, such as chatting up Jackson when he had work to do.

I waved to Jackson and pointed to Zeke. He shrugged, knowing what had happened. "Bring him over to meet the boys." Qigong, and two dachshunds we'd rescued together named Columbo and Rockford, spotted me and scurried over to the bottom edge of the paddock that Jackson had reinforced with chicken wire so that they'd stay inside and safe. I met them there and patted their heads, while their little tails went back and forth like metronomes.

Jackson stepped out of the paddock and came over to us. He had on his usual working clothes—flannel shirt, jeans, and boots—and looked hunky and hand-some with his short-cropped hair, scruffy beard, and piercing blue eyes.

"Hi, honey; hi, Zeke." He gave me a kiss and scratched Zeke behind the ears, which he loved. "So, Simon couldn't handle having a dog. Did you say, 'I told you so'?"

I shook my head. "No, I was nice. He felt kind of bad about it, I think. Both he and Cassie are super-busy right now."

"Unfortunately, I hear that all the time. Best to put Zeke inside the paddock and introduce him to the boys. Neutral ground and all that."

"Good idea." I followed Jackson through the gate. Curious, of course, our dogs scampered over. I put Zeke down on the ground and he immediately rolled onto his back submissively so they could examine him from nose to tail. "Qigong, Rockford, Columbo. Say hi to Zeke, guys."

Dogs are pack animals, so I had no doubt that once they got used to each other Zeke would be happier here with all of us, rather than on his own, alone. His tail was already wagging back and forth.

Zeke stood up and the dogs sniffed him all over again. Finally, they decided he was A-OK, and all four of them began to explore the paddock together. After overhearing the fight between Ivy and David, I couldn't help but think that it would be nice if people could be as accepting as dogs are.

chapter two

Two hours later, at eleven thirty, I headed back to Pure in my mint-green Prius, while Merrily, my chef at Nature's Way, and Lily Bryan followed in the yellow-and-lime-green Nature's Way van with giant sunflowers on each side. We'd packed the van with all the ingredients Merrily would need to make dishes on the spot, along with some that were already prepared. Jackson would arrive later when the cocktail party started at one o'clock.

Pure was the perfect venue for a party. The main area below Simon's office felt expansive and was impressive, with floor-to-ceiling windows on the side that faced the back lawn, a high beamed ceiling, a black bar with silver trim, polished hardwood floors, elegant black tables with white tablecloths, and a large black Steinway piano in the corner, where the pianist was warming up.

We lugged the boxes into the kitchen, which was behind the bar, while I texted Simon to let him know that I was here. He replied with a "thumbs-up" emoticon.

We went back and forth to the van several more

times until we finally had all the boxes and supplies in the kitchen, which was a chef's dream—new, modern, with all the gadgets and shiny appliances you could ever need. Simon had spared no expense since he had planned from the outset to host events at Pure to raise its profile in the wine community.

Merrily and Lily quickly went to work and spent the next hour and a half preparing several choices of *amuse-bouche*—bite-size hors d'oeuvres—and the appetizers that would follow. Meanwhile, I focused on the dining room. The tables had been set, but I wanted to add little pumpkins to each table, and pots of locally grown yellow, orange, and pink mums to add fall flavor.

I'd just about finished when Jackson arrived with the first wave of guests, who oohed and aahed at the room and the view. They headed for the bar, or the servers Ivy had hired who were circulating with glasses of Pure wine while classical music was played on the piano. Other servers offered tasty *amuse-bouche*, including broiled oysters with lime butter, shrimp seviche with mint and mango, and cream-cheese pancakes with smoked salmon.

Jackson looked handsome in a crisp aqua-blue dress shirt, black cords, and boots. It had only been a few hours, but I felt so happy to see him again, the same way I'd felt when we first started dating. That's something.

"You look nice." He gave me a quick kiss. I'd changed into a black cotton turtleneck and a long gray skirt, with a brown vegan belt and vegan boots. I resembled my late aunt Claire, and like her I was tall and slender with long blond hair, high cheekbones, and good teeth. The teeth of the tiger, my aunt would always say.

"You do, too," I said, handing him a seltzer with lime. Jackson had been a member of AA for over ten years now. He'd realized he had a drinking problem after his back injury on the job and had luckily sought help and recovered. "How are the dogs doing?"

"Like they've been together forever. How are things here?"

Before I could answer, Nora Evans, the editor of *Wine Lovers* magazine, pushed past us, wearing a long magenta cape over a burgundy-colored dress, and thigh-high boots, along with Ramsey Black, the head of the East End Wine Council. The three other judges, including one from the New York Wine Council, followed them to the bar.

I quickly texted Simon to tell him that the judges had arrived, and he emerged from his office and hurried downstairs. Moments later, David Farmer and Gerald Parker, the assistant winemaker, exited the tasting room.

But Gerald was scowling. In his late thirties, Gerald had a mop of blond hair and an athletic build and was dressed casually in jeans, a Henley shirt, and flip-flops. He came from Oregon and had moved here to take a job at Vista View Vineyards, now renamed Pure. He said something to David, who reacted by storming off to the bar.

Simon went over to calm David down, then walked over to Nora Evans and the other judges and introduced himself. They chatted for a few minutes, and then Simon led them back to meet David. Crisis averted.

But only temporarily, because Ivy and her identical twin sister entered the main area from the tasting room. Both women were striking, with cupid-shaped faces, pert features, and big blue eyes. Ivy had changed into a sleeveless satin trompe l'oeil designer dress with a cropped pink popover top and a gray skirt with a flared hem, her hair twisted up into a French braid.

I'd learned about high-end clothes when I'd lived with Simon in L.A. He liked to buy them for me, and I didn't mind wearing them then. Now, I dressed more like Amy, who wore a simple but pretty halter dress with a beige, red, navy, and turquoise Southwest print, smocked bodice, and skater skirt, under a comfy-looking denim coat. Her makeup was minimal, except for bright red lipstick, and her hair was up in a loose ponytail.

The two women were arguing. "I wear what I like," Amy said. "I'm sick of you trying to control me, and my money."

"If it wasn't for me, you wouldn't have any money left. Now smile, Nora Evans is here."

"There you go, trying to control me again. Stop it!"

Simon left David and the judges and scurried across the floor to break up the fight by separating the two. He took Ivy over to meet Nora, and Amy went to the far end of the bar.

"Simon's going to wear himself out breaking up fights," Jackson said.

"If he doesn't keep the peace, the event will be a big

bust. They need Nora Evans to enjoy herself, and to love Falling Leaves, Pure's entry in the competition."

Several other vineyard owners moved in for introductions, including Camille and Carter Crocker of Crocker Cellars, Derek Mortimer of St. Ives Estate Vineyards, Harrison Jones of Wave Crest, and Carla Olsen of Sisterhood Wines. Maybe they were here to charm Nora Evans, spy on the competition, or also get some face time with Ramsey Black, who had moved in to chat with Ivy.

Slender, tall, and lanky, and an aficionado of handmade Savile Row suits, Ramsey Black had been an easy choice to be head of the East End Wine Council because he came from a region in southern France that produced wine similar to ours. With his vast knowledge of wine and winemaking, even though he was only in his early thirties, and his flare for promotion—it had been his idea to team up with *Wine Lovers* magazine for the competition—he was widely liked and respected.

"Wonder what that's about?" Jackson said, and nodded to Ivy and Ramsey, who had taken her hand and was whispering in her ear as she smiled and giggled like a little girl.

"Me, too," I said. "But it may indicate that Ivy's marriage is in trouble. That and the argument she and David had this morning that I happened to overhear."

"Sure you weren't eavesdropping?"

"Me? No way." I gave Jackson a Cheshire-cat grin.

The group by the bar chatted for a few moments more, and then David led them to the tasting room. Simon spotted us and waved us over.

But before we could join him, a short, bald man with glasses hurried up. He and Simon had a brief conversation, and then the man walked off, not looking too happy.

"Who was that?" I said when Simon walked up to us.

Simon made a face. "Leonard Sims, the former owner. He keeps hassling me about selling. He wants the place back, now that he's flush again."

"That's not going to happen, is it?" I said.

"Are you kidding? No way. Listen, David and Ivy are giving Nora, the editor of *Wine Lovers*, and the other judges a guided tour of the barn and our winemaking process, and a tasting of Falling Leaves. Thought you'd want to come."

All the servers were circulating, and people were chatting, enjoying the selection of *amuse-bouche* and glasses of wine. Merrily's appetizers would come out next. I could take a quick break.

"We're good." I took Jackson's hand. "Let's go."

After a tour of the winemaking operation, we turned to the tasting room. As opposed to the main space, this room was all wood—the walls, the floors, and the barrels of wine. Simon had added seven large canvases of local nautical and farming scenes in wooden frames by Richard Fiedler, a favorite local artist, which added to the rustic ambience.

Once we'd gathered at the large circular mahogany bar, David uncorked a bottle of the vintage that would be entered in the contest, a pinot noir named Falling

Leaves. The tension and anticipation in the room were palpable as David poured a glass each for Nora Evans, Ramsey Black, and the three other judges.

They sniffed, they sipped, they savored, then Nora Evans pronounced, "Your best yet, David."

"Agreed, well done, David," Black said, smiling. *"C'est magnifique!"*

The rest of the judges smiled and gave it a thumbs-up.

David burst into a big grin, and Simon slapped him on the back. "That's my boy! Way to go, David!"

But Gerald Parker, the assistant winemaker, sulked. The scowl he'd had on his face earlier had turned into a frown. He threw David a nasty look, but quickly assumed a neutral facial expression once he noticed that I was looking at him. He obviously wasn't happy about being demoted from head winemaker under the previous owner, Leonard Sims, to David's lowly assistant.

The other vineyard owners, including Carla Olsen, Derek Mortimer, and Camille and Carter Crocker, weren't happy about Evans's opinion of the vintage either—although our friend Harrison Jones of Wave Crest seemed pleased for David and Simon—but they all plastered on fake smiles. Next, we were all given a taste of the vintage. I had to agree that it was good. I was no expert, but it seemed crisp and clean and tasted, if this was possible, like fall and was indeed evocative of falling leaves.

Once the tasting was over, Evans and Black needed to go to another event, so David and Simon escorted them and the other judges to the door. When the two returned, both of them felt like celebrating and went over to the bar along with Ivy, Amy, and Gerald to ask that bottles of Falling Leaves be opened so everyone could enjoy it.

As I walked past to check in with Merrily and Lily on the ETA for the appetizers, David and Gerald were arguing again.

"I am sick and tired of you taking credit for my work," Gerald said, downing a glass of wine, and promptly grabbing another from a passing waiter.

"You're drunk, Gerald," Simon said. "Time to go."

Instead, Gerald stepped closer and poked David in the chest. "Not until you admit that Falling Leaves was my creation."

"Not true," David said, pushing him away. "And why don't you try showing some gratitude instead of this poor-me act."

"For what?"

"For the fact that Simon, Ivy, and I kept you on when Sims sold to us, when it would have been really easy to get rid of you."

"But we still can," Ivy said. "So don't push it, Gerald. You're lucky you have a job."

"I had an unbreakable contract, and you know that. So cut the bull."

"Try to calm down, Gerry, please," Amy said.

"Don't start, Amy, or you either," he said, giving Ivy a nasty look. "My contract isn't up until next month, and you can't do a damn thing about me until then."

"That's enough," Simon said. "Time for you to go and sober up. We'll talk about this later."

"Screw you, Simon."

Worried that the fight would escalate even more, I waved Jackson over. While Simon had all the physical conditioning of a bunny rabbit, Jackson, a former cop, kept in shape and was fit and strong, and much more formidable.

"What's going on, Simon?" Jackson said. "Need help?"

Gerald sized him up and decided to back down. But after he did, he turned and said to David, "Screw you! Screw you all!" He downed the rest of his glass of wine and stormed off.

Thankfully, Gerald Parker did not return, and we were able to begin serving appetizers to the guests, a mix of seafood, vegetarian, and vegan appetizers, including freshly caught broiled scallops, stuffed garlic mushrooms, double tomato bruschetta, citrus shrimp cocktail, oven-roasted cauliflower bites, eggplant wontons, and vegan veggie quiche. Between the *amuse-bouche* and the appetizers, Merrily had outdone herself today. At first David and Ivy had wanted a more conventional menu, but I'd convinced them that this mix was truer to the concept of their vision at Pure: natural, organic, and sustainable. The menu was based on my personal preferences—I'd gone vegan last year, after being a vegetarian for most of my adult life—and to try to entice others to adopt a more plant-based lifestyle by exposing them to tasty alternatives. But instead of my being able to enjoy the guests' reactions to the food, Ivy and Amy were arguing again, loudly enough to be heard from across the room.

"I was trying to support you, Ivy," Amy said. "Chill out."

"I don't need it. I can handle Gerald, and everything else."

"Oh, I know, that's why Grandfather left you in charge of all his money and holdings, because you've always been his favorite, so together, so responsible."

"And if you'd ever acted like a grown-up, he would have changed his mind. But we see what happened with that."

"I never had control over my own life, so how could I do anything but go along and be what you and Grandfather wanted? So just shut up!" Amy turned and tried to grab a glass of wine from Lily as she went by. Lily was doing double duty in the kitchen and on the floor. But as Lily stopped abruptly, the tray tipped over and the glasses fell to the floor, shattering into tiny pieces.

"You are an idiot," Ivy snapped. "You know that?"

"No, Ivy," I said. "You do not speak to my servers and friends like that."

"I'm paying you, Willow, so stay out of it."

"I absolutely will not."

"Stop it, Ivy. Be nice," Amy said, turning to Lily. "It was my fault. Please be careful when you clean this up. I don't want you to hurt yourself."

"I'll go get the broom," Lily said, visibly upset.

I hurried ahead of her into the kitchen and grabbed one along with a dustpan, and handed it to her. "If you take care of that, I'll get the drinks. Don't worry. It wasn't your fault. You're doing great. If she says anything else like that to you, find me, and I'll take care of it. I'd like to walk out, but I can't do that to Simon."

"I know, but it's okay, really."

I often counted on Lily, who was not only a talented

chef but a speedy and efficient server. Lily was sweet and lovely—a beautiful young woman inside and out—and I hated the way that Ivy had spoken to her. Obviously, Ivy thought that she was superior to everyone else. Amy, thankfully, seemed more enlightened.

While Lily cleaned up the mess, the rest of the guests enjoyed pairing glasses of Falling Leaves with the appetizers. Things were going smoothly again in our catering job, so I went over to talk to Jackson, who was with David and Simon near the entrance.

We chatted for a bit, and I complained about Ivy, but then David's father, Walter, and David's brother, Kurt, pushed open the door, and it hit the wall with a *thwack!*

Both of them wore overalls with T-shirts underneath and boots crusted with mud. Neither had shaved, and they smelled of dirt, grass, and manure.

"What are you two doing here?" David said, pulling them aside.

Simon leaned over to us. "This is going to be trouble. Like I said, they fight, all the time."

"Jeez," Jackson said, "haven't we all had enough for one day?"

"I had hoped so," I said. "But between Gerald and David and Ivy and Amy, this hasn't exactly been a relaxing event."

"This isn't right, David," Walter said, his loud voice booming across the hall. "You need to help your own family, not this place."

"Listen to Dad," Kurt said, and gave Simon a nasty look.

"We're in position to win this thing," David said, "and after a lot of hard work here, I'm not coming back."

"Our farm is going under," Walter said. "But if we won the two-hundred-thousand-dollar prize, it would turn things around for us—for all of us."

"Forget it." David's voice dripped with disdain. "I'm not backing a losing horse. I'm riding a winner all the way to that prize. Besides, Dad, you should sell the farm, then at least we'll all get something out of it."

"You take that back," Kurt said, his hands balling into fists. "I mean it."

"Shut up, Kurt," David said. "With you around, no wonder Dad is going under."

"You shut up," Kurt said.

"Walter, I think you and your son should go now," Simon said. "Or you're going to ruin our event. This is a big night for David, and Ivy, and me."

"There are lives at stake here, why don't you go to hell!" Kurt said.

"Go," Jackson said. "Now."

Kurt sized him up just as Gerald Parker had and came to the same conclusion. "Okay, we'll go, but we'll be back. This isn't over."

"Don't bother," David said. "If you really want to do some good, stop by a real estate agent on your way back to the farm."

Walter headed for the door, but as Kurt swiveled to go, he brought his fist up and clocked David in the nose.

David yelled, then held his nose as blood dribbled into his mouth. "You little bastard!"

"Kurt, that's enough." Walter grabbed him by the arm and they quickly exited.

I grabbed a napkin from the top of the piano and handed it to David. "Are you okay?"

He nodded and dabbed his nose and face. "Fine."

I examined his nose. "I don't think it's broken. But if it begins to really hurt, you should go to the emergency room and get an X-ray."

Simon blew out a breath. "It's a good thing Nora Evans wasn't here."

"Come with me and I'll get you some ice." I led David toward the kitchen, while Simon and Jackson followed.

"Time to smooth things over," Simon said, and when he reached the front of the hall, he announced to the crowd, "Sorry about that, folks. Emotions are running high since this is an important week for all of us in the East End wine business. Please forgive the disruption." He looked around the room. "Now, if the servers could please make sure everyone has a glass of our latest vintage, I'd like to propose a toast."

When we returned from the kitchen, where I'd given David a dish towel filled with cubed ice, the servers were circulating with bottles of wine. The three of us went over to Simon, and he handed David and me glasses of wine from the bar and gave Jackson club soda in a wineglass.

"Thanks, everyone, for coming today," Simon said. "As most of you probably know by now, Nora Evans, the editor of *Wine Lovers* magazine, and Ramsey Black, head of the East End Wine Council, and the rest of the judges gave our new vintage Falling Leaves a very enthusiastic thumbs-up."

The crowd clapped.

"So, if you'd raise your glasses, I'd like to propose a toast to Nora, Ramsey, and the rest of the judges, and to David for creating such a magnificent vintage. *Salud!"*

Everyone raised a glass, and for a moment the mood felt buoyant and light, like a real celebration, which was what we'd all hoped the party would be. But then a bloodcurdling scream shattered the air.

The scream came from the tasting room. Jackson, David, Simon, and I ran in, and in front of the bar we found Ivy, standing over the body of her sister, Amy, who was lying on the floor, her face pasty and white, her big blue eyes sightless, her bright red lips pursed into an *O*, as if she'd been surprised. Next to her, her wineglass was smashed to pieces and the amber liquid pooled under her hair.

"Is she . . . ?" I said, not believing what I was seeing.

Jackson knelt down and felt Amy's pulse. He shook his head. "I'm sorry, she's dead."

chapter three

Jackson called the police, and twenty minutes later my favorite duo, senior Detective Koren and his junior partner, Detective Coyle, arrived. I had a contentious relationship with the two men, in large part because I had a knack for solving murders before they did. Since Jackson and Simon helped me in my investigations, the detectives didn't like either of them much either. So when they walked into Pure and found all three of us, they were not pleased.

"You three . . . again?" Detective Koren said.

"The Three Stooges, right?" Detective Coyle laughed.

We all ignored him, but Detective Koren said, "Show some respect, Coyle. A woman is dead."

"The body is in there." Jackson pointed to the tasting room. "I'll show you. Your coroner is already here."

Jackson and I followed Simon and the detectives back into the tasting room, where the coroner was hunched over the body. We were joined by David and Ivy, who was pale and trembling, and Simon made introductions.

"I'll have questions for both of you, so stay put. That goes for you three as well." Detective Koren gave us a pointed look. "Now, has anyone been in here since you discovered the body?"

Jackson shook his head. "No, I've been here since it happened, until the coroner arrived."

"Playing cop, huh, Spade?" Detective Coyle said. "Having fun?"

Jackson was no longer a cop, but he still had a cop's instincts and was better at it than Detective Coyle or Detective Koren could ever be. "No, Coyle. A woman is dead. I don't think anyone is having fun right now."

"Shut it, both of you," Detective Koren said, snapping on gloves. "Everyone step back. Okay, Bob, what have we got here?"

Ivy began crying hysterically, so David led her out of the room to the backyard. Through the window I could see him giving her a hug, then offering her a cigarette, and both of them started smoking.

Inside, Bob, the coroner, spoke with the detectives, then jotted down notes, while Detective Koren began examining the body. He checked her hands and opened her mouth, stopped for a moment, and asked Coyle for an evidence bag.

Detective Coyle handed him one. "What've you got?"

The two of them put their heads together, and from my vantage point at the edge of the room, I couldn't make out what he'd found. But whatever it was, Detective Koren thought it was worth bagging. Detective Coyle stepped back, and his partner plucked something out of the body's mouth with his gloved fingers and slipped it inside the evidence bag.

"What did you find?" Simon said.

"None of your business, Lewis," Detective Coyle said.

His partner finished looking at the body and signaled to the coroner, who bagged her hands and then with his assistant lifted her body onto the gurney and pushed it toward the entrance.

"Can you take her body around back instead?" Simon said. "I'm afraid it will really upset our guests."

"I'm not having her body taken out over some rutted field and possibly losing trace evidence," Detective Koren said, pointing in the direction of the hall. "Life is tough, Lewis, or didn't you know that?"

"He doesn't know about that, he's from la-la land." Detective Coyle smirked.

I could see the color rise in Simon's face; he was angry now.

Jackson noticed it, too, and grabbed his arm. "Stay cool. Don't complicate things."

"Fine," Simon said through clenched teeth.

The coroner's assistant pushed the gurney into the hall, where guests huddled together at tables looking upset and scared. Upon seeing the body, several gasped, and a low murmur of whispers followed it as it traveled to the door.

Detective Koren went to the front of the room and broke the silence. "I'll need everyone here to stay put. No one leaves without being interviewed and leaving contact information." He turned and looked at me, Jackson, and Simon. "I'll start with you three."

• • •

While Detective Coyle secured the crime scene and supervised the guests' statements being given to uniformed officers, Detective Koren herded us up to Simon's office for an interview. Simon sat behind his desk, while Jackson and I sat on the sofa.

Detective Koren remained standing and paced around the room as he talked. "Now, tell me, how is it that you three are involved in what looks like a murder again?"

"We're not involved," Simon said. "This was a party to kick off North Fork's UnCorked! week, and to welcome the editor of *Wine Lovers* magazine, and the head of the East End Wine Council, and do a tasting. That's it."

"Exactly," I said. "Then it all went very wrong."

"Well, why don't you tell me exactly how that happened." Koren pulled a slim notebook and a pen out of his inside jacket pocket.

Jackson took Detective Koren through the chain of events, starting with what happened at the party and ending with our discovery of the body. When Jackson finished, the detective said, "So who do you think did this?"

Jackson shrugged. "No idea."

I'd already reviewed the events in my mind and couldn't come up with a solid suspect either. If David had been the victim, instead of Amy, I'd have plenty, starting with Gerald Parker and ending with his wife and brother, Kurt.

Detective Koren closed his notebook. "Okay, we'll

take it from here. I may have more questions for all of you, though, so stay local."

He turned to go, but stopped when he reached the door. "And if you have any ideas about playing detective again, especially you, Ms. McQuade, forget it. You've caused enough trouble already."

"She's solved three cases," Simon said. "That's causing trouble?"

"Maybe she helped us get there, but she's no cop." Detective Koren looked at me, then at us. "I'm warning you to stay out of it. All of you."

Despite what Detective Koren had said, Jackson and I discussed the case into the wee hours of the morning. Jackson didn't want me to get involved, but I had a sneaking feeling that Simon would want our crime-fighting team—the Three Musketeers, as he called us—to reunite and solve the crime. Especially if it had the potential to impact his new business venture.

Monday morning, I slept in, and it was almost eight thirty by the time I got back to Nature's Way, did my yoga routine, took a quick shower, and made it downstairs, as Qigong trailed behind me. He took off for the office, where he'd left a bone under a couch cushion yesterday, while I made my way down toward the kitchen and the smell of organic coffee and freshly baked bread, scones, and muffins.

With the success of Nature's Way and the sales of my aunt's popular Fresh Face cream, along with royalties from all her bestselling natural health books, over the past year and a half I'd been able to update the kitchen and spruce up the store and the café.

I'd hired a local contractor to add a large picture window over the sink—so that I could see the medicinal herb garden—and a new farmhouse sink, spider-burner stove, and industrial-size refrigerator, and I'd hired the local flooring company to put in new counters and an eco-friendly bamboo floor.

Once that was done, Jackson and I painted the kitchen a nice buttery yellow, and the rest of the store and the café a vibrant Tuscan orange, with lime-green, black, and purple accents. It was funky, but it worked. The store felt comfy and cozy, just the place to linger over which natural remedy to try or what natural foods to eat.

What hadn't changed were the aisles packed with natural cures and natural foods, and in the middle of the store, a center checkout area that also featured lip balms, organic chocolate bars, and natural health magazines.

Jackson had installed bookshelves opposite the counter, and now they groaned under volumes of vegan cooking, country home remedies, yoga, and superfoods, and my first book, *Cures from Aunt Claire's Garden: 28 Medicinal Plants to Know, Grow, and Use*, which had been released in May.

The book had sold well both locally and all over the country, and since its publication in the spring, I'd held numerous book readings and workshops in the store and in the garden to promote it. It had been fun to talk about my first book and to autograph it for interested readers. I pulled a few copies off the shelf and placed them on the counter within easy reach for customers, and went into the kitchen.

There, I found my chef, Merrily Scott, in the Nature's Way outfit of khakis, a white T-shirt, and a lime-green apron, whipping up batter for buckwheat pancakes, while the blender whipped up vegan strawberry smoothies.

Merrily had the energy of the Energizer Bunny and was cute and perky, her short blond hair now in a pixie cut that suited her. My customers loved her and her food, and over the past few years, she'd developed a healthy following, especially for her award-winning pies.

"Morning, Merrily. That smells really good."

Merrily turned to me, smiling. "Someone's hungry." She stirred the batter one more time, then moved to the stove and poured the liquid onto the hot griddle. The lemon-colored batter accented by bittersweet chocolate chips pooled onto the surface and quickly began sizzling. "Vegan chocolate chip pancakes, get 'em while they're hot."

"Yummy. Thanks, I'll need the energy. I'm going to finish putting up the decorations today. Halloween is only five days away." So far, I'd decorated inside by putting cornstalks in the corners and cobwebs in the windows; today I'd move out front and finish the job.

"It's better to keep busy, I guess. Lily told me what happened." Lily was busy serving food and taking orders in the café. All the tables were occupied by the usual morning crowd. "It sounds absolutely awful." Merrily turned over the pancakes as they began to bubble. "So are you going to investigate again?"

I'd solved three crimes in almost as many years, and Merrily had been working for me the entire time, so she was familiar with the routine. "I hope not. Maybe the police can figure it out this time."

Merrily chuckled. "I wouldn't count on it. If it wasn't for you, they'd still be chasing their tails over those cases." She pulled organic maple syrup and vegan spread out of the refrigerator. "You are good, Willow, and they know it."

"Still . . ." I went to the fridge, grabbed the soy milk, and poured myself a glass. "It would be nice for once to stay out of it."

"If Simon lets you, you mean." She slid the spatula under each pancake, placing them on a plate. "Are we still doing the dinner tonight? If so, I'll need to get busy." She handed a plate to me. "Enjoy."

"Thanks, Merrily. These look amazing." Using a knife, I put a big fat pat of spread on the stack and added a generous amount of syrup. "And, yes, Simon and I discussed the dinner last night, and he said it's too late to cancel. It's full speed ahead."

The Nature's Way dinner to benefit Jackson's animal rescue sanctuary was one of many in the Village of Greenport Monday night. When visitors purchased a ticket for $100, they received an orange bracelet that would open doors to the best restaurants in Greenport and the surrounding area, and a complimentary North Fork UnCorked! logo wineglass. The ticket doubled as an entry for the grand prize of $25,000.

As Lily entered the kitchen, Merrily said, "Lily, Willow says the dinner is still on. So once breakfast is done, I'm going to get started. Can you handle the café?"

Lily nodded. "I'm good."

But when Lily went back out into the café, Merrily shook her head. "I think she's having a tough time handling what happened yesterday. You might want to talk to her."

"Okay, I'll do that."

But by the time I finished breakfast, Lily was busy with four new tables. So I resolved to check in with her later. For now, I grabbed the big box of Halloween decorations from my office and stepped outside.

Nature's Way Market & Café was located on Front Street, across from Mitchell Park, which featured the village green, a refurbished merry-go-round, a camera obscura, boat slips, and in warm weather theater productions by local groups. The Nature's Way building, a three-story yellow Victorian with red trim, featured outdoor seating on the porch, which was nice if you wanted to catch the sea breeze. A black wrought-iron fence surrounded the property and flower beds, and newly planted David Austin English roses in hues of pink, peach, and salmon accented the walkway. To the east of Nature's Way was the new medicinal herb garden that I'd created in honor of Aunt Claire.

Today, the Village of Greenport was already buzzing with excitement over the North Fork UnCorked! event. Banners were festooned across Front Street, and signs were plastered in every window announcing the festivities. Visitors crowded the streets, checking out the sights and the shops before lunch and dinner, when chefs at restaurants would pair signature dishes with local wines.

I'd put pumpkins and gourds painted white with faces to look like ghosts on the steps and strung black-cat minilights around the door. I had just attached a large cobweb to the porch when my cell phone pinged. It was a text from Simon telling me that the police had remained at Pure until after nine o'clock the night before interviewing guests and in particular Ivy, since she had found Amy's body. He added, I may need your help on this.

I didn't text him back and instead finished the task at hand. I needed time to figure out exactly what I was willing to do to help Simon. It depended on the nature of the case. If it was an accident, I wouldn't get involved, but if it was a murder—and it certainly looked that way—it would be a different story, especially if it meant that Simon would be affected.

After I finished decorating, I stepped down onto the walkway and looked back at the porch. It looked fun and festive, just what I was aiming for. When I went back inside, Merrily met me at the door. "The police just called. They've given the go-ahead for us to pack up our stuff in the kitchen and the rest of our equipment and supplies."

The idea of returning to the scene of the crime wasn't appealing, but we needed our stuff. Besides, I had to admit that the amateur detective in me wanted to check it out. "Okay, I think you're better off staying here and getting ready for the party tonight. Maybe Lily can go with me."

A half hour later, Lily and I arrived back at Pure. I'd

texted Jackson to tell him what was going on and where I'd be. He'd reminded me to let the police handle the investigation, and to try to stay out of it.

Pure looked much as we'd left it, although the tables in the atrium were now gone, and the Steinway piano was covered with a sheet and pushed against the wall. All the tiny pumpkins and gourds that had been on the tables were in a big box on the bar. I texted Simon to let him know that we'd arrived and went into the kitchen to pack up the extra food, supplies, and cooking equipment.

While we did, I decided to talk to Lily and see how she was feeling, as Merrily had suggested. So as I handed her items from the refrigerator, I said, "Are you okay? Merrily was concerned that you were upset about what happened yesterday."

Lily shrugged. "It was just a shock. I've never seen anything like that before, and Amy seemed nice, not like her sister at all, and I felt bad that David and Simon's big day was ruined as well."

"I know. Hopefully, the police will figure out what happened soon."

She handed me several small Tupperware containers that held the few leftovers. "But Merrily said that you investigate these kinds of things. Can't you find out what happened?"

Before I could answer, Detective Koren entered the kitchen and came over to us. "Ms. McQuade. Here to pick up your things?"

"We got a call saying we could." I placed the containers in a box.

"Yes, you can, and I hope that you'll do so and

leave." He gave me a pointed look. "Where are Simon and David?"

"I don't know. I just texted Simon to tell him we were here."

A moment later, Simon pushed open the door and stepped inside. "Hey, Willow, Lily."

"I was looking for you, Lewis," Detective Koren said. "I need to talk to you, David, and Ivy."

"We can talk to you." Simon texted David. "But Ivy is exhausted. The doctor just gave her a sedative."

A few minutes later, David stepped in the rear door of the kitchen. Detective Koren waved him over, and the three men headed out into the dining room.

I pulled the last of our food out of the fridge and handed it to Lily. "I think we have everything from here. Let's do the supplies and equipment next."

I grabbed another large box from under the counter and put it on top, then stashed the Cuisinart and a big box of quinoa inside. "If you finish loading this, I'll check the bar to see if any of our stuff is out there."

Truth be told, I also wanted to try to overhear Detective Koren's conversation with Simon and David. I was here, why not?

As I stepped out into the atrium and slipped behind the bar, I spotted the three men talking in the middle of the room. Thanks to excellent acoustics, I could hear every word.

"So what did the autopsy report say?" Simon asked.

Detective Koren hesitated. "It looks like she was poisoned."

"Poisoned," David said, a look of shock on his face. "With what?"

Lily came out of the kitchen just in time to hear David and came over to me, her eyes wide. I put a finger in front of my lips.

"We're not sure yet. We found the remains of a scallop and some plant. The coroner thinks that it's poisonous. We'll know when we get the tox screen, which should be very soon."

"Oh my God," Lily whispered. "Do you think that it was one of the edible plants that I picked yesterday morning to serve as a garnish on the scallop appetizer? Did I make a mistake and pick a poisonous plant instead?" Her face went white. "That means Amy's death could be my fault!"

"You don't know that. You are always super-careful. We both are."

"I think I'm going to be sick."

I put my arm around her and tried to console her. "Don't jump to conclusions, Lily. We don't know anything for sure yet."

"What are you two talking about?" Detective Koren said. It seemed that the good acoustics worked both ways. "You picked a poisonous plant by mistake?" He walked over to us, followed by Simon and David.

"No, I think that's highly unlikely," I said. "But it doesn't mean that someone didn't switch the garnish for the poisonous plant that killed Amy."

"Killed Amy? It could have killed me!" David said, freaking out.

"What are you talking about?" Simon said.

David went over to a spot near the window. "Amy and I were at this table together talking and drinking wine. I offered her a scallop appetizer because I had more than one, and I knew that she loved scallops from when we were together. At first, she refused, but I pressed her, and she ate it. I was just trying to be nice. Ivy is so tough on her all the time."

"Did you eat yours?" Detective Koren said.

David shook his head. "No, Nora Evans, the head judge, phoned. She wanted to tell me again just how impressed she was with Falling Leaves, our entry in the competition. So I just put the plate down, left it, and took the call. But if I'd eaten it . . . I'd be dead. Someone wanted me dead!"

chapter four

"I can't believe someone would try to kill me. I need a drink. Willow, grab me a beer from the fridge next to the sink, will you?"

I did as David asked and placed a cold beer on the counter. But Detective Koren pushed it back to me, giving me a stern look. "Calm down, Mr. Farmer. We don't know anything yet, not really, and I need you to keep a clear head."

"But it makes sense that I was the target, don't you see?" David looked at Simon. "Right, Simon? The texts, it all makes sense now." Despite Detective Koren, David grabbed the beer, twisted off the top, and took a good, long swig.

Simon shrugged. "I don't know, but you'd better tell him."

David put down the beer and pulled out his phone. "Detective, I've been getting death threats, both in texts and e-mails for the past week now." He handed his phone to the detective. "All the messages say for me to drop out of the North Fork UnCorked! competition or else. We're the front-runner in this, and I think that someone wants me out. Maybe whoever killed Amy is the same person who's been sending the messages, and who tried to kill me."

Detective Koren scrolled through David's texts and e-mail history. "I see what you mean. But why didn't you report this to us immediately?"

"Because at first I didn't think it was real, just a hoax, or a bad joke. I figured I could handle it myself. I've been trying to figure out who it is. I've even got a tech guy trying to trace the activity, but it's coming from several different burner phones."

"It sounds pretty elaborate for a bad joke," Detective Koren said. "I think I should keep this and have our guys go over it, too."

"Go ahead, keep it. I'm sick of the messages, especially now, and I was planning on upgrading to a new iPhone anyway."

Detective Koren put the phone into a plastic baggie, then looked at me. "Where is the leftover food that you served yesterday, Ms. McQuade? We need to check it to see if it contains any more of these poisonous plants, and if so, bag it."

"I'm pretty sure that we ran out of the scallop appetizer early, but we were just packing up in the kitchen, if you want to take a look."

In the kitchen, I pulled out the containers of ingredients for the dishes. There were only a few leftovers, just a couple of stuffed garlic mushrooms, and oven-roasted cauliflower bites, and a few slices of veggie quiche. The rest of the ingredients in the box were such things as gluten-free breading, cooking oil, and unused veggies such as tomatoes and eggplant.

Detective Koren quickly went through the box. "I don't see any scallops here."

I nodded. "It was very popular. It didn't last long."

"Why did I have to offer one of mine to her?" David shook his head.

"There's no way you could have known," Detective Koren said.

"And the garnish you picked? What is your name, please?"

"I'm Lily Bryan. I work for Willow in her store and café." Lily pulled a handful of dandelion greens out of a box.

I took them from her. "These aren't poisonous, Detective Koren. These are just simple dandelion greens, and I saw Lily pick them yesterday morning in our class. We like to use them because they're edible and nutritious and they taste good."

Detective Koren took all the greens and put them in a large baggie. "Would it have been easy for someone to substitute a poisonous plant for these greens, Ms. McQuade?"

"Very. They would just need a good reason."

"Like trying to kill me," David said.

Detective Koren left after telling Lily to stay put because he might have more questions for her and after telling me again to stay out of it. But the minute his car pulled out of the parking lot, Simon said, "We've got to do something about this, Willow."

I turned to Lily, who was clearly upset. "It's going

to be okay. Why don't you load the van? I'll be right out."

She hesitated, so I went over to her and gave her a hug. "You're okay, just take a few deep, cleansing breaths."

She brushed away her tears, took a few breaths, and put on a brave face. "I'll get our stuff."

"Thank you, Lily." I motioned Simon and David to the door. "Let's go outside."

We headed out to the lawn and sat down at a picnic table. I took the side with a view of the front lawn, and the tree line that hid the cliffs and the blue-green Long Island Sound. The sun still felt warm, but the breeze off the water caused a slight chill, so I zipped up my LIFE IS GOOD orange sweatshirt.

"I can't believe that someone tried to kill me," David said as he sat down across from me. "And I thought those messages were bad."

Simon didn't sit down, but instead paced back and forth. "And whoever it is, he's still out there. He may try again."

"Oh, God. No, this can't be happening." David got up, pulled out a pack of cigarettes, lit one up, and started pacing as well. Watching the two of them move back and forth was like watching a Ping-Pong match.

"Willow, you and I and Jackson have got to work on this together, like before. Now that it's a murder, we have to. David's life is in danger and so is Pure. Someone wants to keep us from winning this competition."

"Simon told me you three have a good track record on this kind of thing." David blew out a stream of smoke. "That you're smarter than the police."

"I don't know about that," I said. "But we have had good results. We do work well together."

"Yes, we do," Simon said. "The Three Musketeers."

"Jackson doesn't want me to get involved," I said.

Simon waved that notion away. "So what else is new?"

Lily and I returned to Nature's Way and spent the rest of the day getting ready for the dinner that night. I'd left a message with Jackson but hadn't filled him in yet on the latest developments. I was pretty sure what he'd have to say about it, but I was also pretty sure what I wanted to do—namely, help Simon.

While Lily helped Merrily prepare the evening's dinner in the kitchen, Wallace and I set up the café to accommodate more guests. To that end we'd moved some of the tables and chairs out onto the porch and lawn and added heat lamps to create more usable space. Out beyond Front Street, Mitchell Park was now crowded with people as they crisscrossed their way across the Village of Greenport enjoying North Fork UnCorked!

We'd just moved the last set of table and chairs to the lawn when Wallace said, "I know that you have a lot of things on your mind, Willow, but can we talk?"

I pointed to the chair he'd just put down and sat in the other. "Of course."

"I'm worried about Lily. She's a sensitive girl, and that business yesterday at Pure, and today with the police and the news about that poisonous plant, I just don't know."

"I understand, Wallace." I suddenly realized that, yes, I might need to investigate for Simon, but quite possibly for my employee Lily, too. I knew from experience that once the police zeroed in on someone, it could be extremely difficult to shake them.

"Wallace, it is normal for the police to have questions since she prepared that particular appetizer and had foraged for the garnish, the dandelion greens. But the fact is, anyone could have switched out the greens for a poisonous plant at just about any time. I do think the police will see that and eventually work on other leads."

"Eventually? But how long will that take?"

"I'm not sure."

"I've been here long enough to know that you have a knack for solving murders, Willow." He gave me a pleading look. "Can you help her?"

I told Wallace that of course I would help Lily, but first I needed to discuss it with Jackson. Once most of the setup work was done, I slipped away upstairs to take a shower and change into a black cotton shift dress with quarter sleeves, decorated with small white butterflies, and black heels.

As I got ready, I took the time to mull over the events of the past twenty-four hours. No clear suspect for Amy's murder presented itself. But, really, it was too early for that. I needed to investigate—gather the individual pieces—to solve the puzzle of this murder.

• • •

Jackson arrived around six o'clock, looking good in a yellow T-shirt, jeans, boots, and a black blazer. Between his short-cropped hair, stubble beard, and blue eyes, I wanted to take him back upstairs and fool around, but that wouldn't make us very good hosts for his farm's fund-raiser.

By this time, the café, porch, and lawn were completely ready. We had tables in and out, and even space on the steps—we were casual here—so plenty of room to mingle and talk. In addition to the Halloween decorations, we'd strung pretty white lights all around the checkout stand, on the doorway of the kitchen, and outside on the pink and purple rose of Sharon bushes in the yard.

Meanwhile, Merrily and Lily worked toward the 7:00 p.m. start time to begin serving the vegetarian and vegan entrées, including fall-vegetable curry, Swiss chard with chickpeas and couscous, brown-butter gnocchi with spinach and pine nuts, linguine with capers and green-olive sauce, and gemelli salad with green beans, pistachios, and lemon-thyme vinaigrette.

Since we had a few minutes before the event started, Jackson and I stepped outside onto the porch, so I could fill him in on the latest news. Most significant was that Amy's death would probably be classified as a murder because of a poisonous plant, and that Lily was a person of interest because she had foraged for the dandelion greens that were used on the scallop appetizer.

"Do you think she *could* have done it?"

"No. Besides, someone has been threatening David, sending him texts and e-mails and telling him to drop out of the competition. I just can't see her doing that. What's her motivation?"

"I agree. More likely it's one of the rival vineyards that were at the party, or Gerald Parker, or Kurt Farmer."

"Regarding the vineyards, yes, the cash prize is substantial. It could motivate someone to go to the dark side."

"Yes, Obi-Wan." Jackson smiled. Both of us were big *Star Wars* fans, and looking forward to the next movie. "Does Detective Koren know about the texts and e-mails?"

I nodded. "Yes, David showed them to him, after he started freaking out that someone wanted him dead, since Amy ate one of his scallop-and-greens appetizers. David had someone trying to trace the messages to their source, and now Koren will do the same, so we'll see. What do you think?"

"It seems like a reasonable theory that if David's food had been tampered with, the killer wanted him dead, not Amy. There is a lot at stake." Jackson got quiet for a minute and watched the evening crowds of people heading to different restaurants, up and down the street. Finally he said, "And because it involves Lily and Simon, and his winery, you're going to want to investigate, right?"

"How did you know that?"

Jackson gave me a "get real" face. "C'mon."

"But it would be different this time."

"Really, how?"

"The killer is after David, not one of us. It's a little more removed."

Jackson couldn't help but laugh. "It isn't. Not once you get involved and things start to unravel. You may find out that person you thought least likely to be a killer is the one. Believe me, I've seen it before on the job. It would be much better if you just let this one go. It's too dangerous. It always is."

"That's true."

"Our lives are good. We're happy. I'm making a difference, and so are you. The medicinal plant garden and your new book were a hit, and you're doing good work here, and I'm doing my thing at the farm. Plus, you heard what Detective Koren said."

"I know that, but I really feel I need to do this, and I am pretty good at it. Actually, we're good *together*, the three of us."

Jackson shook his head. "Honey, you are good, but Simon should just hire a private investigator instead. It's easier, it's safer, and I can give him a couple of names."

"Did I hear someone mention my name?" Simon bounded up the stairs, wearing a denim blazer, orange button-down shirt, black jeans, and loafers, without socks, of course, and came over to us.

"Yes, you did," Jackson said. "We were just talking about what happened today at Pure, and the fact that I don't want Willow involved in this investigation."

"Yeah, I get that." Simon took off his sunglasses. "But I could really use her help and yours, Jackson. This is important. David is scared out of his mind, and it could impact our standing in the competition. We've worked so hard to get to this place, and it could all be for nothing."

"What about a private investigator?" Jackson said, not giving up so fast. "I know of a few really great people."

"Are they from out here? Do they understand Greenport and the people and the North Fork winery business and all that?"

"Well, no. They're retired cops that I know from the job, in Nassau County."

"I just don't think someone like that, an outsider, can crack this case. I need you, both of you." Simon gave us a pleading look. "So will you do it?" He got down on his knees. "I'm begging you, please."

I looked at Jackson, and he shrugged—that Simon was up to his usual antics—and said, "Up to you, McQuade."

"Thank you, honey," I said. "Simon, I'll help you, of course I will."

"Whew." Simon got up. "I was a little worried that you weren't going to have my back on this one."

Now I gave Simon a "get real" look. "C'mon, Simon, you knew I'd help you. I'm sure Jackson will, too, when he has time away from the animal sanctuary, right, honey?"

Jackson blew out a breath. "Sure, I've got to protect you from yourself. That goes for both of you."

Simon put an arm around each of us. "Just what I was hoping for! It's the Three Musketeers, together again!"

chapter five

I decided to start the investigation by going back
to basics, in this case finding out if David had any
enemies. After I was sure everyone was taken care of,
I headed over to talk to him. David, wearing a brown
corduroy jacket over a faded yellow tee, jeans, and red
high-top sneakers, was flirting with Carla Olsen, a
petite redhead, and the owner of Sisterhood Wines.

He spotted me and said something to Carla, who
moved on. When he turned back to say hi, he almost
ran into Lily, who was serving glasses of Falling Leaves.

"Sorry, Lily."

"It's fine," she replied frostily. "Wine?"

He pointed to his almost-full glass. "I'm good." He
pecked me on the cheek. "Willow, nice party."

"Thanks. Everything okay?"

"Yeah, fine." David watched Lily walk away. I wondered what was going on between them—did they have
a history that I didn't know about?

"I wanted to tell you that I've decided to help you
and Simon, Jackson, too."

"Wow." David smiled. "Thank you. That's a relief."

"First off, we need to know the basics, like if you have any enemies? Anyone we should talk to or check out?"

"As you saw at the party, I don't exactly get along with Gerald or my father and brother, but besides them and whoever is sending those texts and e-mails, I don't know." David shrugged. "I really try to get along with everyone."

I wondered if this was true, and if he was faithful to his wife, Ivy. "David, I know this is probably a touchy subject, but I have to ask. Is there someone else in your life, I mean, besides Ivy. I noticed that you were chatting with Carla and . . ."

"People always take it that way." David sounded frustrated. "I like women, period, but I don't fool around, Willow. I'm a married man."

"Okay." I put my concerns about other women on the back burner for a moment. "So no one else comes to mind who has a grudge against you or anything?"

He shook his head. "Nope."

"And you and Ivy are okay?" I was thinking about the fight I'd witnessed at the corn maze. "Yesterday morning you two seemed upset."

"We're fine, Willow. Don't worry about me tonight, take care of your other guests."

"I can do both." I noticed that he wasn't eating. "Can I get you a plate of food?"

His eyes opened wide. "No, I grabbed something before I came. I'm feeling a little anxious about eating out after what happened. I mean, I'm sure the food is fine, but I'm just being careful."

"It is fine, really, David. You should eat. Ivy, too."

"Oh, she's eating." He gestured to Ivy, who was chatting with Simon, in between bites of gnocchi. "She's always hungry. Both of them are, I mean *were*, the same way."

I glanced at Ivy. "I guess that comes from being twins. She must miss Amy so much, even more so than a regular sibling."

"They loved each other, for sure. Even though they didn't always get along." David sipped his wine. "They were just very different people—personality-wise, the way they acted, even the way they dressed. Ivy's more uptight, Amy was more easygoing. It rubbed both of them the wrong way at times." He patted his jacket pocket. "I'm going outside for a smoke. I'll see you in a bit." He squeezed my hand, smiled, and headed for the door.

Jackson came over to me. "How's it going, McQuade? Learn anything new?"

"Not really. Besides Gerald, and his father and brother and whoever is sending those messages, he can't think of anyone who would want to hurt him, but I'm not sure if he's being completely honest about his love life or his marriage. I'm going to talk to Ivy next."

"Okay, but go slow. You don't want them to know exactly what you're up to."

"But I'm investigating for them."

"You're helping Simon, a friend. We really don't know David, and Ivy, especially, all that well."

I kept his warning in mind as I made my way across the room to Ivy, who had finished eating and was talking to Gerald. But as I walked over, Gerald stepped away.

"I'm very sorry about your loss," I said. "This must be a really difficult time for you."

"It's a terrible shock. I'm not quite sure what I'm going to do without her."

"I just wanted you to know that Simon asked me to help out with the investigation."

She arched an eyebrow. "I don't understand. I thought you were some kind of holistic doctor and ran this health food store, certainly not a detective."

"Actually, I do both. I got involved in amateur sleuthing when my aunt Claire Hagen was murdered, and I've solved several cases since then, with Jackson's and Simon's help."

"Really?" She gave me a look as if she didn't believe me.

I ignored her tone and plowed on through. "Besides Gerald and his family, does David have any other enemies?"

"I think it's one of the rival vineyards, which is what I'll tell the police when they interview me."

"So you and David are good, I mean, after your fight yesterday morning?"

She stared at me. "Eavesdropping is an ugly habit, Willow. But if you must know, my husband and I are just fine."

By ten o'clock Monday night all the guests had gone home—along with Merrily, who was exhausted. Jackson was upstairs with the dogs, and Lily and I were left alone to finish the cleanup. This wasn't a coincidence.

I'd sent her uncle Wallace home as well, since I wanted to talk to her about David Farmer.

Merrily had cleaned up the kitchen before she left, and Lily and Wallace had cleared and reset all the tables in the café, so the only thing left to do was to move the rest of the furniture on the lawn back inside.

We were setting up the last table on the porch when I said, "So what's going on with you and David Farmer?"

Upon the mention of David's name, Lily, startled, dropped four settings of silverware on the floor. As it clattered, she sucked in a breath. "How did you know?"

"I'm a pretty good observer and I noticed that you two didn't seem very comfortable around each other. In my experience, that usually means something is going on or something's over."

She went pale, and I pushed back a chair and helped her sit down. "It started when we began planning for the party for Pure. Remember, I had to go up there a lot?"

I sure did. There was plenty to do to get ready, from the list of whom to invite—which Ivy supervised and scrutinized and changed constantly—to planning the menu, to hiring extra help, to, even, the playlist for the pianist. Since I'd been busy in the medicinal herb garden, Wallace was managing the store and serving customers, and Merrily was cooking in the Nature's Way kitchen, I'd often send Lily up to Pure.

"David was usually there and we started talking and, over time, we got, well, close, and then . . ."

"You slept together." So much for David's protestations about being faithful to Ivy.

Lily looked embarrassed. "I knew it wasn't a good idea to sleep with a client."

"No, it's not."

"I'm so sorry, but he kept pursuing me. Finally, I gave in."

"What are you saying?" I sat down opposite her and took her hand. "Lily, did he force you to have sex with him?"

She shook her head. "No. Not at all. It was mutual, for sure."

"And the fact that David was married didn't bother you?"

She shrugged. "Before we got together, he told me how unhappy he was with Ivy, that his marriage was a sham and that they didn't even share a bed anymore. Then he told me that I understood him in a way that she never could."

I wondered just how many married men had used that approach on prospective lovers. But I didn't say anything except "Are you still seeing him now?"

"No, he broke it off on Sunday, before the party." Her eyes started to mist up. "We were together for almost three months and then he just tells me it's over. It was pretty devastating. I'm still upset."

Would being dumped make Lily into a murderer? I doubted it, but I had to ask. "Lily, you didn't do anything you regret, did you?"

"Try to poison him, you mean?" She stood up and pushed the chair back. "No, of course not! How can you even ask me that?"

"Because I'm investigating Amy's murder, and it

looks like there was a mix-up between the dandelion greens and some type of poisonous plant."

"I'm angry over what he did, but I could never do that. No, Willow, never."

"You're going to have to tell the police about you and David, you know."

"But they're already suspicious of me after they found that poison hemlock. Willow, I can't! They'll think I had a motive to kill David and put me in jail! I couldn't handle that, not at all."

"But if it comes out later, Lily, it will look worse for you."

"I don't know, Willow." She wiped away tears.

I went into my office and grabbed a box of tissues and brought it back out to her. She grabbed a few and wiped her face.

"I talked to David about his love life and he said that he was faithful to Ivy."

"That's a lie. And I wasn't the only one either."

"Carla Olsen?"

Lily nodded. "Even though he told me he wasn't seeing anyone else after we slept together. I just don't know what to believe anymore."

Me either. Already the circle of possible suspects had widened beyond rival vineyard owners, and I wondered if a jealous lover or even Ivy had tried to kill David and killed Amy instead.

chapter six

Tuesday morning the weather was crisp and clear, a perfect fall day. Jackson left Nature's Way early to take care of the morning feeding of his animals and took all the dogs with him, so I did my yoga routine in the second-floor studio, then showered and dressed in jeans, a lime-green Nature's Way tee and matching hoodie sweatshirt, and vegan sporty sneakers, then headed downstairs for breakfast.

Luckily for me, Merrily had just baked a tray of gluten-free blueberry muffins, so after I fed the two cats, Ginger and Ginkgo, I grabbed a muffin and a cup of organic Fair Trade coffee and went into my office to catch up on some work, including writing blog posts about cures from my new book for my publisher's website.

After that, I went over my agenda for my 10:00 a.m. Edible Plants Workshop, featuring the calendula and yarrow that we had harvested on Sunday. Both herbs were versatile, and I was looking forward to teaching my class how to make calendula and yarrow teas; a calendula, yarrow, and oatmeal facial; and other beauty and health treatments.

I gathered all my materials, including the plant cuttings from Sunday that I'd stashed in the oversize fridge in the back of the kitchen and previously dried flowers, and set up a table in front of the counter. Even though I was teaching a class, customers would still be able to shop for groceries and eat in the café.

At nine forty-five, all but two of the people who had attended the foraging workshop had arrived, and by ten fifteen we were all in the kitchen and I was teaching them how to make freshly brewed calendula tea, one of my favorite natural remedies.

"Calendula is pretty amazing. It has anti-inflammatory *and* antiseptic properties." I poured boiling water over dried calendula blossoms. "Even a simple calendula tea can be used to treat lots of common complaints like a sore throat, or a urinary-tract infection or indigestion, along with minor wounds and burns, skin irritations like insect bites, acne, athlete's foot, itchy scalp, and even flea bites and hot spots on pets. Just keep in mind that the correct ratio is a tablespoon of petals to one cup of water." I finished pouring the water and put the teakettle back on the stove.

"Now, we'll need to let this steep for at least fifteen minutes, but I've also got a batch that is ready to go to the next step." I pulled a saucepan off the stove and grabbed a mesh strainer. "First, we'll need to use this strainer to catch the blossoms and other parts of the plant." I poured the warm brew through the strainer and into a clear glass bowl. "And that's it. You can use it warm or cold, but it does have a short shelf life, so be sure to keep it in the fridge and to use it within two days."

The class clapped.

"Thanks. Now I'll teach you how to use calendula in specific skin-care products, like for diaper rash, for example. All you'll need to do is add coconut oil, beeswax, and zinc oxide powder to make a salve. Let's try that first, and then we can move on to wound-healing salves. First we'll put coconut oil, which is solid at room temperature, over a low heat to liquefy it, then add the calendula and let it infuse." But as I reached for the coconut oil, my phone buzzed.

"Excuse me." I pulled out my phone. It was Simon, probably calling to discuss the strategy for our investigation, but maybe not. "I need to take this, but I'll be right back. Grab a blueberry muffin and coffee if you like."

The class eagerly dug in.

I stepped outside the kitchen. "Simon?"

"Willow?"

"Yes, I'm teaching a class. Everything okay?"

There was a long pause. "No, I'm afraid not. There's been another attempt on David's life."

"Is he all right?"

"He's pretty freaked out."

"I'll bet." David was already anxious about his safety after Sunday; now this. "I just have to finish up my class and I'll be right down."

An hour later, after I left a message for Jackson to meet me at Pure, I headed east. On a normal Tuesday in October at eleven twenty-five in the morning, Pure's parking lot would be sparsely populated, but thanks to North Fork UnCorked!, it was almost full for today's scheduled events. David would be giving a walk and talk among the vines about making organic, bio-dynamic wine, and Ivy was teaching a seminar about tasting and purchasing the right wine, preferably one of theirs.

Jackson, wearing jeans and a faded long-sleeved orange LIFE IS GOOD T-shirt and boots, was waiting for me at the door, watching as Simon escorted the former owner, Leonard Sims, to his car. "What's going on with Simon and Leonard?"

"Sims returned with an even better offer this morning, but David told him that Pure wasn't for sale at any price. He then accused him of trying to kill him to get Pure back. Simon had to intervene."

"Between David's near miss and Sims's visit, it's been quite a morning. Did Simon tell you exactly what happened?"

"No, he wanted to wait for you. But he did tell me that the wake for Amy Lord will be Wednesday afternoon and evening, and the funeral is Thursday morning."

"Okay, I'll go with Simon to provide support, and check things out," I said.

"Probably a good idea. I don't think I can get away."

"He knows that you're busy. We'll report back."

Sims drove away in his black Jaguar, spewing up dirt with his tires as he went, and Simon walked over to us, wearing khakis, a long-sleeved denim shirt, a dark blue bow tie, and faux-suede driving shoes.

"Hey, thanks for coming, you two." He shook

Jackson's hand and gave me a kiss on the cheek. "David is a mess. When he started attacking Sims, I had to take control, although Leonard kept insisting that everyone had their price. I hope that's the last we see of him."

"I hope so, too—you have bigger problems to deal with," I said. "So what happened to David?"

"I'll show you. Follow me."

We went through the tasting area, where we found Ivy giving a seminar to potential customers, who were rapt with attention, including Camille Crocker, which was curious since she owned Crocker Cellars, a rival vineyard. Various vintages in shades of gold and amber were already poured into glasses that lined the counter.

"Okay, now everyone pick up a wineglass, but don't drink it just yet." Ivy smiled. "We need to go over the basics of wine tasting. First, we check out the color, opacity, and viscosity. Next, we use our sense of smell to pick out aromas." Ivy and the participants put their noses into the glasses. "You'll notice fruit, herb, and flower notes."

Ivy seemed better today, although I knew from experience that grieving was messy, which I'd experienced when I lost Aunt Claire. One was prone to peaks of "I'm feeling better" and plenty of valleys—such as not wanting to get out of bed. Ivy nodded to us as we rounded the bar and headed out back to the barn.

Next to the bed-and-breakfast, we found David among the vines, giving his talk on grapes and the growing cycle, along with biodynamic and organic farming methods in living soil. He was one of many vineyard owners who were doing the same type of talk this week.

"How is he?" I said.

"Better," Simon said. "He's in his element now, so it takes his mind off everything." We watched as David smiled and chatted with the customers. Behind him, workers harvested the crop, stuffing succulent grapes into big yellow crates at their feet.

"What are they harvesting today?"

"They're working on grapes for the cabernet sauvignon, and then we're done for the fall."

"Which is that one?" I said. "I can't keep them all straight."

"It's a red wine with a nice black-cherry fruity flavor, along with licorice, black-pepper, and vanilla notes. It's a cross between cabernet franc and sauvignon blanc."

"Red wines can give me a headache, but I guess since this is all organic, with no sulfites, it probably wouldn't."

"Correct, no sulfites, or yeast nutrients or genetically engineered yeast. Organic is the way to go," Simon said. "In fact, new research out of UC Davis shows that organic fruits and berries have up to fifty-eight percent higher natural antioxidants than nonorganic do."

"Organic farming is really just so much better for the planet and people," I said. "I'm proud of you for going in this direction, Simon."

"You inspired me." Simon smiled. "And it's paying off. If we can just figure out Amy's murder, and who's out to get David, it'll be smooth sailing."

"Yes, that." Jackson sounded a little bit impatient.

"To that end, can you please tell us what happened this morning? I need to get back to the farm."

"Your wish is my command." Simon walked over to the fire-engine-red barn door and pulled it open. "The scene of the crime is just inside."

We went inside the barn, and Simon flipped on the overhead lights. It felt stuffy and warm and smelled of oak. Huge wooden barrels and even larger steel tanks were on either side of the barn, while bottled wines were on each end in massive racks on the cement floor.

We followed Simon to the south end of the barn, where police tape partitioned off a yellow forklift, a section of the wall with two ragged, gaping holes, a large wine rack that had been smashed into pieces, and shards of glass and puddles of wine on the floor.

"This is where it happened."

"Walk us through it, Simon," Jackson said. "Give us the details."

"Okay, David was picking out a few bottles for a customer, and he had his back to the rest of the room. But when he heard the forklift coming, he turned around. He said a guy in a white jumpsuit with a hard hat, wearing large sunglasses, was the one driving. David yelled at him to stop, but whoever it was kept coming at him. Luckily, David managed to move out of the way, and the forklift went right into the wine rack, the bottles, and the wall, and missed him by inches. Then, whoever it was jumped off and ran out of here."

"Could he identify who was on the forklift?" Jackson said.

Simon shook his head. "Nope. It happened too fast, I guess."

"Could it have been Leonard Sims?" I said. "After all, he was here."

"No, he arrived afterward. I saw him pull in."

"And you also escorted him out," Jackson said. "When did the police get here?"

"Around nine, a little while after it happened. It was just Detective Coyle; he said that Detective Koren was busy working on something else."

"Glad I missed him," Jackson said. "So what did he say?"

"David went through the series of events and then said he had to start his talk. After he went, I mentioned to Coyle that I thought that the two-hundred-thousand-dollar prize for the competition was a good incentive for a rival vineyard to want to hurt David, and that maybe one of them did this and was behind those nasty texts and e-mails as well. Of course, I didn't mention David's love life."

"So you think that could be a factor, too," I said.

"Definitely."

"Okay, and what did Detective Coyle make of that?" I said.

"Not much. But he did ask if Lily had been around when it happened."

"So they're zeroing in on her to the exclusion of any other theories or suspects," Jackson said. "Sounds about right—neither of them is very good at big-picture thinking."

"I know Lily didn't try to kill David or do this," I said.

"Was she at work this morning?" Jackson said.

"No, she has the day off." I suddenly felt my

stomach drop. Despite my instinct that Lily was no murderer, I felt a frisson of doubt.

"Don't do that." Jackson put his arm around me. "Just because she has the day off doesn't mean that she did this."

"He's right," Simon said. "And I didn't see her anywhere."

"That's something, I guess," I said.

"Did Detective Coyle say anything else?" Jackson said.

"He asked if we'd found Amy's cell phone, but I told him no, and he told me that they had no info yet about the texts and e-mails, and then he left to talk to Ivy as well, since she entered the barn right after the accident."

Something Simon had just said prompted a thought about Ivy, but I couldn't quite grasp it. I let it go, hoping that it would come back if it was important.

Simon continued, "The crime-scene people were here for about an hour after he left. But I don't know what they found."

"So no tox screen yet?" Jackson asked.

"Not that I heard. Coyle wasn't exactly sharing information."

Jackson checked his watch. "I need to get going. I have a vet coming at twelve thirty for two of my new rescue horses, but first, I need to talk to a horse rehab expert from the Farm Sanctuary in Watkins Glen."

"Are they going to be okay?" I always worried about the state of the animals that Jackson rescued. But I also knew that if anyone could bring them back to health, it was Jackson and his team of vets and volunteers.

"I think so, with some tender, loving care. I got them from a horse farm that's being investigated for abuse. It was bad, really heartbreaking. The rest of the horses went up to the Farm Sanctuary."

Animal abuse, especially when done for money and higher profits—think puppy mills to supply pet stores, horses and greyhounds for racing, and farm animals for food—upset me more than any other issue. But I tried to be productive with my anger by going vegan, offering delicious vegetarian and vegan dishes at Nature's Way, and helping Jackson as much as I could.

"Okay, I know that's important, you need to go— but what's our next step in terms of investigating?" Simon said.

"I think we focus on the wine auction tonight in Mitchell Park," I said. "All of the most prominent vintners will be there, and it might yield a few more suspects."

After Jackson left, Simon and I went to his office to discuss the case. On the way upstairs Simon took a call from his contractor to discuss a new covered pavilion for the back lawn that Simon was planning for next season. Once it was done, guests would be able to listen to live music on the weekends while sipping a Pure vintage.

We entered the office, Simon finished the call and went over to his desk, and I walked over to the window in the office that faced the east side of the property. From there, I could see David move up and down the rows of vines as he gave his class, while workers continued to harvest grapes around him.

"He doesn't seem upset at all now."

"I told you." Simon sat down in his desk chair and put his feet up. "He's in the zone." He pointed to his phone. "Oh, by the way, I found a tech guy in the city to go over David's texts and e-mails. So far, he hasn't found the source, just like the cops."

"Did your tech guy say whether there were calls from other women, besides Ivy, on the phone?"

Simon put his phone down on the desk. "No, but I can ask him. What are you thinking?"

"I talked to David last night, and I asked him about other women and he denied it, but you said that wasn't true. Who exactly is he seeing—Carla from Sisterhood Wines?" I decided to leave Lily out of the discussion for now.

"That's been going on for a while, but there have been others. Last summer, he had a new woman every weekend."

"Does Ivy know?"

"Hard to say, but she's supersmart, so it's very probable."

I wondered if Ivy knew about Lily. "Do you think that Ivy could have tried to kill him out of jealousy or maybe one of his disgruntled lovers did it?" *Not Lily*, I thought, *please don't let it be Lily*.

"Carla was at the cocktail party, not to mention . . ." Simon's voice trailed off.

I walked over to the desk and drilled him with a look. "Not to mention who, Simon?"

He blew out a breath. "Your assistant, Lily. They spent

a lot of time together in the time leading up to the party. I hate to say it, Willow, but I got a definite vibe that their relationship didn't end when the workday was over."

I nodded. "Okay."

"You knew?"

I shrugged. "She told me last night and said he ended it on Sunday. But, of course, the police don't know."

"Sure, because if they did, she'd be in jail right now since she prepared the appetizers."

I heard a blip and Simon pointed to his wrist and a watch with a bright blue band. "It's my new Apple watch. It's got a stopwatch and a heart-rate sensor, and a bunch of other stuff. Pretty cool, huh?" He turned it toward me and I read a text from Kate, at Salt: Supplier is out of bay scallops for Wed dinner. Change menu?

Suddenly, I realized what I'd forgotten.

But before I could tell Simon, his watch rang—a weird phrase, but in this case accurate. He punched a button, said, "Simon," and listened for a few moments. "Yes, I got your text, don't panic. We'll figure it out. I was planning on swinging by today anyway. I'll be down in a few." He said good-bye and signed off.

"Kate's super-busy right now," he said. "I'm hosting the reception after the funeral, too, so she's got her hands full."

In addition to buying the vineyard, Simon had last year purchased a seafood restaurant, located at the end of Preston's dock in Greenport, renamed it Salt, renovated the interior and exterior, revamped the menu, and reopened to great reviews.

The place was always packed, and Jackson and I only were able to get a table because we knew the owner. Wednesday night, Simon was hosting a sold-out event at Salt that featured his vintage Falling Leaves and Kate's signature dishes. We would be there, but first I needed to tell him what I remembered.

"Like I said, cool, right?" He pointed to the watch. "I really like this thing."

"Very, but—"

He grabbed the keys to his Mini Cooper. "Walk me out?"

"Wait a minute. When you got that text, I just remembered what I had a glimpse of in the barn before."

"Go. Lay it on me."

"You're not the only one with that kind of watch."

"Right, Ivy has one, too. The black-and-gold one. I looked at that, but I like this sporty model better."

"Simon, focus?"

"Okay, go ahead."

"So the other day when I overheard them in the corn maze, I noticed a message on Ivy's watch, just like the one you just got."

"From who?"

"I don't know, but the text on her watch said, 'You bitch! You'll pay for this!' "

"Really?" Simon's eyebrows arched.

"Really. Obviously, David isn't the only one who is getting nasty messages."

When we reached the main floor, I spotted my late aunt Claire's longtime boyfriend, Nick Holmes, dressed in his usual garb of polo shirt, yoga pants, and purple Crocs, come in the door, followed by his students, who held yoga mats, straps, and blocks. Nick taught popular yoga and meditation classes at Nature's Way and a program here called Yoga on the Vine.

Nick had trained in various places in the UK and USA, including the Kripalu Center for Yoga & Health, and his goal was always to provide a safe and welcoming place for beginners and longtime practitioners. He encouraged students to above all enjoy the practice while they learned how to awaken untapped resources, including calmness, creativity, compassion, and vitality. He felt the benefits, too. Nick had just turned seventy-two, but was still fit and in excellent health and looked at least ten years younger than his calendar age.

"In the meantime, I wonder if Nick has any insights into Amy's murder," I said to Simon, whose cell rang a moment later.

"Good idea. Ask him. I have to take this—it's Kate, again."

While Simon talked to his chef, I followed Nick into a large room with floor-to-ceiling windows to the right of the tasting room and the twins' office. It had a spectacular view of the vines, which spread from this building to the main road.

"Hi, sweetie!" Nick gave me a warm hug. "Are you okay? I heard about Amy. How awful! I thought she was a nice girl."

"I'm fine, but I'm helping Simon figure out who killed her."

"So you're on the case, good! Those cops need your help." He beamed at me like the proud uncle he was.

"They don't seem to think so."

"Ignore them, but be careful. If there's any danger, take that wonderful boyfriend of yours with you. But fill me in, what exactly happened here?"

I told him, then asked, "Do you have any idea who might have wanted to kill David?"

Another gaggle of students came in the front door in yoga attire, holding sticky mats, and came over to Nick. "*Namaste.* Make yourselves comfortable." He gestured to the other women and men spreading out mats and doing warm-up poses. "I'll be right with you."

He took my arm and we stepped outside the room. "I'm afraid I can't be of much help, honey. David is a bit of a charmer, though. He likes women and they seem to like him. As for Amy, she seemed sweet, exactly the opposite of Ivy, who was just awful to her, and all the employees here. She's actually not very nice to me either."

"I don't like to hear that. You're so wonderful, Uncle Nick."

"Thank you, sweetheart, you're incredibly biased, and I love it." He smiled at me. "But I'd better get started. Be careful, okay? Love you."

"Love you, too."

He gave me a bear hug and went inside.

I walked over to Simon, who had just ended his call. "What did Nick have to say?"

"That David is charming and Amy was nice, and he loves me."

"That's all true."

"I know."

Suddenly, we heard screaming from the kitchen.

Moments later a red-faced Gerald Parker, the assistant winemaker, stormed out into the atrium, followed by David, who screamed, "Go ahead and quit, we're not changing the label!" David spotted Simon. "Tell him, Simon. He wants credit on the label for Falling Leaves. I told him he's nuts and we're not doing it! It's just not done! It's a *Pure* vintage, not a Gerald Parker vintage!"

Gerald didn't reply, just headed for the tasting room.

"I'll talk to him," Simon said. "Why don't you have a drink, David, try to calm down, buddy."

Quickly, I checked my watch and said softly, "Simon, it's not even one o'clock."

Under his breath Simon said, "Willow, he doesn't have a problem." Simon walked over to the bar, went around, grabbed a Corona, stuck a lime in the top, and handed it to David. "I'll go talk to Gerald."

I tagged behind Simon, and we found Gerald out back in the barn, stocking more bottles of Falling Leaves, but at the opposite end of the building from the forklift and the police scene. "What do you two want?" He shoved another bottle in, the scowl back on his face.

"You two need to cool it," Simon said. "You work well together as a team, but when you pressure him for credit, things go sideways."

"That's how you store wine, Simon." Gerald shoved another bottle of wine into the wine rack. "It's all *Sideways*, just like the movie."

"What do you mean?" I said, wondering if his life mirrored, even if only in his mind, the events of the film.

"Nothing."

"How about if we give you a raise?" Simon said. "Let me see what we can do."

"I don't know." *Clunk*, another bottle went into the wine rack. *Clunk, clunk*, two more. "I have to think about it. I may need to make a change."

"What kind of change?" Simon said.

"Don't know." Gerald pushed two more bottles into the rack.

Simon stared at him for a few moments. "I know you're upset about David taking credit, but you wouldn't do something stupid, would you? Like trying to knock him off?"

"What? No, that would be crazy." Gerald shoved another bottle into the rack. "No, I wouldn't hurt him, but it makes me nuts that someone tried to get at him and killed Amy instead."

chapter seven

When I arrived back at Nature's Way, a police car was in front. I parked in the back and took a few deep breaths to center myself before I went inside. When I did, I found a frantic Wallace Bryan, who told me that Detective Koren and Detective Coyle were in my office interviewing his niece, Lily.

"What's going on?" I said, looking at Lily, who sat slumped on the couch, crying. The coffee table was littered with used tissues. "What are you doing here, Lily?"

"I came to get my check," she said, sniffling. Wallace went over and put his arm around his niece.

"Are you harassing her?" I pulled out my phone. "I'm calling a lawyer."

"It seems that your employee had a relationship with David Farmer." Detective Koren tapped his pen on his notebook.

"That can't be true." Wallace looked at Lily. "Lily?"

But Lily just grabbed a few tissues from the box on the table and blotted her tears.

"Who told you that?" I said.

"Let's just say it was someone close to the source."

Immediately, I thought about what Simon had told Jackson and me—namely that Detective Coyle had interviewed Ivy about the accident. I was sure they had discussed other topics as well, maybe even David's wandering eye.

"Ivy."

Detective Coyle blanched. "What? How did you know that?"

"Shut up, Coyle," Detective Koren said.

"And you believe her?" I wasn't going to confirm or deny the rumor.

"We do." Detective Coyle smirked. "It seems that it started when Lily was working on that event you had over the weekend. Yeah, she got real chummy with David."

"It's over now." Lily turned to Wallace. "I know it wasn't the right thing to do, to get involved with a married man—I just got caught up in it."

"I'm sure it was David Farmer's fault," Wallace said, squeezing her hand. "He seems like a very charismatic man."

"Regardless," Detective Koren said. "Someone tried to kill David Farmer, and your niece prepared the appetizer that he almost consumed but instead offered to Amy."

"And there's more," Detective Coyle said. "The tox screen is in. . . ."

"Correct," Detective Koren said, taking over. "Amy Lord died from poison hemlock. That's the same poison that killed Socrates in 399 BC."

"Right, that ancient guy."

"Coyle, you're not helping." Detective Koren gave him a disdainful look. "Symptoms from the poison typically appear twenty minutes to three hours after ingestion. And from the time frame we've constructed, Amy Lord was dead about half an hour after she ate the scallop appetizer."

I thought about this for a minute. "Whoever did it must have topped the dandelion greens with chopped-up hemlock. In fact, hemlock is known as poison parsley. Anyone looking at the plate wouldn't notice the difference."

"So anyone could have done it," Lily said, drying her eyes.

"Yes," I said. "Anyone at all."

"That may be so, Ms. Bryan, but we'd still like you to come down to the station for further questioning," Detective Koren said. "You were involved with David until he ended it, so you do have motive, and you can't account for your movements this morning either, when the second attempt took place."

"I took a long walk on the beach this morning with my dogs. I wasn't at Pure, and I didn't try to kill David either time! I love him!"

I blew past her outburst. "Simon Lewis said he didn't see her at Pure today. You can check with him."

"Oh, we will," Detective Coyle said.

"Lily didn't do this," I said. "There are plenty of other reasonable suspects, like Gerald Parker, for one. Just this morning he and David had a big fight over who should get credit for their entry in the *Wine Lovers* magazine contest. Not to mention his father and brother or any of the rival vineyards. The list of suspects is long, Detectives." I left out David's lover Carla Olsen, since that would reinforce Lily's motive.

"That may be true, but right now, Lily here has a means, motive, and opportunity, the trifecta," Detective Koren said. "She's coming with us."

Lily wiped her eyes and stood, a resolute look on her face. "Let's go."

"You're not going to interview my niece without a lawyer," Wallace said.

I pulled out my phone and began to punch in numbers. "I know exactly who to call."

Simon immediately got in touch with Shawn Thompson, a Harvard-educated, top-notch criminal attorney who practiced in New York and had helped us when Jackson had been falsely arrested a year and a half ago. Since Simon was such a good client of the firm's, Thompson cleared his schedule, hopped on a helicopter, and headed east to represent Lily Bryan. He'd arrived around three o'clock and had immediately gone to the Greenport jail, and Lily had been released a few hours later. But we weren't sure what was going to happen next.

A few hours later, Jackson and I met Simon in Mitchell Park for the first East End wine auction. Although wine auctions were common in, say, Napa and New York City, and wine was also often sold online to enthusiastic buyers, this was our first one and would benefit East End Community Veterinary Care, a new program to help the pets of low-income residents and the animals in shelters. The three of us agreed to go because Simon had his eye on an expensive bottle of wine, and to continue our investigation, since many of our suspects such as various vineyard owners would be there.

The air was cool and crisp as Mitchell Park began to fill up with people who savored local wines, including collectors and sommeliers. The setting was the green crescent of land down stone steps and just beyond the merry-go-round, with a view of the marina and Peconic Bay.

The organizers had placed folding chairs facing the podium, while next to it was a large table with bottles of fine wine on top of a crisp white tablecloth. A sound system pumped in classical music.

Derek Mortimer of St. Ives Estate Vineyards, Harrison Jones of the Wave Crest Vineyard, and Camille and Carter Crocker of Crocker Cellars sat down in front and opened their programs. The Crockers were relatively new members of the East End wine community, but had already won several regional awards and were widely considered a close second to Pure in quality.

Before the bidding began, we grabbed three seats down in front on the right, and I filled Jackson and Simon in on the police's visit to Nature's Way to see Lily. "She was really upset. I felt bad for her, especially because her uncle was there and the police brought up her affair with David."

"That's rough," Jackson said. "How did that even happen?"

"She spent a lot of time down there because I was busy with other things. I almost feel responsible."

"No way," Simon said. "You can't control what goes on between two people."

"But it's over now?" Jackson said.

"I don't know," I said. "She said she loved him, in front of Koren and Coyle, no less."

"That's not good," Jackson said.

"I know, and it's obvious that she's still upset about the breakup. But David denies he was even involved with anyone."

"That's just not true. Case in point." Simon gestured to Carla Olsen of Sisterhood Wines, who had just taken a seat across the aisle from us.

"So he's got a roving eye, and then some," Jackson said.

"You got that right," Simon said.

"The good news is that Shawn got her out of jail," Jackson said. "But will they bring her in again? That's the big question. If I know Detective Koren, he's not done with her."

"I think you're right," I said. "Which makes it even more important for us to solve the case." Gerald Parker took a seat next to Carla, and they started talking.

"Exactly," Simon said, glancing over at Gerald. "Hey, we need to tell Jackson about Gerald's blowup with David about the label, too."

Jackson gave me an inquisitive look. "What happened?"

"Gerald wanted credit on the label of Falling Leaves, and of course David said no, but afterward we followed him out to the barn. He said he couldn't get over the fact that someone tried to kill David and killed Amy instead."

"Maybe he tried to kill David and killed her by mistake and feels guilty," Jackson said.

"That's a very good point," I said. "Plus, Gerald told us he's now considering a change."

"If that gets around, the other vineyard owners will want to hire him so he'll share Pure's secrets with them, and they can dominate the market," Simon said. "But I won't let that happen. Gerald signed a nondisclosure clause, and if I get a whiff that he's doing something shady, I'd go after him, hard."

"Still, there's nothing to stop him from using his talents as a winemaker for another vineyard and creating the next big thing," Jackson said.

"Without David? Doubtful. Although it won't stop others from trying." Simon gestured with his program. "But let's put it on hold for now. Here's Ramsey Black, our host and auctioneer."

We watched as he walked up to the podium, dressed in a sharp-looking black suit and tie. "Actually," I said, "we might learn something."

"You focus on that." Simon glanced at his program. "I need to pick up a few cases tonight to add to my collection. Word around town is that several local and wealthy wine lovers have gone into their private cellars to donate to the cause."

"So this could get exciting," I said.

"Yes. In my experience you can't get what you want unless you're willing to outspend every other collector or sommelier in the crowd. So it could get very expensive." Simon picked up his paddle, which had the number 57 in bold.

"Fortunately, that's not an issue for you," Jackson said.

"No, of course not. But I don't want to go crazy either."

"Good evening, everyone," Black said. "And thank you for coming out tonight to bid on celebrated wines and support a very good cause. All the proceeds will go to East End Community Veterinary Care, a new program that will help low-income residents by providing free medical treatment for their pets, and for animals in all the shelters on the North and South Forks who are in need of preventative, emergency, and long-term care."

The crowd clapped.

"Tonight, I'll be auctioning off a wide variety of wines, including those from local vineyards, from the United States and around the world, at a variety of price points. Given the important work of East End Community Veterinary Care, I encourage you to dig deep!"

The crowd clapped again.

Two volunteers joined Black at the podium, each holding a bottle of wine. "Let's begin with a prestigious vintage that I'm sure will be of interest to those of you who are avid collectors." He pointed to the bottle on his right. "From the collection of Fred Eaves, I put on offer a complete lot of Romanée-Conti 1990 Domaine de la Romanée-Conti." He picked up the gavel from the podium.

Several people in the crowd gasped, including Simon. "Oh my God. I have to have this."

"Don't go crazy," I said.

"I'm gone. I did not expect this lot."

"We'll start the bidding at sixty thousand dollars," Black said.

"Sixty thousand dollars for a case of wine?" Jackson shook his head. "That is obscene. But at least it's for charity."

"That's right, Jackson." Simon grasped his bidding paddle tightly.

Carla raised her paddle.

"I have a bid for sixty. Do I have sixty-two?"

"Carla has that kind of money?" Simon said.

"I don't know," I said.

Simon thrust his paddle in the air. "Sixty-five."

Carla countered, "Sixty-eight."

"Seventy," Simon said.

Black nodded. "I have seventy. Do I hear seventy-two?" He looked at Carla.

She shook her head.

Simon grabbed my hand and squeezed it. Jackson rolled his eyes.

"Anyone else? I'm selling this very prestigious lot at seventy thousand dollars. Anyone else? No?" Black waited a moment. "Going once, twice . . . sold!" He slammed the gavel down onto the podium, where it made a satisfying *thwack*. Simon released my hand and gave me a hug. "I got it! Wow!"

"Good for you," I said.

"Good for pets and people," Jackson said. "This new program will make a big difference for a lot of animals."

"Just like you do," I said.

"She's right." Simon was absolutely giddy with excitement. "And I've got a great idea. How about if I match my bid and gift your rescue?"

"Simon, you don't have to do that," Jackson said.

"I want to. And I can afford it."

"That's very sweet of you, Simon," I said. "Are you sure?"

"I'm sure. You'll have a check tomorrow night when

you come to Salt for the dinner. Okay?" He put his hand out to Jackson.

Jackson smiled and shook it. "Thanks, this will do a lot of good. Really, thanks, Simon."

"You are very welcome. I can't wait to see what's for sale next!"

Ramsey Black was true to his word—the auction featured a wide array of wines, from the prestigious to the more moderately priced. By the end of the night, Simon had picked up two more prestigious lots, and Black announced that the auction had raised almost $500,000. It was a good night for animals and the people who loved them.

A reception followed with various local vintages, including those from Pure, St. Ives Estate Vineyards, Sisterhood Wines, Wave Crest, Crocker Cellars, Farmer's Vineyard, and others.

Unfortunately, when we went up to sample the various vintages, David's father, Walter Farmer, and David's brother, Kurt, were nearby talking to Carla Olsen and Ramsey Black, along with Harrison Jones of Wave Crest and Derek Mortimer of St. Ives.

Kurt seemed to be taking a special interest in Carla. I had to admit, now that he had shaved and showered and changed into a suit, he was a lot more appealing. Carla laughed at something he said.

David scowled. "What is Kurt up to with Carla?"

"Just ignore them. Let's take a taste of the competition." Simon asked for a glass of Crocker's wine, while

I tried Farmer's, and David got Carla's. We tasted each one, then switched glasses.

"What do you think? Besides ours, I like the Crocker vintage," Simon said.

"Me, too," I said.

"Agreed, but I'd have to say that my father's is the best of the lot," David said. "Still no competition for us, though."

"That's because you should be working with us, your family, and not this out-of-towner," Walter said as he moved over to our group, while Kurt and Carla continued talking.

"Dad, I'm not coming back."

"We'll see. You just need to get your head straight." Walter pushed past David.

"I need a drink." David headed back to the wine-tasting table, where he grabbed two glasses of Crocker's wine and slugged them down in rapid succession.

"I think your friend might have a problem," Jackson said. "Willow told me that he's drinking at lunchtime."

"That's ridiculous," Simon said. "He just likes Crocker's wine. It's my favorite, too, after Pure. Believe me, Jackson, David couldn't function the way he does if he had a drinking problem."

"That's a common myth, Simon," Jackson said. "Many alcoholics are high functioning."

"No offense, Jackson, but I still don't believe it. I have to pay for my lot. I'll be back." Simon set his glass at the table and headed for the cashier.

"He doesn't want to hear it, Jackson."

"I know, that's pretty common, too."

"You're here if he needs you, that's all you can do for now."

As Simon walked off, Camille and Carter Crocker came up to us. "Hi, *chérie*," she said, and kissed me on either cheek. *"Comment allez-vous?"*

"I'm fine, and you?"

"Bon!"

"Good to see you," Carter said, shaking Jackson's hand.

"Did you enjoy the seminar at Pure today, Camille?"

"I did. It's always fun to see what the other guy is doing."

Camille, a petite brunette originally from Paris, had met Carter, a big guy with a penchant for jeans, plaid shirts, and cowboy boots, and with a big personality, at a wine auction in NYC five years ago. The couple, both in their early thirties, had moved to the North Fork two years later and opened their winery in Mattituck, fifteen minutes west of Greenport. We'd met the couple last year at the grand reopening party at Pure, and Camille and I had quickly become friends, since we both shared a passion for organic gardening.

"You guys did well tonight," Jackson said. The couple had scored several bottles of pricey wines.

"Sure did," Carter said. "Although not as well as your friend Simon."

"Simon is enthusiastic about wine," I said.

"That's an understatement." Carter sounded somewhat annoyed. Simon had outbid him more than once.

"But he's done a great job revamping Pure," Camille said, quickly smoothing things over. "It's impressive."

"I'll tell him you said so," I said.

"Terrible business about Amy Lord, though," Carter said.

"Yes, we feel so badly for Ivy and David," Camille said. "Do you have any idea who did it, Willow?" She knew about my penchant for amateur sleuthing.

"Not yet. In fact, it would be good to talk to you about the local vineyard scene to get some background. I also want to talk to several specific owners who were at the party."

Carter checked his watch and tugged on Camille's arm. "I'd better pay, and then I've got to get home for that conference call." Carter headed his own investment banking firm in New York, but spent most of his time out here. "Why don't you stop by to see us? We'll talk."

"That sounds like a great idea," I said.

Camille squeezed my hand. "Okay, *chérie*, we'll see you soon."

The Crockers left, followed by the Farmers, and Carla, Derek, Harrison, and Gerald. Ramsey Black had strolled down to the waterfront with Ivy.

"Those two are being chummy again," Jackson said. "Something is going on with them. Shall we walk down there and try to find out what?" He put his hand out and we headed in their direction across the cool grass. While we walked, I told him about the message I'd remembered from Ivy's watch.

"That's not very nice."

"No, it's not. Someone is obviously pretty upset, but who? It couldn't have been David. You said he and

Ivy were together in the corn maze," Jackson said as we reached the dock pilings. "You'd have to get the watch to know for sure, and that's tricky."

Now Ivy and Ramsey Black were less than three yards away and in a heated argument, contrary to their cozy conversation at the cocktail party.

"Maybe it was a message from Ramsey. They don't seem to be getting along tonight."

The night was clear, with no wind, so it was easy to overhear the conversation. "I thought you knew what you were doing," Ivy said. "I can't have him leaving, and spilling secrets."

"He won't. I took care of it." Black glanced in our direction. "But I can talk to him again. Try to smooth things over."

"Please, we have to win on Sunday, and I don't want him causing trouble for us."

"He won't." Black took her arm. "Let's go."

We watched as the two of them headed away. "Now, what was that about—controlling Gerald?" I said. "What is he, some kind of ad hoc adviser? I don't think that Simon knows about this."

"If Ramsey's having an affair with Ivy, David probably doesn't know either."

chapter eight

We left the party early after Jackson got a call from one of his volunteers—someone usually stayed the night, especially with new arrivals—that one of the horses seemed sick. After Jackson called his vet, we headed to his house.

Fortunately, the horse was only dehydrated and was put on IV fluids overnight. By Wednesday morning she was doing much better. The weather was glorious, slightly cool, with blue skies and amber light bathing the fields behind Jackson's property. So after I did my yoga routine at the foot of Jackson's four-poster bed, and while he took care of our dogs and the rest of his charges, I decided to go for a walk.

I needed to get back to basics. I'd been up half the night thinking and reviewing what I knew so far. Finally, I'd realized that the simplest way to figure out who had poisoned Amy was to find out where the poison to do the deed came from.

I didn't know whether poison-hemlock was common on the East End. If it wasn't, that would help me narrow down the field, which included Ivy, and perhaps even Ramsey if the two were involved, and

Gerald, along with jealous vineyard owners, including David's father and brother. Other suspects, too, might reveal themselves over time.

I'd done some preliminary research about the presence of poison hemlock with the help of the East End Botanical website, which said that it could be found in fields usually in sunny areas, which wasn't much help. But the plant was over eight feet tall and featured hairless hollow stalks with purple blotches and lots of umbrella-shaped flower clusters, so it would be hard to miss.

Having often walked Jackson's and Simon's fields, I was reasonably certain they had no eight-foot poison-hemlock plants, but I had to check. Even though Lily and I had been super-careful and only foraged for safe plants, if it was here, somewhere, it might mean that someone close, such as Ivy or Gerald, had found it and tried to use it on David.

Anyone could have procured the poison from anywhere, but I'd start here and go on from there. If the plants weren't here, it might help Lily, too.

Starting out at the west end, next to Jackson's barn, I walked east, down the field toward Pure, making sure not to miss anything. Mostly, it was a combination of wildflowers, weeds, bushes, young trees, and my favorite: edible plants. Since I planned to lead another walk and workshop in two weeks—this weekend we'd be busy with crowds from North Fork UnCorked!—I'd brought a bucket along, and as I went, I scanned the ground for new edibles and plants for use in remedies.

I'd only walked a few yards when I quickly spotted a dandelion patch. Because of what had happened, the

plant I loved now seemed to take on a darker connota-
tion. I bent down to examine it more closely. But it
confirmed what I'd already known: Lily could not have
mistaken this genial herb for an eight-foot-high poison-
hemlock plant.

Continuing on, I passed more dandelion patches,
then a few yards away I spotted chickweed, a plant with
small green leaves and delicate tiny white flowers that
sprouts in the fall. Small in size but mighty in power,
the chickweed was chock-full of vitamin C, perfect for
cold-and-flu season.

I plucked up a few plants to experiment with before
the next class, thinking it would make a nutritious
ingredient for a tofu stir-fry, a salad, or raw soup. As a
natural remedy the chickweed had anti-inflammatory
properties, for a soothing salve. So I'd show the class
how to make this cure as well.

A few minutes later, I reached the other end of the
field, by Pure's corn maze, turned, and headed back to
Jackson's. On this pass, I quickly came upon the versatile malva. The plant featured a single white or pink
flower with five petals and circular or kidney-shaped
leaves. Malva leaves are anti-inflammatory and high in
beta-carotene and are thus used in teas and syrups for
coughs and sore throats, so it was also a good choice for
the upcoming cold-and-flu season. The leaves can be
eaten raw or added to soup, so I could combine it with
the chickweed to make a raw concoction.

But I still hadn't spotted any poison hemlock. So I
continued along the field, walking back and forth until
I finally reached the forest's edge opposite the barn,
and beyond that Long Island Sound. As I headed back

toward Pure for the last time today, I kept my head down and my eyes sharp, looking for edibles and poison hemlock. But when I reached the far end of the corn maze, I hadn't spotted any.

Since I was there, I decided to check in with Simon and David, but as I turned to go, I noticed a hole in the ground at the edge of the trees. The hole was empty except for a crisscross of roots and leaves that had fallen inside. What had been here? I stood up and moved around in a tight circle to try to find any indication of what had been planted here and removed. At first, I didn't notice it, but then it seemed impossible that I'd missed it at all. But once I followed the scattered leaves, branches, and roots from the now-gone plant, it led me to another poison-hemlock plant growing less than two feet away.

Sucking in a breath, I considered the implications of my find. Since I believed Lily was innocent, this had to mean that someone else, someone who knew or looked for and found the tree, had taken it and used it to try to kill David. However, the police weren't going to think that. No, they'd surmise that Lily had found the plant and used it to do the same thing.

I called Jackson but he didn't answer, so I walked over to Pure to tell Simon what I'd found, and what I hadn't found because someone had taken it. Inside Pure, it was quiet, but I texted Simon to tell him I was here. When he didn't answer, I wandered into the tasting room and, finding no one, continued on to the storage barn. As I was passing the bed-and-breakfast, my pal Allie, a tall, energetic redhead, our resident masseuse at Nature's Way, came out the door. Seeing me, she smiled, leaned her massage table against the porch railing, and came over to me.

"Hi, honey." She gave me a hug. "How are you? I just can't believe what happened to Amy. Are you investigating again? The police need your help."

I'd known Allie since college, and she and her best friend, Hector, had moved out from NYC shortly after Aunt Claire's death to set up shop in Nature's Way, to support me and expand their client base. Allie knew all about my adventures as an amateur detective.

"I don't think that the police would like hearing that. But Simon asked me to investigate. We think that someone wanted David dead and killed Amy by mistake." I explained how David had offered one of his poisoned scallop appetizers to Amy.

"If it's about another woman, it might be Ivy taking revenge," Allie said. "I'm not just saying that because I don't like her. David really runs around, and right under her nose."

"She's right about that," Hector said as he joined us. Hector was a gifted acupuncturist, and a wonderful human being, sweet and kind. Jamaican, his skin brown like a cocoa bean, he was fit and handsome, with a shaved head that made him look like some kind of superhero. If he hadn't been gay, he and Allie would have been a couple long ago. They kind of were, without the sex, since they lived together and did most things as a twosome.

He pulled me in for a hug. "Are you doing your investigating thing again, sweetheart?"

I nodded. "Have to. Simon asked, and I couldn't say no."

"That's because you are friends now, better than lovers, right?" Hector smiled.

"Yes, much better. So you both have seen David sneaking around?"

Hector nodded. "More than once I've seen him meeting women inside." He gestured to the bed-and-breakfast.

"And that's not all," Allie said. "We've seen him at the bar at Harry's Half Shell on Main Street near our house with other women, too, multiple times. He doesn't even seem to worry about being caught."

"Maybe it's because Ivy is cheating on him, too," Hector said. "One time, I was called in to do a treatment very early, during the week, and I heard her next door with someone."

"Do you think it could have been Ramsey Black?"

"Who's he?" Allie said, her forehead crinkling in thought.

"He's the head of the East End Wine Council, and I think something is going on between them."

"I did see a man outside afterward, when I was done with my appointment. He went into the barn, and a few minutes later Ivy came out and followed him. So maybe that was him?"

"What did he look like?"

"Very handsome, and well dressed—if I had to guess I think he was straight because he didn't check me out." Hector laughed.

"I believe it," I said.

"Thank you, sweetheart," Hector said. "So they both

went in, but I had to leave so I don't know what happened next." He checked his watch. "Allie, we'd better get going. We have appointments at Nature's Way."

I said good-bye to them and took a quick look inside the barn, but no one was there. Simon was probably at Salt, but where were David, Ivy, and Gerald? I headed back outside, and this time when I walked past the bed-and-breakfast, the door was open. Inside, one of the maids was cleaning the room in front.

"Help you?" she said as I walked inside. A pretty petite brunette, she was dressed casually in black pants, sneakers, and a rose-colored shirt with three-quarter sleeves. Her name tag read ZOLA.

"I'm a friend of Simon's and I was wondering where he was. Do you know?"

"I haven't seen him today." She pulled the comforter and the sheets off the bed and deposited them into a bin on the cart.

"What about David or Ivy or Gerald?"

"I don't know." Zola pulled the pillowcases off. "Ivy was here earlier telling us what to do, but then she left. As if we don't know by now what needs to be done."

"So she's hard to work for?"

"Always, and now since Amy is gone, she's even worse. Yes, a death like that is really hard, but she is not the only one with problems."

"Have you ever seen Ivy staying in one of the rooms, maybe with a friend?"

Zola arched an eyebrow. "You ask a lot of questions. Who are you?"

"I'm Willow McQuade, and Simon has asked me to look into Amy's death."

"You're a detective?"

"No, I'm not a cop, I'm an amateur sleuth. Simon and I have worked together before."

"You find killers?"

"Yes, we find killers."

"That's amazing. Good for you."

"Thank you. We have a theory that someone was trying to kill David and killed Amy instead."

"Oh my, that's terrible, but why, how?"

I explained the switched appetizer scenario.

"So maybe someone had the grudge for David?" Zola put fresh sheets on the bed.

"Yes, and what we're wondering is, if maybe Ivy was having an affair. We have heard that David was pretty busy with other women."

"You could say that. Half the time I am covering up for him, and half the time for her. I like him better." Zola laughed.

"Me, too. There is one man I'm wondering about in particular. His name is Ramsey Black and he's French, very handsome and well dressed."

"Oh, yes, I know Mr. Black." Zola explained that while David had various lovers—she described one woman who sounded like Carla but no mention of anyone who looked like Lily—Ivy used the bed-and-breakfast to meet Ramsey Black, and only him, usually early on weekday mornings. Ivy must have been meeting Ramsey the day Hector overheard them next door.

Simon had still not returned, or anyone else, so I called his cell phone, but had to leave a message. After stopping by to pick up the dogs from Jackson, I headed back into town and took them all for a walk on the village green. Once they were tuckered out, we headed back to Nature's Way, where I helped all four dogs onto the oversize couch with lots of comfy blankets, in front of a faux electric fireplace that I'd put in last winter, thanks to money from Aunt Claire's royalties. She was taking care of all of us, even now. Zeke had quickly been assimilated into the pack and fell asleep with his head on Qigong's neck, while Columbo and Rockford lay back-to-back, like two tofu hot dogs in a bun. The two cats, Ginger and Ginkgo, came in to check the scene out but quickly scampered off upstairs.

While all the dogs took a nap, I put the investigation into Amy's death on the back burner for a bit and turned my attention to bills that needed to be paid and ordered natural products, including supplements, gluten-free breads, and cruelty-free vegan beauty products. By the time I'd finished and had lunch, I still had not heard back from Simon, so I called him, again. I wanted to find out where he was, and also to make arrangements to meet him at Amy's wake, which was to take place tonight from 5:00 to 7:00 p.m. He didn't call back.

Finally, at six thirty Wednesday evening, I left Simon a message that I'd meet him downtown at the funeral home. But when I got there, police cars were on both sides of the street, so I went around the corner, parked, and quickly walked back. I got there just in time to see David's brother, Kurt Farmer, being led out in handcuffs, while David, Ivy, and Simon stood outside the door. Simon spotted me, and I waved him over.

"What is going on? And where were you today?"

"Dealing with David and his brother."

"What happened?"

"David and I went to do a radio interview at K-BAY, in Southold, this morning. Good publicity, reaching the local market, you know?"

"Yes, right, so that's where you were. I stopped by but no one was there."

"Yeah, Gerald called in sick, too, not that I believe it. He's just sticking it to us."

We watched as a policeman I didn't recognize pushed Kurt into the backseat of a cruiser and slammed the door.

"Simon, focus. How did Kurt get into the picture?"

"He was waiting for David when we got back to Pure."

"Why, what happened?"

"His father got a call that the bank had decided to foreclose on the house, and Kurt blamed it on his brother. He thinks if David had worked with them, the vineyard would have been profitable and it wouldn't have happened."

"You can see why he might think that," I said.

"Except he's nuts. They got into a fight, and David thought he'd broken his wrist. Ivy was at Salt, helping me with the wine pairings for the party tonight, so I brought him to the emergency room. We were there all afternoon because they were all backed up—some boating accident, I think. Good news—his wrist is just sprained."

"So how did Kurt end up back here tonight?" We watched as the cop car took off in the direction of the police station and the jail. David reacted by lighting up a cigarette, and Ivy threw him a nasty look and went back inside.

Obviously, they still weren't getting along. Given this, it wasn't difficult to believe what David had told Lily, namely that he and Ivy no longer shared a bed. It couldn't be any fun working together either.

"I guess he wasn't finished with David," Simon said. "He showed up about fifteen minutes ago, and we thought he just came to pay his respects, but then he and David went out back and started up again. Ivy is furious with both of them, but especially David, because he couldn't control his brother at her sister's wake. It was a bad scene." Simon checked his watch, where a message bubble said, Crazy busy—need you—Kate. "I've got to get to Salt now. You two are coming, right?"

"I'm meeting Jackson there at seven. And I have something important to tell you."

He and Jackson both needed to know about the poison hemlock at the edge of the forest.

chapter nine

It was always a good thing to know the owner of a new and popular seafood restaurant, especially during a busy week such as this. Simon had reserved a table for the two for us, outside on the deck, and under a heat lamp, with a view of sailboats, motorboats, and yachts moored to the dock, and of Peconic Bay and Shelter Island. He'd placed just ten tables on the deck, so while the inside seating accommodated up to two hundred, outside felt almost like a private oasis. The dinner at Salt would benefit the North Fork Animal Welfare League, which ran exemplary shelters in Southold and Riverhead.

The event featured an oyster-themed menu—instead of the scallops, which was probably a good thing—paired with various vintages from Pure, including the contender for the big win, Falling Leaves. We started out with raw oysters and hot sauce that Ivy had paired with sauvignon blanc, then moved on to oyster stew and pinot noir, oysters Rockefeller and chardonnay, and finally to fried oysters, with skinny sweet-potato fries, creamy coleslaw, and a secret tartar sauce blend that had a kick, and Falling Leaves.

Jackson, though, was quite content with iced Perrier, with a slice of lemon. As he said, it was dry, refreshing, and didn't detract from the flavor of the oysters being served. While we enjoyed our meal—seafood was the one thing I had a hard time giving up as a vegetarian/vegan, having grown up on it on the East End—I filled Jackson in on what I'd learned during the day, starting with finding the poison hemlock.

"So the plant that you found was right next to the empty hole? I've never seen that plant out there, anywhere, and I've walked all over with the dogs."

"I almost missed it, too, but it's there. The question is, who dug it up and how do we find out?"

"Good question." Jackson slurped down a raw oyster. "That is so good. It tastes like it just came out of the water."

"Glad you like it," Simon said as he pulled a chair up to our table but remained standing. "Everything good?"

"Excellent," Jackson said. "I'll say."

"Good, well, I had a few minutes so I thought I'd find out what you wanted to tell me." Simon put down his glass of wine and pulled a crisp blue check out of his inside blazer pocket. "And I also wanted to give you this. For your animal sanctuary, and for taking Zeke in." He handed it to Jackson, who took it and shook his hand.

"This is great, Simon. Thank you, man, really."

"You're doing a very good thing, Simon," I said. "Thank you."

He put an arm around each of us. "What is the point of being rich, if you can't help your friends, and the causes they believe in?" He grabbed his glass and raised it. "Cheers to you, Jackson. Keep up the good work."

We raised our glasses and toasted. "To you, Simon," Jackson said. "For being a good friend to both of us."

Simon sat down and leaned toward me. "Now, what's the latest?"

So I explained how I had found the hole where a poison-hemlock plant had been and an actual living plant right near it, along with the idea that it might mean that Ivy or Gerald or someone else had used it to try to poison David.

"But Lily had access, too," Simon said. "That's not a point in her favor."

Jackson shook his head. "No, it's definitely a good-news, bad-news kind of thing."

"But now that we know it's there, we need to figure out who used it," I said.

"How do we do that?" Simon said.

"We can search their offices at Pure first," I said. "And you can get us into David and Ivy's house, right?"

"Sure thing." Simon plucked two keys out of his wallet and laid them on the table. "I have an extra for the house in case they get locked out. The code is 44501." He pointed to the second key. "And this is the master to all the offices at Pure. You could go after dinner and search Ivy's and Gerald's offices and then go to Orient and search the house. It's just off Village Lane on the water."

"Good idea," Jackson said. "Everyone is here now."

"Exactly, and I'll keep an eye on them," Simon said. "But what about looking into David's brother and maybe even his father, and the other vineyard owners?"

"I want to talk to Camille Crocker, too. Can you go tomorrow?"

"Yes, definitely," Simon said. "But we'll have to do it in the afternoon. Amy's funeral is in the morning, followed by a gathering here."

"That's right," I said. "I'll go with you."

"Thanks."

"I won't be able to go," Jackson said. "Late this afternoon I found out that we're expecting a pig, a cow, and a goat, and maybe two greyhounds. All out of pretty terrible situations, so you'll have to report back to me."

"No problem," I said. "We also need to find out about Ramsey Black." I told Jackson and Simon about what my friends Allie and Hector and Zola the maid had said about Ramsey's meeting Ivy at the B and B at Pure.

"That's pretty close for comfort," Jackson said. "Right under David's nose. Wasn't she afraid of being found out?"

"Obviously not, and neither was David, Allie said. She and Hector have seen David in Harry's Half Shell more than once with women other than his wife."

"Including Lily?" Jackson said.

"No, they didn't mention Lily and neither did Zola. They must have met elsewhere."

At Pure, we started with Ivy and Amy's office on the first floor off the tasting room. The space featured high ceilings with rustic beams, and a large picture window with views of the vineyard. The room was decorated with more of Rich Fiedler's paintings—one of the crab shack perched on the edge of the wetlands, and two close-up studies of stones and shells on the beach.

The art complemented the plush rose-colored couch, driftwood coffee table, and sleek desk with a glass top. They'd opted for a large wall-to-wall industrial-looking steel bookcase behind the desk, which held a variety of wine-themed works from *A Good Year* to *The Billionaire's Vinegar* to *Nose*.

"Where do we start?" I said.

"Definitely not the desk." Jackson circled it. "No drawers."

I laughed. "And not a scrap of paper in sight." The top of the desk was clear, and there were no file cabinets or other places to store anything they wanted or needed to hide.

"But here's something interesting." Jackson pushed a few books out of the way and reached back to grab a laptop. He opened it and booted it up.

"Good find." I went over to him.

"This is Ivy's computer." Jackson placed the laptop on the desk, put the cursor on the entry icon with a butterfly and her name below it, and pressed it. "We're in. Let's see what we've got."

The laptop only had five folders: "New Wines," "Orders," "Press Clippings," "Party," and "Employees."

"Try opening the one that says 'Employees,'" I said. "Maybe it mentions Gerald."

Jackson clicked on the folder, and we examined the

contents. "There's a document labeled 'Gerald,'" he said, and clicked it open.

"What is it?"

Jackson blew out a breath. "An employment contract."

"Click on that e-mail." I pointed to one with the subject line that read, *Need your help—Gerald*, and was dated this morning. The e-mail opened, and an employment contract and a confidentiality agreement were attached.

Ivy Lord To: Ramsey Black
Re: Need Your Help—Gerald

I still don't like it. Let's discuss tonight. Ivy

On Wed, Oct 28, 2015 at 8:19 AM, Ramsey Black
<ramseyblack@gmail.com> wrote:

Ivy—I've examined the documents and they seem in order. Between the contract and the confidentiality agreement I believe if he were to share any of his knowledge of any of your vintages, you would have legal grounds to sue him for damages. But you would also have to provide proof that he has done so. I'm not sure how easy this would be to do. The best course, especially during this sensitive time, is to keep him at Pure and keep him happy. If you win the competition, you'll be on higher ground. Ramsey

From: Ivy Lord Sent: Wednesday, October 28, 2015
8:05 AM To: Ramsey Black

Attachment: Contract; Confidentiality agreement
Subject: Need Your Help—Gerald

Ramsey—I'm worried about Gerald. He seems
determined to let people know that he created Falling
Leaves, not David. I attached his contract and our
confidentiality agreement. Can you review? Ivy

"It seems very businesslike," I said. "You'd never
know that they were involved."

"I'd guess that's the point. If anyone looked at this,
they'd think she was just asking him for his opinion,
nothing more."

"I'll bet they get a lot more personal when they sext."

"I'm sure."

"So this is why Ivy wanted to talk to him tonight
and they ended up arguing. That's what we saw in the
park."

"Exactly." Jackson scanned the contents of the folder.
"I don't see anything else there that can help us." He
closed the folder.

"What about her e-mail?"

"I'll try." He clicked on the mail icon. The mailbox
opened and filled up with new messages. "It looks like
it's mostly business stuff."

"I see what you mean." There were e-mails from
Wine Lovers magazine about the time for the tasting,
a bill from vendors for the tables and chairs, the e-mail
from Ramsey Black, and a reminder about her AmEx
bill. "Can you go further back?"

Jackson scrolled down farther and found e-mails
from Lily to Ivy about the menu for the party, Amy to

Ivy about the tasting for *Wine Lovers* magazine, and from Ivy to Simon and David about the need for more publicity for Pure. The junk mail and deleted folders were both empty.

"She's either deleted anything sensitive, or she has nothing to hide, besides Ramsey," I said.

"Wait a minute. Look at this folder in the in-box. *IL* for 'Ivy Lord.'" He clicked on it. Only one e-mail came up—from David. "It's from Sunday, the day of the party."

> Ivy Lord To: David Farmer
> Re: Our conversation
>
> You're threatening me? Don't make me laugh. IL
>
> On Sunday, Oct 25, 2015 at 12:05 PM, David Farmer
> <davidfarmer@Purevineyard.com> wrote:
>
> Your behavior is reckless and has put everything
> we've worked for at risk! Find a way to fix it or I will
> tell Simon. David

"Tell Simon what?"

"Maybe David found out about Ivy and Ramsey Black. Black is one of the judges for the *Wine Lovers* magazine contest," Jackson said. "Say Pure wins and someone finds out. They'd be disqualified. David and Simon would lose everything."

"So to keep David from telling Simon, or anyone else, Ivy and Black plot to kill David and kill Amy by mistake?"

"Could be. But this e-mail was sent at twelve oh five and the party started at one o'clock. That's a pretty tight time frame to plan and execute a murder. Not to mention that they would have had to procure the poison hemlock."

"It's right out back," I said. "I found it."

"But we don't know if they knew that. Still, I'm going to print this out."

"But why leave this e-mail on the computer where anyone could find it, including Amy?"

"She did make some effort to hide it." Jackson put the laptop back in the bookcase and plucked the page with the e-mail messages out of the printer on a lower shelf. "Besides, Sunday was busy, maybe she just forgot. It doesn't look like she uses the laptop that much at all. She probably relies on the watch. She also doesn't know that she's under suspicion."

"Should we show this to the cops?"

"It's not enough. We have no way of proving that Ivy did anything at all." He folded up the page and stuffed it into his back pocket. "It could be important but we have to keep looking."

Gerald's office was out back in the barn, which made sense considering that's where he spent most of his time. Tucked in the northwest corner and half the size of Ivy's, the office still had a terrific view of the vineyard from the oversize window. He'd shoved a desk and chair in and added a computer that had seen better days. Every square inch of the desk was covered with paper. Bookshelves on either side of the desk were full of books about growing grapes and making, collecting, and selling wine. Above each shelf were whiteboards, which had been wiped clean. A battered couch was to the left of the doorway, and next to it an overstuffed file cabinet. In every way, this was the exact opposite of Ivy and Amy's office.

"You want to start with the desk drawers and the computer and I'll start with the filing cabinet?"

"Sounds good." I pulled the desk drawers open, one by one, but soon realized they only contained reams of copy paper and office supplies, including pens, highlighters, a glue stick, a stapler, staples, and Post-it pads. When I opened the bottom drawer, at first it looked empty, but then I noticed a sealed plastic baggie that contained several dried-up white flowers and leaves in the back right corner. Grabbing a pen, I used it to pull the baggie out. "I think I may have something."

"What is it?" Jackson came around the desk. Carefully, I opened the baggie and looked inside.

"I think this is poison hemlock."

"Really?"

I found a clean piece of paper, put it on the desk, and slowly emptied the baggie onto it. "Can you look up poison hemlock on his computer?"

"Sure." Jackson pulled the keyboard toward him and did a search. "Got it." He turned the screen so I could see a photo of a poison-hemlock plant that featured bunches of delicate white flowers. "Looks like it to me."

"Me, too. So this means Gerald did it," I said. "He tried to kill David and killed Amy instead."

"Not so fast. First, we're not absolutely sure it's poison hemlock, and second, it would have been really easy for anyone to put it in his desk to incriminate him. Ivy is already angry that he's talking about leaving, so why not pin a murder on him?"

"But that would mean she *did* have access to the poison."

"Or maybe Ramsey did and helped her by planting the evidence. Remember what he said to Ivy after the wine auction: 'I took care of it.'" Jackson minimized the poison-hemlock website window and clicked on the folder labeled "Research" on the desktop and scanned it. "Okay, but take a step back. What if none of that happened and the stuff in the baggie does belong to Gerald. What would be his motive for killing David?"

"That David wouldn't give him credit for Falling Leaves," I said. "They were already fighting before Amy's murder."

"Still, is it enough to kill for? I don't think so."

"There is Amy to consider as well. When Simon and I talked to Gerald, he seemed upset by the randomness of her death—that someone had tried to kill David and killed her instead."

"Maybe he was in love with her. It doesn't mean he killed her by mistake."

I examined the flowers and leaves more closely. "Can I see that photo again?"

Jackson minimized the folder and switched back to the website. "What are you thinking?"

I compared the flowers and the leaves to the plant in the photo again. "I don't think this is poison hemlock after all. I think it's yarrow." I poured the flowers and leaves back into the baggie. "Maybe whoever put it in the drawer thought it was a good enough match for poison hemlock—you know, just to stir things up with the police."

"So it doesn't help us." Jackson exited the site and scanned the desktop. "There's a ton of stuff here, but nothing jumps out at me, except for his résumé, which probably means he was looking for a new job." Jackson clicked it open. "What's his background anyway? Is he local?"

"No, he's originally from Oregon. He moved to the East End to work here. Or at least that's what I thought." I pointed to the screen. "But it says here that he interned at Farmer's Vineyard in the summer when he was in high school."

"Maybe his family had a second home on the North Fork. Lots of people do. Too many, if you ask me."

"And when he got older, he came back to work here."

"Right. Take a look at this letter." Jackson clicked a new doc labeled "Résumé Letter" open. "It's dated yesterday and it's addressed to David's father, telling him he always enjoyed working for him and how he appreciates all he taught him and asking him to keep him in mind if he needs a new winemaker. He ends it with, 'It would be good to work for a place where I'm treated like family.'"

"If Gerald left Pure and went back to Farmer's, David, Ivy, and Simon would be very upset."

"That's for sure. Especially if he helped the Farmers with what he's learned from David."

"Simon's lawyers would put a stop to that."

"They'd certainly try."

"Can you look at his e-mail account, too? Maybe there's more info about it there."

Jackson tapped a few keys. "Unlike Ivy's, this one is password protected. No go. Let's finish up the sweep of the office and move on to David and Ivy's house."

We thoroughly searched the office but didn't find anything else of interest. Forty-five minutes later, we were on our way to David and Ivy's house in Orient Point. We were about a mile off when my phone rang. It was Simon. "Hey, what's up?" I said. "We're almost to David's house, and we found a few things at Pure." Briefly, I told him about Ivy's e-mail correspondence with Ramsey Black and what we'd uncovered in Gerald's office.

"Good," Simon said. "But you'd better come back. Ivy and Ramsey left after you two did to go to Whitman's bar, but she just came back here alone to go over the arrangements for the reception after the funeral. Now she's on her way home."

"Was she with David?"

"No, and that's the other reason I called." Simon blew out a breath. "I can't find him, and I need your help."

chapter ten

We arrived back at Salt fifteen minutes later to find the place empty, except for two waterfront tables and Simon behind the bar, mixing a martini in a silver shaker. "Thanks for coming back, you two."

"What's going on?" I said.

"I don't know. I tried David on his cell and his home phone and even went to his favorite bars in Greenport, but I can't find him. I'm getting worried, especially with what's been happening."

"Did Ivy have any idea where he might be?" I said.

"No, and she didn't much seem to care. She just wanted to get home."

"Maybe he reconciled with Lily or he's with someone else, Simon," Jackson said. "It could also be nothing."

"I suppose you're right. I'm definitely on edge." Simon turned around and looked at the shelf where the glasses were supposed to be stocked. "Crap. No more glasses. Roger, the waiter, already took them all into the back to run through the dishwasher." The door to Salt opened and a couple came in. "I'd better handle this," Simon said. "We are closed for the night."

"I'll get you a glass in the meantime," I said. "So you can have your drink."

"Thanks. You're a pal."

Jackson and I walked toward the back of the restaurant to the kitchen. "He's really having a hard time," I said. "We've got to figure out what's going on here."

"We will. We made good progress at Pure tonight."

"True." As we passed the freezer, I noticed that the door was ajar. "What's this doing open?"

"Roger or another member of the waitstaff probably forgot to shut it."

"Maybe." But something made me take a step back, and I opened the door. Through the frosty air, I spotted a body slumped in the corner of the freezer next to the gelato, and it was chillingly familiar. "Oh my God! It's David!"

Jackson peered inside. "And he doesn't look good."

The two of us went over to him, and I checked his pulse. "He's alive."

"Help me move him out of the corner," Jackson said. Each of us took an arm and moved him toward the middle of the freezer.

"What's going on?" David mumbled.

"We're getting you out of here," Jackson said. "Can you stand up?"

"Think so." David tried, but he dropped to his knees.

"Let's try this again," Jackson said, and grabbed David's arm and put it around his shoulder, put his arm around David's waist, and helped him out the door into the warm air of the corridor. While he did, I called 911 and asked for an ambulance and the police.

Twenty minutes later, both had arrived, and while

the medics tended to David, the crime-scene people secured the scene, and Detective Koren talked to us.

"I suppose I shouldn't be surprised to see you three here," he said.

"Simon is our friend," I said. "We came to Salt for dinner, as his guests."

"Yes, and it was damn good," Jackson said.

"Thank you, Jackson," Simon said.

"Okay, enough for the Zagat guide review, Spade." Detective Koren flipped open his black notebook. "Now, Mr. Farmer tells me that he'd been going to get more bottles of that wine Falling Leaves when someone knocked him on the back of the head and shoved him into the freezer. He estimated that he'd been inside for over an hour—from ten o'clock to eleven—and would have remained there and probably frozen to death if you hadn't found him. Can you take me through the chain of events?"

Jackson told him about eating dinner here, then created an on-the-spot lie, saying that we'd taken a drive to the Narrow River Marina beach in Orient to take a walk in the moonlight. We'd returned, he said, when Simon called to say that David was missing around 11:00 p.m. It sounded good to me. I hoped it did to Detective Koren.

"When did you leave to go for this walk?"

"Right around nine o'clock. An hour before David disappeared."

"Given that it takes approximately twenty to thirty minutes to get to Orient and back, this clocks your walk in at what—an hour and a half—at night? At the end of October?"

"Our schedules are very busy right now," Jackson said. "We like our alone time. But the point is, we were gone well before David, Mr. Farmer, was struck on the head and put into the freezer."

"Okay, Spade, okay," Detective Koren said. "You weren't here. I get it. But keep your nose clean and out of whatever this is."

"What is it?" I said. "Do you think that someone is trying to kill David, and that they tried before at Pure, at the party, and killed Amy by mistake? Are you still after Lily?"

"You've sure got a lot of questions, Ms. McQuade. Not that I'm answering any of them." Detective Koren waved to a uniformed officer, and the two of them headed toward the kitchen.

"Lovely fellow," Simon said.

"Isn't he just," I said. "Let's go check on David."

Outside, we found David sitting in the rear of the ambulance, shivering underneath several blankets and sipping hot coffee.

"How are you feeling now?" I said as we walked up to him.

"I'm glad to be out." He pulled the blanket up to his neck. "But now, I'm really dizzy and nauseous, and my brain feels like it's swimming in my skull. They think I have a concussion. They're going to take me to the emergency room to check it out."

"I'm so sorry, David."

"Don't be sorry," he said, brightening. "You two saved me."

"Did you see anything? Do you know who hit you?" Jackson said.

"No. I was just walking past the freezer to get more wine from the storeroom when someone knocked me on the head and shoved me inside. If you hadn't found me, I'd be dead by now. I don't know how to thank you."

"You just did," I said.

He shivered and clutched the blankets even closer. "Did you talk to Detective Koren yet?"

"Yes, we're all good," Simon said.

"He interviewed me, too," David said. "But I couldn't help him much."

"That's understandable considering what happened," Jackson said. "But I think he has what he needs."

"He did tell me that they found a ladle in the freezer with blood on it, so I guess that's what he or she used." David took another sip of coffee, warming his hands on the cup.

"Try not to think about it right now," I said.

"Right," Simon said. "Just chill out, buddy."

"Did you call Ivy?"

"Yes," Simon said. "She's on her way."

"This is all she needs after Amy's death."

But when we'd arrived, Simon had said that Ivy didn't seem concerned about David at all. The marriage was obviously in trouble.

"She's tough," Simon said, smoothing things over. "She can handle it."

The ambulance driver—a burly guy in jeans, a long-sleeved T-shirt and vest, and boots—came around back and said, "We're okay to go."

"Take care, David," I said. "We'll check on you tomorrow."

"Tomorrow is Amy's funeral, but I don't know if I'll be able to go now."

"Just take care of yourself," I said. "We'll hold a good thought for you, too."

"Okay, thanks. You guys are really great."

The driver helped David lie down on a cot in the back of the ambulance, and then slammed the back doors shut.

We watched the ambulance pull away and went back inside, where Simon headed directly for the bar. "Now I really need a drink. Want one?"

"I'm good." I followed him over and sat down on one of the stools that surrounded the rectangular bar on four sides. The bar had been built with teak from an antique sailboat, while the reclaimed-wood floors and rustic beams in the ceiling came from a weathered barn, giving the interior the feel of a ship's cabin.

"Jackson? Seltzer?"

"No, thanks." He sat down next to me.

"Forget the glass." Simon strained the drink, rubbed a twist of lemon peel around the edge of the martini shaker, dropped it in, and took a good, long swallow. "Nice."

"So who do we think did this?" I said. "Ivy, maybe? Or Ramsey? When did they leave originally?"

"I think it was nine thirty or so," Simon said. "Definitely after you two left around nine. I even followed them over to Whitman's bar to make sure she wasn't headed home."

"But they could easily have come back and tried to kill David later," Jackson said.

"Sure," Simon said. "I watched them for a few minutes, but then I had to get back here."

"Right," I said. "Then she shows up around eleven to discuss the arrangements for the reception after the funeral and said she didn't know where David was when you asked her."

"*If* she did it, it was a nice act." Simon took another sip from the shaker. "Leonard Sims, the guy who wants to buy Pure back, was here for dinner, too, and he stayed awhile. And he left about the same time that Ivy did. A lot of people were in and out tonight."

"So whether someone was here or not, it might not matter," Jackson said. "Anyone could have come in through the kitchen and attacked David."

"It wouldn't have been easy, though," Simon said. "The kitchen was rocking up until almost eleven o'clock." He took another drink from the shaker and put it down. "So you found some interesting stuff at Pure?"

"I think so," Jackson said. "Ivy's laptop gave us the e-mail exchange between her and Ramsey Black, and there was also an e-mail from David to Ivy that we didn't tell you about."

"What?"

"David told Ivy that her behavior was reckless and was putting everything they'd worked for at risk," I said. "He told her to find a way to fix it or he would tell you."

"Tell me what?"

"We think David may have found out about Ivy and Ramsey," Jackson said. "If anyone else did, it would put the competition at risk for Pure because he's a judge. David wanted her to stop."

"That makes sense," Simon said. "And it also gives me something else to worry about."

"I know," I said. "Sorry."

"If you win, they'd have to prove that he made it happen," Jackson said. "So don't get carried away just yet."

"But maybe Ivy or Ramsey or both may have tried to kill David tonight before he told you or anyone else. Just to keep it quiet."

"I don't know," Simon said. "Ivy is a control freak, but I really don't think she would kill David. Without him, Pure isn't worth much."

"True, but we've got to connect these dots somehow," Jackson said.

"What about Gerald's office?" Simon said. "Anything you didn't tell me?"

"No, we told you about finding what I thought was poison hemlock but is probably yarrow," I said. "And that it could have been planted there by Ivy or Ramsey. And Gerald's letter to Mr. Farmer, and the fact that he worked for them before."

"And if he goes to work for them, he could try to share our secrets," Simon said. "Terrific."

"Again, it hasn't happened yet," Jackson said. "So try to remain calm. But I do think that David should consider hiring a bodyguard. I could recommend a few."

"Okay, but right now, I need to go to the hospital and see how he is."

At ten o'clock on Thursday morning, Simon and I sat in a pew at the Methodist church in Southold, several rows behind David, Ivy, and various family members, including her grandmother Emily Lord, the family's ninety-two-year-old matriarch and widow of Walter Lord, the family's patriarch, who had died in 2012, leaving Ivy his fortune. David had been released from the emergency room at the Eastern Long Island Hospital a little after one o'clock in the morning, diagnosed with a mild concussion and freezer burn. In the short time between the attack and the service, Simon had called Jackson and asked him to find a bodyguard who could start immediately, and now that man, Scott Peters, sat next to us.

Scott, forty-eight, six feet four, and heavily muscled, had retired from the village police force six months ago, but soon became bored with puttering around his garden and playing golf. Now, his job was to see to it that David came to no further harm.

Funerals are always difficult, but the church was interesting because of its historic past. It dated back to the 1640s, and the simple interior reflected its colonial beginnings.

White wooden pews lined with worn red velvet faced a simple altar with a large standing gold cross on top, while a red carpet ran down the length of the room. Stained-glass windows depicting scenes from the Bible were on either wall, and soaring above were hanging lights with embellished crosses. The smell of incense lingered in the air.

Gerald sat in the row behind us, apparently recovered from whatever illness he had been suffering from, and next to him was Ramsey Black. Farther back, on both sides of the aisle, were members of the community showing their support, and on either side by the exit were vineyard owners, including Carla Olsen, Derek Mortimer, Harrison Jones, and Camille and Carter Crocker. Leonard Sims, the former owner of Pure, had made an appearance as well to pay his respects or perhaps to try to buy back his vineyard one more time.

Unfortunately, David's father, Walter, and David's brother, Kurt, had decided to show up as well, scrubbed up and looking presentable, and they, too, sat in the back. Hopefully, there wouldn't be any more trouble between the two brothers.

Detective Koren was here, too, keeping an eye on things. I spotted him up in the choir loft, talking to someone on his phone. "Detective Koren is here," I said.

"I guess that's standard procedure," Simon said as he texted someone on his watch. "He's checking out who's here, and how everyone acts."

"It may be a good sign that he came," I said. "It might indicate that he isn't sure that Lily did try to kill David."

"Or that he is."

The service went by quickly with just a short homily by the pastor and a eulogy given by Ivy, who broke down several times in tears. Gerald also was emotional, snuffling back tears as she spoke.

"He seems pretty upset," I whispered.

"No kidding," Simon said. "He and Ivy are crying the house down. Her, I understand, but what is up with him?"

"Maybe they were closer than any of us thought."

A few minutes later the service was over, and Simon and I followed the crowd outside, where we were surprised to find Jackson, dressed in a suit and tie.

"I didn't know you were here," I said.

"I slipped in after the service started. Thought you two could use the support."

"Thanks, man," Simon said. "And thanks for hooking David up with Scott. He seems great."

"He is," Jackson said. "I got to know him at a PBA fund-raiser when I first moved out here. He's solid. David's in good hands now."

As the steeple bell clanged from the tower above, Scott guided David and Ivy into a limo parked in front of the church, along with the rest of the immediate family, including the grandmother, Emily Lord.

"I can see that," Simon said.

"Lily was here, too," Jackson said. "I sat behind her. She stayed for about ten minutes and left."

"Why would she come?" I said.

Jackson shrugged. "For David? I don't know. But I spotted Detective Koren up in the choir loft, and he was watching her."

"I saw him, too. Lily's actually supposed to be at work," I said. "But Wallace probably covered for her."

"Understandable, she is his niece," Simon said. "But she shouldn't have come here."

"No," Jackson said. "It just reinforces the fact that she still does have feelings for David to Detective Koren, which goes directly to motive."

Almost everyone else had gone to their cars, including David's father and brother. "I'll talk to her. But shall we go?" I said. "We can take my car to the cemetery." The three of us got into my mint-green Prius and followed the hearse, the limo, and the rest of the mourners. But Walter and Kurt Farmer veered off in a different direction. At least there would be no confrontation today.

The rest of us headed around the corner to the church's cemetery, which would be Amy's final resting place. The Lords had been second-home residents in Orient for years, and upon retirement had settled here permanently and purchased a family plot.

Jackson turned to look in the backseat at Simon, who had two bouquets of roses. "What are those for?"

"Ivy asked us to pick them up so people could say good-bye and lay one on her grave."

"Nice."

We drove into the cemetery across from Southold High School and down a dirt road to the gravesite and parked behind David's limo. When we got out, we walked over to Amy's grave, which was next to Walter Lord's, her grandfather, both of which had elaborate marble headstones. Once we had all gathered, the pastor led a brief ceremony.

Once he was done, I helped Simon hand out the roses to all the mourners. Ivy went first, with her mumbling something we couldn't hear, then dropping the rose on the coffin and falling to her knees on the dirt crust around the grave. David dropped his rose, then helped her up. He and Scott guided her to the limousine.

One by one, we stopped by Amy's grave, said our good-byes, and placed a rose on the coffin. Gerald, who was last, lingered by the grave longer than most. When he finally tossed the rose in, tears were in his eyes.

Before the crowd began to disperse, Simon said, "Please join us at Salt now for light refreshments."

The crowd mumbled back thank-yous and headed for their cars. But when we got back in the Prius, Simon pointed out the window. "Look, Gerald is still standing there, by the gravesite."

"He looks like a statue," I said. "Like he's frozen."

Most of the mourners had decided to come to Salt, but David's father and brother thankfully were not among them. Gerald was also missing; perhaps he was still at the gravesite. Obviously, there was more to that relationship than we'd thought. The other vineyard owners weren't here either, since it was North Fork UnCorked! week.

But this wasn't a worry, as Simon and I would begin interviewing them all later on our self-styled tour. For now, Simon's staff had prepared a light lunch of chowder and sandwiches for everyone, although Ivy and David weren't interested in eating and instead kept to themselves at a table in the corner.

Jackson grabbed a table nearby while I went to the bar to get something to drink. Emily Lord, Ivy and Amy's grandmother, had taken a seat at the bar and was sipping a manhattan on the rocks. She wore a simple black shift dress, with sturdy heels, glasses, and her hair in tight white curls. "I'm sorry for your loss, Mrs. Lord." She turned to look at me. "Thank you, dear. And you are?"

"I'm Willow McQuade, a friend of Simon Lewis. I

own a health food store, Nature's Way, in Greenport. I catered the cocktail party at Pure on Sunday."

"My poor sweet Amy. The family is shattered. She was so young." Even though Emily was elderly, she definitely seemed clearheaded and cogent.

"I know. This must be very difficult for all of you."

"Amy had so much potential. If only her grandfather and Ivy didn't try to dominate her so, she might have found her way." Emily took a sip of her drink. "I stood up for her more than once, but there was only so much I could do. It's no wonder that David ended up with Ivy, instead of Amy. Ivy knows how to get what she wants—she learned that from her grandfather, and my husband, Walter Lord."

chapter eleven

The buzz of the crowd inside Salt continued, but I stared at Emily Lord, trying to digest what she had just told me. "David and Amy used to be a couple?"

"Of course, all through college. David, Amy, and Ivy all met out here and eventually attended Boston University. The date for the wedding was set for the middle of June right after graduation in May, but then something happened and it was called off. By Christmas of the following year, David and Ivy were engaged to be married."

"What happened, do you know?"

Emily shook her head. "But David and Ivy have made a good marriage, so I suppose it worked out for everyone." Obviously, Emily Lord hadn't had a close-up view of that marriage in a long time. Before I could probe any further, she had taken her glass, grabbed her walker, and wandered off.

I stepped up to the bar and waited to order two seltzers with lime wedges. No drinking for me today. Simon and I had decided in the car that we would begin our wine-country tour this afternoon, and I needed to remain clearheaded to try to find some answers. As I stood there, Gerald finally arrived and headed directly for the bar.

I approached him when he reached it. "Are you okay? You seemed pretty upset during the service and afterward."

"I told you, Amy was good people. Not like her sister, or David. Now, if you'll excuse me, I need a drink."

I decided to push it a bit. "But to be that upset, it seems like it was more personal. Were you and Amy involved?"

"That's none of your business." He raised his hand to get the bartender's attention and, when he came over, said, "Give me a glass of Farmer's cabernet, please."

"Farmer's? Not one of your own wines?"

The bartender returned with the glass of wine. Gerald took the glass, turned back to me, said, "I seem to have lost my taste for it," and stormed away.

I ordered the seltzers and returned to our table, where I found Jackson talking to Simon. At the next table, Ivy was talking to Ramsey Black.

"What did you find out up there?" Simon said.

"Interesting stuff," I said. "Did you know that Amy and David were an item in college at BU and were supposed to get married, but called it off and no one knows why? And that by Christmas of the following year, David was engaged to Ivy?"

"Wow," Simon said. "No way. Really? That had to cause some hard feelings all around."

"I know, and on another front, Gerald definitely does not want to talk about his feelings for Amy, and he ordered a glass of Farmer's wine instead of yours. He said, 'I seem to have lost my taste for it.'"

"So something is up," Jackson said. "Maybe Walter Farmer made him an offer after he e-mailed over the letter and his résumé that we found on his computer last night."

"Maybe, but where is David? And what's up with Ivy and Ramsey? Did you manage to overhear anything?"

Jackson nodded. "David left the table right after you went up, and I don't know where he is. But Ramsey came right over to talk to Ivy. At first, he expressed his condolences, but it quickly changed into a discussion about Gerald and the possibility that he might be leaving, and the fact that David knew about the two of them, and how it might affect the competition if the word got out."

"Really? You heard all that?"

"I have supersonic detective hearing. Even though I'm retired, I don't miss much."

"You are good." I gave him a smile.

"Thank you, hon," Jackson said. "But we still have lots of gaps that need to be filled in. Personal relationships are one thing, but so is money."

"I guess you're right," Simon said. "Two hundred K is a good chunk of change. It could be life-changing to some. Not to me, of course."

"We know, Simon," I said.

"I'm just saying."

"Focus, you two. So this means that it's really important to check out the other vineyard owners to see if one of them wanted David dead, and if they are trying to lure Gerald away. They were not happy at the tasting."

"Not at all," I said. "We also need to check and see if any of the vineyard owners who were at the Pure party have access to any poison hemlock. So besides asking questions, we need to be on the lookout for that as well." I checked my watch. "It's twelve fifteen. I say we leave right after we finish eating."

"Where do we start?" Jackson said.

"Are you coming?" I looked at him. "I thought you didn't have time."

"Everything is under control at the farm. And I thought you could use my help."

"Always."

Simon smiled and clapped his hand on Jackson's shoulder. "Let's do this."

"We'll start with Camille and Carter Crocker at Crocker Cellars. I think she may be able to shed some light on the other vineyard owners."

An hour later, on Thursday afternoon, we all piled into Simon's fire-engine-red convertible Mini Cooper and headed to Crocker Cellars, which was located in Mattituck, fifteen minutes east of Greenport. Camille was closely connected to most members of the local wine community and had indicated a desire to help, so it was the logical place to start.

The so-called North Fork Wine Trail began in Baiting Hollow and ended in Orient Point, but instead we would be hopping from vineyard to vineyard, not to taste every wine but to interview those owners who had been at the party at Pure on Sunday.

Ten minutes later, we drove past the former Hargrave vineyard, now Castello di Borghese, in Cutchogue. Louisa and her now ex-husband, Alex Hargrave, cofounded the LI wine industry in 1973 when they were the first to plant grapes out here, on this land, and eventually produced several different award-winning varietals, including cabernet franc, cabernet sauvignon, chardonnay, merlot, and pinot noir. Thanks to the glacial soils and cool maritime climate, grapes thrived both on the North Fork and the South Fork, i.e., the Hamptons, and the winemaking business grew, eventually catching the attention of wine aficionados across the country and around the world.

Crocker Cellars was located north of Route 48, five minutes west of Castello di Borghese. Simon took a quick right, and we traveled down a rough cement road that was badly in need of repair. Because farmland bordered both sides of it, when gusts of wind from Long Island Sound blew in, the air became filled with yellow-brown particles of dirt.

Crocker Cellars was an oasis in the middle of the brown farmland. The twenty-five-acre estate featured over $1 million in landscaping, including lush gardens and a man-made pond, with half the land dedicated to growing the grapes to make merlot, cabernet franc, chardonnay, and cabernet sauvignon vintages.

The tasting room was fashioned after a Tuscan farmhouse, made out of pale yellow brick accented with wrought iron, a red-tile roof, and a wooden double door with heavy metal door knockers. This nod to Tuscany was thanks to Camille Crocker's heritage—her grandfather had an olive-oil business in this region of Italy.

My favorite part, though, was the beautiful plants in front of the building, a mixture of blues, violets, and pinks, from flax, sage, and rosebushes, which were just about done for the season. Camille had taken the tour of Aunt Claire's medicinal herb garden more than once, and I knew she had faith in natural cures, such as the lavender found here.

Lavender was my all-time favorite herb—the Latin root of the name is *lavare* or "to wash" because of its clean aroma—and I often used it as a tonic for stress relief and to help me sleep since it's a natural sedative. I often picked off a few dark purple blossoms and rubbed them together to release the soothing scent.

Simon pulled into the parking lot and took a spot near the door. But as he did, Leonard Sims, the former owner of Pure, backed out in his Lexus. Simon jumped out of the car and went over and stopped him before he could go.

"What are you doing here, Sims?"

"It's a free North Fork, Simon. I can go where I please. Have you reconsidered my offer to buy Pure?"

"No, of course not."

"Then I was right to explore other options. Now if you don't mind, I need to be going."

Simon stepped away from the car. "What other options?"

But Sims drove off and left Simon there. "What was that all about?"

"Maybe he was here to do business with the

Crockers." Through the window of the tasting room, I saw Camille inside talking to Carter. "They're in the tasting room."

"So what's our approach?" Simon said.

"Camille knows that I'm looking for information so I say we get the general lay of the land, the feelings about David and Pure in the community. See if anyone is especially disgruntled."

"And why Sims was here."

But as we got closer, it became clear that Camille and Carter weren't talking, they were arguing. As Jackson opened the door, we heard Camille say, "I told you I'm not selling! We can figure this out."

Carter, who was facing the door, saw us and said something to Camille, who turned around with a smile plastered on her face. "*Chérie!* You made it!"

The interior of the tasting room was rustic, with stone floors, stucco walls, a pitched wooden ceiling, and rows of barrels, with several round high-top tables and stools, accented by colorful murals that depicted Tuscan vineyards and villages.

Several Crocker Cellars wine bottles of various vintages had been placed on the tasting station next to pretty crystal glasses, ready for customers. Through an arched doorway, a corridor led to crates of wine that were ready to go.

I went over to her and we exchanged air kisses. "Is this a good time?"

"Sure thing," Carter said. "In fact, I have something I wanted to show you, Simon." Carter walked over to the tasting bar, picked up an impressive-looking bottle of wine, and handed it to Simon. "Got this little beauty at an auction in New York yesterday. Whatcha think?"

"A Chambertin, nice."

"It's not nice, it's amazing. I had to get my own back after you beat the tar out of me at that East End Community Veterinary Care auction."

"Right." Simon handed it back. "I see."

"There's still the matter to be settled on Sunday by those *Wine Lovers* magazine judges."

"Sorry, buddy, that one is in the bag."

Carter gave Simon a hard look, but then broke into a broad grin. "We'll see about that. Now, if you'll excuse me, my day job is calling. Good to see you folks."

"Shall we do a little tasting?" Camille turned away, went over to the wine bar, and picked up a bottle of cabernet sauvignon.

"Sure," Simon said. "Love to."

Camille picked up the corkscrew, opened the bottle, and began to pour.

"None for me, thanks," Jackson said. "I don't drink." We were both grateful for his recovery in AA.

"No problem," Camille said as she filled three glasses, and handed one to each of us.

Simon sipped his. "Very nice, Camille, thank you."

"Simon, let's take a look around," Jackson said, motioning to the archway. It would give me time to talk to Camille privately.

Once they moved away, I said, "Camille, are you okay?"

"What do you mean? I'm fine."

"But you two were arguing about selling the winery, and we saw Leonard Sims outside."

"That man is a leech. We've just had some problems this year, and some unexpected expenses, and our winemaker just quit, so it's been, well, tumultuous. But I believe that we can make a real go of it. We've already won several prestigious competitions, and despite what Simon said, we do have a chance of winning on Sunday. We're nipping at Pure's heels. He knows that— everyone does."

I took a sip of the wine. "Your wine is very good."

"Thank you, but unfortunately, Carter is only focused on the bottom line. We've had a lot of money going out, and not enough coming in. So he asked Sims here."

"It takes time for a business to become profitable. Surely Carter understands that."

"Sometimes he does, but today is not one of those days. But I'm working on a solution. I won't sell."

"What are you going to do?"

She took a generous sip of her wine and placed it on the bar. "Enough about me. How can I help you?"

"I'm trying to get a feel for things in the vineyard community. I'm hoping that it will help me figure out who killed Amy. It may have been a mistake."

"What kind of mistake?"

"David offered one of his scallop appetizers to Amy, and she ate it and died. He didn't eat his. We think, and the police do as well, that David was the actual target, that somebody wanted him dead."

"No! How horrible." She downed the rest of her glass, and as she put it back on the bar, her hands were shaking.

"So I guess my question is, have you ever heard any

chatter about David or know of anyone who really had a grudge against him or Pure?"

"Pure has done well, so naturally there is a lot of jealousy, but I can't point to anyone specifically, no." Her cell phone on the bar rang, and she went over and looked at it. "I need to get this. It's an important call from a new distributor. If it works out, it could really help us."

"You'd better take it then. Thanks, Camille, and good luck with everything."

"*Merci*, Willow, *merci*." Camille blew me a kiss good-bye.

"Something's up," Simon said as we walked out the door.

"What do you mean?"

"Simon noticed that they had a lot of inventory," Jackson said.

"Doesn't that make sense since the wineries have just harvested and bottled most of their wines?"

"Not that much of a reserve, and not from last season," Simon said. "We certainly don't have that kind of volume left over. It can only mean one thing—that it's just not selling."

"The wine tasted pretty good to me," I said. "But I'm no expert."

"It is good, not as good as ours, but right up there. I don't get it."

"She got that call from that new distributor. Maybe that will help, but she did say that Carter wants to sell.

They've had a lot of bad luck this year. That's why Sims was here."

"He did say he was exploring his options," Simon said.

"But she doesn't want to sell," I said. "She said something about working on a new solution, but she changed the subject before I could get any details. She did say that they had lost their winemaker as well. So I wonder if they've approached Gerald, too." I noticed something near the corner of the building and walked over to see what it was.

"Terrific," Simon said. "That's all we need—our closest competitor stealing our number two winemaker with all our secrets."

"Don't panic," Jackson said. "You don't know anything for sure yet." The two of them walked over to me. "What are you doing, Willow?"

"Checking this out." I pulled out my phone and took a photo. "If I'm not mistaken, this is poison hemlock."

chapter twelve

Before anyone at the vineyard could see me, I plucked part of the plant off and shoved it inside my jacket pocket. Then we scurried to the car.

"If that's real, it means that Camille or Carter could have done it, tried to kill David to get him out of the way, and killed Amy instead," Simon said as he pulled out of the winery, took a left onto the cement road, and headed east again.

"I'll need to take a closer look first."

Jackson grabbed his phone and did a search. "When you get up there a bit, pull over so Willow can examine the plant and try to match it to this." He held up a photo of poison hemlock.

"Will do," Simon said. Moments later, when we reached the end of the road that fed back to Route 48, he pulled over onto the dirt shoulder.

Once we'd stopped, I carefully took the plant out of my jacket pocket and examined it. "Can I please have the phone?" Jackson handed it to me and I considered the two plants, the one in my hand and the one on the screen.

"Do you think it's the real thing this time?"

"Well, is it? Is it poison hemlock?" Simon leaned over to try to see.

"Yes, this time it is. I'm sure of it." I showed the plant to Jackson and Simon and held up the plant. "Do you two agree?"

Jackson nodded. "Looks right to me."

"Me, too," Simon said.

"Since Crocker Cellars is operating in the red, Camille and Carter do have a motive to kill David," Jackson said. "Getting rid of him won't affect the two-hundred-K prize from the competition, which it seems like they desperately need, but it would put a big dent in their main competition, which is Pure, and boost their sales in the long run."

"You said they were good, Simon," I said.

"It's true," Simon said. "Besides us, they are the most recognized vineyard out here, with the most awards even in the short time they've been open. Just like us, really."

"Which means they had good reason to be threatened by David, and Pure, and the most to lose by coming in second," Jackson said. "Think about it. If you're way back in the pack with no hope of succeeding, it doesn't make much sense to take out your main competition, but if you're running neck and neck, it might."

"It's even possible that if David were dead, it might sway the *Wine Lovers* judges to vote for the Crockers instead," I said. "You never know what will change people's thinking. It might have been a risk that the Crockers thought was worth taking."

"Not to mention that Carter's supercompetitive," Simon said. "Did you see how he tried to rub in that sale of Chambertin in my face? I saw that sale, I could have scored big online, but I was busy with other things."

"Forget it," Jackson said. "There will always be another bottle of expensive wine to chase. You'll get it next time."

"Sure you will," I said. "But I'd like to drop this off at the EEAC."

"In English?" Simon said.

"The East End Agricultural Center. It's on the way back and I'd like them to check it. Let's be one hundred percent sure." I opened Simon's glove compartment, which was neat and tidy and held only the driver's manual. "I'm going to put it in here for safekeeping for now."

"Okay, we'll drop it off," Simon said. "But didn't we need to check out a few other places today—you know, pass the cork, as they say, from one winery to another? We might even get a free tasting."

"Do you have the cork from Crocker Cellars?" Jackson said. "You'll need it to give it to the next winery to get your drink."

"Well, no," Simon said.

"Then you'll have to pay your own way," Jackson said. "But we know you can afford it."

"Because you told us so," I said, and smiled at Simon.

"Yeah, yeah, okay. Where to next?"

We arrived at St. Ives Estate Vineyards, in Peconic, a few minutes later. While Crocker Cellars took its inspiration from all things Tuscan, Derek Mortimer, the owner and vintner at St. Ives, had re-created a traditional granite cottage common to his native seaside village of St. Ives, in Cornwall, England, for his tasting room. Up the road past the cottage, he'd gone even further, building two guesthouses for visitors, an elaborate English garden, and even a medieval castle that would be right at home in a Masterpiece Classic TV show.

The castle had caused a furor when he had proposed building it, but after he gave part of the acreage to the Nature Conservancy and scaled down the size, the plans were accepted by the Town of Southold. Since then, his castle had been featured in lots of glossy lifestyle magazines and on home-and-garden TV shows.

We found Derek Mortimer inside the tasting room, dressed in a three-piece suit and pouring a glass of burgundy for a visitor. The tasting room featured a fireplace that took up one entire wall, rugs on the stone floors, medieval-looking sconces and chandeliers, and a round oak table with all the wines on offer. A TV in the corner ran a short documentary about the vineyard; the building of the castle, tasting room, and guest cottages; and the English garden here, and a look back at Mortimer's first vineyard in Cornwall, Heath Estate Cellars, which he still ran with an on-site partner. Mortimer finished with his customer and came over to us.

"Mr. Lewis, what are you doing here, away from Pure on this busy North Fork UnCorked! week? Shouldn't you be close to base?"

"Just thought I'd stop in with my friends," Simon said. "This is Willow McQuade and Jackson Spade."

"Aren't you the one who catered that ghastly affair

on Sunday? I felt so horribly for poor Amy. She was my favorite in that family."

"Yes, it's very sad," I said. "And we're trying to find some answers."

"Isn't that what the police are for? Besides, I've already spoken to them, and I couldn't tell them anything of interest." Mortimer walked back over to the tasting bar and opened a cigar box. "Care for one? You, too, Willow, I don't discriminate." He smiled and plucked a cigar out of the box, clipped off the end, and lit it.

"I think we're all good," Simon said.

"How do you like my little estate—and my castle? I didn't see any of you during those dreadful village planning meetings. The town was all up in arms; they were against me, you see, but we made a compromise and it all worked out." Mortimer puffed on the cigar, which quickly filled the room with smoke and made me feel quite ill. I moved toward the window, which was open an inch. "When I wake up in the mornings, if I didn't know better, I'd swear that I was at home in Cornwall. Although the air doesn't smell the same and I do prefer our lovely beaches—"

"Mr. Mortimer," I interrupted, "we were wondering if you saw anything on the day of the party. The police think, and so do we, that David Farmer was the real target, because, you see, Amy ate his scallop appetizer."

Mr. Mortimer seemed baffled. "You mean she just took it off his plate?"

"No, he offered it," Jackson said. "And the greens on top turned out to be poisonous."

"Oh, dear, I didn't hear that." Mr. Mortimer puffed a few more times. "That is truly awful."

"Did you notice anything at all?" Simon said.

"That Gerald chap seemed pretty annoyed, and didn't David's family show up, too? David got punched in the face."

"Since then, there have been two attempts on his life," Jackson said. "One in the barn, and another at Simon's restaurant, Salt, in Greenport."

"I don't know anything about that. What a terrible business."

"Have you heard anyone mention that they were disgruntled about Pure or about David?" I said.

"I think everyone knows that Pure is the one to beat, so yes, I think there is some envy and jealousy in our little community. Do I think it would drive anyone to murder? I really can't say."

"What were you two doing?" Simon said, when Jackson and I got back in the car.

"Willow wanted to look around for any poison hemlock so I was talking to Mr. Mortimer. On a hunch, I decided to ask him if Leonard Sims had tried to buy St. Ives, and he said, 'No, not in years. He knows better than to come back here.'"

"That's interesting," I said. "Did they have a fight or something?"

"He wouldn't say. Loose lips sink ships and all that, but it seems like Mr. Sims is not well liked around here."

"Big surprise," Simon said.

"Did you find anything, Willow?" Jackson said.

"No, but I also didn't have time to look all over the English garden. We'll have to come back tonight."

We stopped at the East End Agricultural Center next, to drop off the poison-hemlock plant I'd found. The center was located in a white Victorian building on the main road a mile or so west of Cutchogue village, with offices on the main floor and a counter that separated the front of the room from the desks scattered in back. The high-beamed ceiling featured skylights, and the late-afternoon sun slanted in and made squares on the floor, while dust motes circled in the air. It had the feel of an old library and did have an extensive research library on the flora and fauna on the East End.

I spotted Sara Fletcher working at her desk in the back and called her over. Sara, in her late twenties, had shoulder-length blond hair and with her distinctive black glasses looked like the biodiversity researcher and expert in viticulture she was, with a PhD from Cornell University. She'd started working here last year, and I'd met her when she'd taken a tour through Aunt Claire's Memorial Medicinal Garden. She was also pretty, with a knockout figure, which I knew would register with Simon.

She gave us a smile and took off her glasses. "Willow, and Jackson! Good to see you!"

Simon gave her a rakish grin. "And I'm sorry we haven't met before. I'm Simon Lewis, I own the Pure Winery in East Marion. I'm also a TV writer, executive producer, and screenwriter."

"Wow, well, I just love your grapes and your wine, Simon. You've chosen well. Falling Leaves is a real winner."

"We think so, too. Just waiting for Sunday night. Will you be there?"

"I'll be there, and even though I'm not supposed to say, I'm rooting for you to win."

"We appreciate your support. Perhaps we can share a glass of wine together? And of course I'd love to give you a tour of Pure when you have time?"

Jackson rolled his eyes, and I smiled.

"Yes to both, thank you, Simon." She turned to me. "So, Willow, how can I help you?"

I pulled the plant out of my jacket pocket and put it on the counter. "I found this and I was wondering if it's poison hemlock."

Sara leaned over to look at it. "It's pretty common around here. Grows like a weed, you know." She grabbed a book from under the counter, opened it to a page with a glossy photo of poison hemlock, and slipped her glasses back on. She studied it for a few moments before saying, "It looks like the real thing to me."

"How come you never told me about Sara?" Simon said as he pulled back out onto the main road, Route 25, and headed east. Our next and last stop for today was Ramsey Black's office in New Suffolk, just south of Cutchogue village, and only minutes away. "She's smart, and beautiful, and a real knockout."

"I didn't know you were looking," I said.

"I'm always interested in meeting someone new, and let's face it, we have a lot in common."

"She thinks you're great and your wine is great and so do you. True," Jackson said, and laughed.

"You two are always giving me a hard time. I should ask for my check back, not that I would," Simon said, petulant.

"You can take on Hollywood but you can't handle us? I remember how you'd deal with studio and network heads, the writers, the cast and the crew. You're tough."

"Yeah," Jackson said. "C'mon. We're the Three Musketeers, remember?"

"You're right, and so is Sara, I'm amazing." Simon laughed. "And so are we."

"We make a good team," I said. "We've learned a lot today already. And we'll learn more tonight at the bonfire and movie at Sisterhood Wines and going back to St. Ives."

"But for now, we need to see Ramsey Black," Simon said. "Should I call ahead?"

"No," I said. "We're almost there."

We pulled into the driveway that led to Ramsey Black's office on New Suffolk Avenue in New Suffolk. The road circled through the woods and up a large hill, and when we parked and got out and looked east, the view of the Peconic Bay was nothing short of spectacular. But the parking lot in front of the yellow

Craftsman-style house with a large porch was empty, and it didn't appear that anyone was around.

"We should have called," Simon said once we reached the porch. "He's not here, or anyone else."

"It doesn't look like it," I said, looking in the window. The lights were off, and the three desks usually manned by Ramsey and his two associates were empty. "Which makes sense since it's a Thursday afternoon during North Fork UnCorked! week, but we could still look around."

"Willow? What are you thinking?" Jackson said. "I'm not helping you to break in."

"I will," Simon said. "I need to know who tried to kill David and, despite his new bodyguard, may try again, not to mention sabotaging our entire business. We may find some answers in there." Simon turned the door handle and it opened. "Hey, we got lucky. These country folk don't lock their doors."

"I do," I said. "Maybe they forgot. Or they'll be right back."

"Then we'd better be quick."

"I'll keep a watch out and text you if someone is coming back." Jackson walked back to the car.

"Thanks, buddy," Simon said.

"Thank you, honey."

"No problem." Jackson threw us a wave.

Ramsey's desk was near the front window and overlooked the porch with a view of the bay. Two files were on the blotter, and a large envelope; both his in-box and out-box were empty, and the computer was missing. I glanced around at the other desks, which had no computers either, leading me to believe that they all used laptops. The folders only contained the schedule of tastings and events this week and W-2 forms for the two employees.

So I moved on to the large envelope, which had been sent via FedEx from Nora Evans at *Wine Lovers* magazine to Ramsey Black at this address last week. He'd opened it, so I carefully pulled the flap back and pulled out several back issues of the magazine, along with a letter from the editor:

Ms. Nora Evans
Editor in Chief, Wine Lovers Magazine
1414 Broadway, Suite 505

New York, NY 10020
10/15/2015

Dear Ramsey:
It was a pleasure speaking with you yesterday. I agree that the front-runners in the competition are, in order, Pure, Crocker Cellars, and Farmer's Wines, followed by Sisterhood Wines, St. Ives, and Wave Crest.

But of course, it's essential that we keep an open mind. Once we begin the tastings at the Pure vineyard on Sunday, October 25th, and visit the other wineries in the competition the following week, we will come to a final decision as to who is the winner of the monetary prize, the award, and the four-page photo spread.

In the meantime, I enclose back issues of our magazine to give you a better idea as to content and style. Since we are a quarterly, I'm thinking that I'll do a Q & A with you about your role at the East End Wine Council and your background, along with a profile of the winner either by me or a freelancer for the April 2016 issue, to kick off the Spring/Summer. We can talk details after the competition is completed.

Best,
Nora Evans, Editor in Chief, Wine Lovers Magazine
212-555-1212
www.farmtotablemag.com

"Simon, take a look at this." I handed the letter to him.

"Wow, this is good news." He smiled. "But I don't like the fact that they mention Crocker Cellars and Farmer's Wines. I knew Walter and Kurt's stuff was good, but not that good. That makes me nervous."

"I think it's interesting that the vineyard owners who were at the Pure party and at the funeral are all mentioned and, coincidentally, are the ones we've been checking. It makes me think we're on the right track. Maybe it is business and not personal." I took the letter, put it on top of the stack of magazines, slid it all inside, and replaced the envelope on the stack of folders. "Did you find anything?"

"No. Did you check the desk drawers?"

"No. You check the left side, and I'll check the right."

"Nothing here," I said, finding copy paper, tape, and pens.

"Ditto. Just office supplies. Check the middle one."

I pulled open the top drawer.

"Hey, that's Ivy's." Simon picked up a silver bracelet embellished with grape clusters and twisting vines. "David gave that to her last Christmas. She must have left it here, or at his house. If we had any doubt, this is proof that something's going on between them."

"Yes, but what's this?" I pointed to a small jewelry case.

"Is it an engagement ring?"

I picked up the tiny box and flipped the top open. Inside, resting on velvet fabric, was a silver engagement ring, with a big diamond. "Wow, this is beautiful." I examined the inscription. "But it's not for Ivy. It says, 'MP, Yours Forever, RB.'"

"Can I see it?" Simon said.

I handed the ring to him, and pulled out my phone. "Jackson just sent me a text to get out. We need to go." I glanced out the window and no one was there, but I guessed that he didn't want to take any chances.

I held out the box and Simon placed the ring back inside. "I don't get it. Who is MP?"

chapter thirteen

On the way home, we filled Jackson in on Nora's letter and the bracelet and engagement ring. All of it was intriguing, although the content of the letter was much clearer than who *MP* was. But we'd have to find out.

In the meantime, I'd planned a fun evening for Jackson and me—movie night at Sisterhood Wines, where we might also be able to gather information. Throughout the summer Carla had hosted a film festival of classic movies every Thursday night, and she'd saved the best for the last one of the season: Alfred Hitchcock's *North by Northwest*, starring Cary Grant. Instead of using a traditional movie screen, however, she'd painted the side of one of her barns white and projected the films onto it.

Carla provided the wine, but we brought along organic popcorn and Honest Tea, along with blankets and chairs, and water for the dogs. We'd scored good seats in the front, and the dogs, Qigong, Columbo, Rockford, and Zeke, tired from a long walk around town and playing together, napped under a woolen blanket. Carla had also placed heat lamps throughout the seating area.

We dressed in jeans and sweatshirts and sneakers because we wanted to be comfortable. We also planned to stop by the St. Ives Estate Vineyards afterward to look for any poison-hemlock plants and needed to be in activewear to move.

As for investigating tonight, Simon was hosting a wine tasting at Salt, another North Fork UnCorked! event in town, and our suspects, Ivy and Ramsey Black, Gerald, the Crockers, Derek Mortimer, and the Farmers, were absent. I'd wanted to chat with Carla about her relationship with David, but she'd been busy with her guests.

Jackson and I both loved this movie—and Hitchcock films in general—so I decided that I'd take a break from the case and just enjoy watching it. But I couldn't help but notice when David got up and followed Carla around the side of the barn right after the film started at eight o'clock. Scott Peters, his bodyguard, followed.

Twenty minutes after that, when a drunk Roger O. Thornhill, aka Cary Grant, almost died in a fiery car crash, my assistant, Lily, drove in, screeched to a stop in the parking lot, jumped out, and ran around the barn.

"That looks like trouble," I said. "She went to talk to David."

"Should we go over?"

"I will. Can you stay here with the dogs?"

"Sure, text me if you need me." Jackson squeezed my hand.

When I rounded the corner of the barn, Lily was

yelling at David. "You told me you were done with her! And here you are!"

David looked befuddled. "I don't understand. What are you doing here?"

"A friend of mine saw you two together and texted me, so I came down."

"Just calm down, miss," Scott said. "It's okay."

"No, it isn't," Lily said, crying. "You know that I love you, and you do this."

"Carla and I are just friends now, nothing is going on. Right, Carla?"

But Carla suddenly looked uncomfortable. She didn't answer.

Lily lunged at David and pummeled his chest with her fists. "You are a bastard and a liar!"

"I'm calling the police, David," Scott said, pulling her off, then taking out his phone. "This girl is out of control."

I grabbed her arm. "Lily, I thought that this was over."

"It was, but then . . ."

Carla looked at David. "Is this true? Did you two hook up again?"

"David?" I said, giving him a hard look.

"This is none of your business, Willow," David said.

"That's true, but this is a complicated situation, and you know that I'm just trying to help both of you."

"I know and I'm sorry," Lily said.

"You should be," Carla said.

I pulled Lily into a hug. "Lily, I know you're upset, but you've got to get yourself together. The police are already interested in you. This will just make things worse."

She pulled away from me and wiped her eyes. "It doesn't matter. The only thing I care about is David."

The police arrived a few minutes later and took down statements from all of us about what had happened. When Detective Koren arrived, he went a step further and took Lily into custody. Her face was blank as he led her to the car. I told her I would call her lawyer immediately.

Movie night was ruined, so Jackson and I decided to head back to St. Ives Estate Vineyards a little earlier than planned to check for poison hemlock. We really needed to figure out what was going on, now that Lily was back in custody. I had wanted to question David, but Scott hustled him off. So we packed up our stuff, put leashes on the dogs, and headed back to the truck.

Jackson had parked in front of the tasting cottage, and once the dogs were inside the truck and we'd packed the blankets and chairs in the back, I said, "I'm just going to take a quick look to see if there is any poison hemlock here. The way Carla was acting, I don't think she's okay with being 'just friends' with David. It was obvious that David and Lily hooked up again, and Carla didn't know anything about it. Maybe this happened before with Lily or someone else, and she got fed up and tried to kill him."

"Okay, use this." Jackson handed me his flashlight. "But keep it low to the ground or she'll see you. Be careful."

"I will. Back in a bit." Using the flashlight, I stepped through the wet grass and circled the tasting shed first, then the barn, and finally Carla's farmhouse, but didn't find anything.

But on the way back, I spotted familiar-looking tall plants at the end of a row near the parking lot. Keeping the flashlight down, I swept it across the ground, watching where I walked since it was so uneven, until I reached the spot. There, entangled in the wires that trained the vines, were four poison-hemlock plants in a cluster. Using the flashlight, I scanned the plants. By now, I knew what the real thing looked like, and this was it. I headed back to the truck.

"It's here, she has it, too," I said as I climbed into the truck, and the dogs jumped up and kissed me.

"So she's definitely in the pool of suspects," Jackson said. He backed out of the lot and took a left, then a right onto Route 48. We rode along in silence for a few miles before he said, "Willow, please don't get upset, but are you sure that Lily could not have done this? Tried to kill David and killed Amy instead? From what you said, she sounded pretty unhinged."

I thought about it for a moment. "She was upset, but I think it's because she really loves him. And I don't think, despite what's happened and how he's acted, that her love has turned to hate. I say we keep looking."

"That's good enough for me. Let's go to St. Ives."

Jackson parked across the street from St. Ives, and after we cracked the windows, covered the dogs with blankets, and said we'd be right back, we locked the truck and headed into Derek Mortimer's estate. We had no idea what kind of security was present, so our plan was to get in and out quickly, so the dogs wouldn't be alone for long.

Having access to poison hemlock, especially when it seemed to be ubiquitous on the East End, might not be damning evidence on its own for a suspect, but it had to be considered, along with other factors. So we went through the gate next to the tasting cottage and headed directly for the English garden that Mortimer had created.

Beyond it, the light gray stone castle, a scaled-down version of Queen Elizabeth's Balmoral Castle in Scotland, stood watch over the grounds, as clouds moved through the air above the towers and the turrets. Keeping the flashlight low, we moved quickly down the paths featuring flowers, bushes, and trees, many of which were now dormant, and checked for poison-hemlock plants.

"I don't see anything, do you?" Jackson said as he swept the light across a large grouping of Montauk daisies, sedum plants, and a grouping of the edible plant lamb's-quarter. It bloomed in the summer, and the green leaves with a white mealy coating were rich in iron, calcium, beta-carotene, and vitamin C. I liked to make a tea by pouring a cup of boiling water over two generous tablespoons of fresh leaves and steeping for ten minutes. Afterward, I cooled the remaining tea and put it in a compress for headaches and sunburn.

"I see edible plants but no poison hemlock, and

those plants are hard to miss. Should we go? I don't want to leave the dogs alone too long. Plus, it's getting cold."

"Just one more row to go," Jackson said as he reached the head of the path and took a U-turn past large pots of mums and a giant pumpkin and headed back to the street. We made it to the large stone fountain at the end of the path, before the tasting room, when suddenly floodlights above the castle gate flashed on, and the sound of barking dogs shattered the silence.

"We'd better move it, McQuade—run!"

Jackson grabbed my hand and we took off, hoping to reach the gate by the tasting room before the dogs caught us. But the grass was wet, and I went down.

"I've got you," Jackson said, helping me up. "Let's go!"

We ran as fast as we could, covering the ground quickly but maybe not fast enough, because the sound of the dogs' barking and growling was getting closer—in fact, they were now just behind us.

I took a chance and glanced back. About ten yards in the distance were what looked like jaguars, not dogs, big, black, and menacing. "They're getting closer!" I said. "I think they're Dobermans! And they're huge!"

"Don't think about it. Just run!"

We double-timed it, but moments later I slipped again. I hit the ground hard and almost took Jackson down with me. But although he stumbled, he didn't fall, and reached down to help me up.

"You okay?"

"I'm fine."

"Okay, let's go, almost there."

He swept his flashlight toward the gate, and we started running again. Suddenly, I spotted it. "The plant! I see it! It's there by the gate! How did I miss it?"

"Forget the plant! Move, McQuade!"

With speed I didn't know either of us possessed, we covered the last few yards and made it to the gate. While Jackson flung it open, I grabbed part of the poison-hemlock plant and tried to tear a piece off.

"C'mon!"

Jackson took my arm and tried to pull me through the gate, but I resisted.

"I've got to get it!" I plucked off a few leaves and part of a stem.

"Willow!" He stepped back, lifted me up, and carried me through, using his foot to slam the gate shut behind us. A moment later, the Dobermans reached the gate and jumped on it, barking, snapping, and growling, mouths wide, spit flying through the air. Our dogs were barking, too, and lights were going on in the nearby houses. We ran across the street, through the inky darkness, jumped into the truck, and took off, leaving the cacophony of the night behind us.

When I woke up early Friday morning and got out of bed, my body protested. I'd gone down hard more than once in Derek Mortimer's English garden, and now my muscles were sore and cramped. I also felt anxious about Lily and her fate now that she was back in jail. So while Jackson slept, I drew a hot bath and emptied in a cup of Epsom salts. Once the tub was full, I added ten drops each of lavender, patchouli, and jasmine essential oils to the water. Immediately, the blissful aroma filled the room and I felt myself relax. Inhaling essential oils through the nose in the practice of aromatherapy works because it stimulates the part of the brain—the olfactory system—that is connected to smell. In turn, a signal is sent to the limbic system of the brain, which influences the endocrine and nervous systems in the body.

The tub was so relaxing that I found myself almost drifting back to sleep, but Jackson, wearing jeans and a T-shirt, padded in and woke me up. "Hey, why didn't you invite me in?" He leaned down to give me a quick kiss. "We like a good bath, don't we, boys?" The dogs wagged their tails and pawed at his pant legs. Qigong put his paws on the bathtub and tried to drink the bathwater. "No, Qigong, down, boy."

"Falling last night took its toll, so I thought I'd try a hot bath. But I need to get out and get going. Did Lily text me? I'm worried about her."

Jackson took my towel from the back door and handed it to me. "No, but Shawn Thompson, her lawyer, did. She's still in jail, they are still questioning her, but he's hoping to get her out by lunchtime."

As I toweled myself off, I said, "She never should have gone to Carla's, or the funeral. She needs to keep a low profile. I'll have to talk to her. But between the attack on David at Salt and the funeral and our outing yesterday, I haven't had time."

"So what's the plan for today? I've checked in at my place and everyone is doing okay, and we aren't expecting any new arrivals, but that could change, of course."

I put the towel back on the door and got dressed in jeans, a long-sleeved white Nature's Way T-shirt, and vegan sneakers. "Since we can't do anything to directly help Lily right now, and we'd planned on going to the Vines and Canines guided walk at Wave Crest Vineyard at noon, we could use some of that time to talk to Harrison." Harrison Jones, the owner, was a friend of ours. "He can give us the scoop on Ivy and Amy, since they grew up together as teenagers. He went to BU with them and David, too. With what Ivy's grandmother had to say, about her always getting her way, I want to learn more about the Lord family dynamics."

We arrived at the Wave Crest Vineyard at twelve thirty and headed down a cypress-tree-lined driveway to the parking lot, which overlooked the Sound. The main building, surrounded by vines, was modern, clean, and white, with glass walls and solar panels on the roof. The wine cellar, where the vintages matured, was connected through sloping tunnels to the contemporary structure above with its offices and tasting rooms.

The Vines & Canines event was a self-guided tour through the vines and along a two-mile path that ran along the top of the cliffs. It also featured, inside a gated area in front of the tasting room, fun competitions such as cutest dog, dog who jumps the highest, and dog who looks the most like its owner, along with agility and earthdog events. All the proceeds went to local animal charities, including Jackson's.

Harrison spotted us and headed over as we got out of the car with all our dogs. In his late thirties, he had a beard and was dressed in cords, a turtleneck, a wool wrap sweater, and loafers. He'd made big money in Silicon Valley, and this was his third home, after Napa and L.A., where his wife, Julie Jones, worked as an up-and-coming actress and had starred in Simon's first TV show, *I.Q.*

After Simon bought his house here, Harrison and Julie came to visit. Harrison had wanted to move back here for some time and get involved in the burgeoning East End wine movement. So they bought a house on the water, and the land for Wave Crest. But his vineyard was small, a hobby, really—a way to create his own vintages to please himself first.

A huge animal lover, he held events of this kind whenever he was in town and often alerted the shelters and Jackson about animals that were in need. Harrison opened the gate and stepped out with his black Lab. "Willow, Jackson, thanks for coming by! This is Marshall. He's my latest rescue from the Southold animal shelter. This makes four so far, but who's counting? Certainly not me." Harrison smiled and scratched the dog behind the ears. His tail went ticktock, ticktock.

"Hi, Marshall!" Jackson and I said, and petted him, too.

"And look at your brood. One is cuter than the next. Who's the new fella?"

"This is Zeke," I said. "He belonged to Simon, but he just didn't have the time to put in as a pet parent."

Harrison made a face. "I hate to hear that. Getting a pet should never be an impulse purchase. I'll have to talk to him."

"I know, Harrison, believe me, we've tried. But Zeke's with us now and we're enjoying him."

"You're right, and good for you. Now, what would you like to do? Compete? Take a photo? Take a walk? I'm afraid Julie isn't here. She's up for a part in a new series and had to stay put in L.A."

"That's okay. A walk sounds good," Jackson said. "I can take the dogs if you want to talk to Harrison, Willow." Jackson grabbed all the leashes and headed toward the path along the cliffs. "C'mon, boys, you'll see Willow in a bit."

Harrison looked at me. "If you're here with me, and not with him and your pups, it must be something serious. What's up?"

"You know about my work as an amateur sleuth, right?"

"Sure do. Are you working on something now?"

"Yes, and I'm having trouble. The police think, and so do Jackson, Simon, and I, that Amy Lord was poisoned by accident at the Pure party."

"How so?"

"Amy ate one of David's appetizers, and it was poisoned. That's why we think she died."

"Poisoned with what?"

"Poison hemlock, and I've been checking the various vineyards out here to see if they had access. So far the places I've found it—at Crocker Cellars, St. Ives,

Sisterhood Wines, and even out behind Pure—all have people who didn't like David."

"What, you're checking me out?" He feigned insult.

"No, I needed to speak with you, get some background info."

"Okay, well, just so you know, I don't have it, and I like David but not Ivy. Simon can be a little out there."

"Yes, we know."

"But poison—that's really terrible," Harrison said. "Amy was always my favorite member of the Lord family. I would have been at the funeral but I had an important meeting in the city with a top exec from Silicon Valley about a big deal, and I just couldn't miss it. Not that Ivy and David and I were close, we didn't socialize or anything, but I was still in touch with Amy. Still, I felt terrible for the family. I did send flowers."

"That's what I'm wondering about, Harrison, the Lord family. I was talking to Ivy's grandmother, Emily Lord, at the get-together at Salt after the funeral, and she told me that David and Amy were originally a couple, not David and Ivy. She seemed pretty sharp and it sounded like the truth. What happened?"

Harrison turned to watch the dogs playing and didn't say anything for a long time. "She is sharp, and she isn't misremembering at all. But no one really talked about it. One minute, David and Amy were together, happily making wedding plans, and the next, it was off. By the next winter, he was with Ivy, and I have to say Amy didn't take it well at all. It took her a long time before she was her smiling self again."

"Do you have any idea about what might have gone wrong? Emily Lord intimated that Ivy is used to getting her own way. Maybe Ivy decided she wanted David and pushed her sister to the side? Is that possible?"

"It is, and it's what I was just going to say to you. Ivy has a stubborn streak, always has since we were friends as teenagers. They had a second home, really a mansion, down the block from our summer house in Orient. If we all wanted to go to the beach at the end of the block, and she wanted to go to the ocean instead, guess where we went? There was just no arguing with Ivy. I think it was tough for everyone, especially Amy. Then, when the grandfather, Walter Lord, died in 2012, and his fortune went to Ivy, along with total control of the estate after providing for his wife, Emily, of course it just made things worse. Overall, it's just a very dysfunctional family."

"With all that negative history and bad blood, it seems strange to me that Amy would choose to work out here with her former boyfriend and her sister."

"I think Ivy wanted her here, where she could keep an eye on her. She also had control of the finances, and I don't think Amy was strong enough to strike out on her own. So Ivy got what she wanted, again." Through the trees, I watched as Jackson slowly made his way down the path that crossed the cliffs, with the dogs running in front of him. "Looks like they're having fun."

"We're like you, Harrison, everything is better when the dogs are along for the ride."

"Why don't you go catch up with them?"

"Just one more thing. Did Amy ever mention that

she was involved with the winemaker at Pure? His name is Gerald, and he seems pretty torn up about her death."

"Yes, she did, more than once, but when I asked her if something was going on romantically, she said she didn't want to talk about it. Maybe she was afraid that if anyone—think Ivy—knew, she'd wreck it for her."

chapter fourteen

After my conversation with Harrison, I felt more confused than ever. Was the motive for David's almost
murder and Amy's accidental killing personal or business? On our way back to Nature's Way, I filled Jackson
in, while the dogs, now tired from their run, slept on
the seat between us. The sun had gone down, and the
temperature had suddenly turned colder, so I turned up
the heat for all of us.

"You're right, the motive could be either business or
personal," Jackson said. "On the personal side, maybe
Ivy wanted David out of the way to pursue a relationship with Ramsey. Business motive? She wanted to be
in charge, although she'd still have Simon to contend
with. Ramsey could have tried to kill David for her, or
for the both of them. So that would be personal. Maybe
the engagement ring was meant for her. But what does
MP mean?"

"Another personal-motive possibility? Gerald could
have tried to kill David because he wanted to be free to
pursue Amy without any chance they might get back
together."

"But he could also have wanted David out of the way so he could take the credit for Falling Leaves and be head winemaker," Jackson said. "So it could be business, too. Same goes for the Crockers, and maybe Derek Mortimer."

"True, all of them had access to poison-hemlock plants. And so did Ivy, Ramsey, and Gerald."

"Maybe Leonard Sims, the former owner, thought that by getting rid of David, Simon might sell," Jackson said. "So that's a business motive. But what about the Farmers? Would they really try to kill one of their own?"

"Depends on how deep the hatred and anger goes. Anything is possible."

"I guess we should check and see if they had access to poison hemlock as well."

I nodded. "You know, Carla Olsen could have a business and a personal motive to try and kill David. She wants to be number one and she also seemed pretty upset when Lily showed up last night. Let's stop by and see her. It's coming up."

When we pulled up, Carla Olsen, petite, with curly red hair, was sitting on the steps of her tasting room, smoking a pipe, wearing overalls over a T-shirt and red high-top sneakers, while two cats lounged on the deck behind her. "You'd better stay here with the dogs," I said to Jackson. "She's got cats, and most dachshunds see cats as prey."

"Don't I know it." Jackson pulled Zeke onto his lap

and grabbed Columbo's and Rockford's collars, so I could open the door. "These three would go absolutely nuts."

Qigong was super-mellow, and when I said, "I'll be right back, Qigong, stay," he snuggled up next to Jackson and promptly went back to sleep. "Same goes for all you guys."

Now that Jackson had the dogs under control, I walked up to Carla, who said, "Back so soon?"

"We were just at Harrison's Vines and Canines walk and thought we'd stop by on the way back. But we have three dachshunds that I think would go crazy over your kitties."

"I'm sure they would. So please don't let them out." She tapped her pipe out and went inside her tasting room, which looked like a log cabin both inside and out. A roaring fire was going in the fireplace, with seating provided by two comfy-looking overstuffed chairs, and her vintages were featured on a rustic-looking bar in the back of the space.

She had several prints of her vineyard on the wall, and a whole table full of marketing paraphernalia, from slickly produced four-color brochures with her on the cover to an expensive-looking catalog of her wines. I'd heard she had a background in PR and marketing in book publishing in New York.

"You've really done a lot to promote your winery. Not everyone is up to this standard."

"It's what I do." She pulled out a bottle of wine and poured two small glasses. "Would you like to try my latest vintage, Drunken Vines? It's the one I've entered in the *Wine Lovers* magazine contest." She held up the bottle. "I went for an antique-vintage vibe." The label featured a quirky painting of the tasting room with its bright red roof, and a stylized rendering of the name of the vineyard in gold letters.

"Very nice, and, yes, I'd love to try it." I picked up the glass and took a small sip. "It's very good. I'm partial to white wines myself."

"Me, too." She put the cork back into the bottle, but left it there. "So what's up, Willow? I know you didn't stop to talk wine. Is it about David . . . or Lily . . . or both?"

"I guess both. You probably don't know, but Lily is still in jail, although she's expected to be released."

Carla shook her head. "That girl is crazy."

"Crazy crazy, Carla? Or just crazy over David?"

Carla blew out a breath. "David, I guess. But there's no need, as you heard last night. David and I were together, but now we're just friends."

"Excuse me, but you seemed pretty annoyed at Lily last night if you and David are just friends." I took another sip of wine to be polite.

"Okay, maybe he ended it and I'm still not happy about it, but I'm trying." She put her finger on her cell phone and spun it around. "I just needed to talk to him last night is all, but between his best-bud bodyguard and his teenage lover, Lily, it didn't go well."

"You wanted to talk to him to see if you could get back together, right?"

She hesitated. "Yes, okay. I was trying to start things up again."

"With a guy who is married and has a girlfriend? Doesn't sound like there is much left over for anyone else."

"Probably not, but I'm used to crumbs, I guess. But after last night, I'm out. It's too much of a mess, and David has got to get his head straight. Between Lily, and that bitch of a wife, Ivy, and Amy dying, he's pretty messed up."

"I'm actually looking into Amy's murder for Simon and David."

"Yeah, I know, he told me. I don't know what you think you can do, though."

"For starters, I've been visiting other vineyard owners like yourself, and I've found something interesting."

"Like what?"

"Like the fact that you and Derek Mortimer and the Crockers all have poison hemlock on your vineyards. That's what was used to kill Amy."

"That stuff is all over the place, Willow, not just here. I spray for it, but it grows back." Carla pulled the cork out and poured herself more wine. "As for the Crockers, and Derek Mortimer, I could tell you some interesting things about them."

"Like what?"

"Derek Mortimer is a pretentious dandy who thinks he knows more about wine than all the rest of us put together. But given the fact that he almost went into business with Leonard Sims, he's not too bright."

"When was this?"

"When Sims was about to lose Pure, or as it was then, Vista View Vineyards, he needed help, and he went to Derek. He knew him from the East End Wine Council meetings. Derek seriously considered it, but before he did anything, he checked Sims's financial records and found out that he was deeply in debt, and his house was in foreclosure. He even owed money to several loan sharks in New York, which is how he ended up here in the first place. He was running away from his past. So the deal was off."

"So that's what Derek Mortimer meant when he said that Sims would never approach him again."

"Exactly. No way."

"And the Crockers?"

"Right before Sims sold the vineyard to Simon and David, or should I say to Simon and Ivy, Camille and Carter tried to lure David away. They offered him really good money, bonuses, the works. It would mean getting away from her, and more time for us—we'd just met then. But Simon matched it all, and more, so he stayed. Now, I hear that the Crockers' current winemaker just quit."

"Yes, she told me that. Who are they trying to hire?"

"Camille would love to get David, but she knows that he won't leave Pure, so she's going for the next-best thing, Gerald. But don't ask me how they're going to pay for it. Rumor is they had a lousy season last year, lots of expenses, mucho debt, and now Carter wants to pull the plug."

"How do you know all of this?"

Carla smiled. "I heard it through the grapevine."

"Right."

"It's very active out here." She tapped the phone. "I'm on this all day. You can't keep a secret for long."

On the way back to Greenport and Nature's Way, I told Jackson about my conversation with Carla. We both agreed that, yes, she was hung up on David—they had been an item for some time—but neither of us were sure that she had it in her to kill. Both of us found it interesting that Carla and probably most of the wine community out here knew about the Mortimer-Sims deal, and the Crockers' troubles. Jackson was just pulling into the back of Nature's Way when I got a text notice.

"Lily?"

"Yes, she says she's been released and is going home. No charges."

"It might be a good idea to text her back and tell her to stay away from David. It's only hurting her."

I quickly tapped out a text. "How about this?" I read it to him: " 'Please stay put and rest. DO NOT have any contact with David, until Amy's murder is solved, otherwise it will continue to draw the attention of the police. We are doing everything we can to clear you. I will update you tomorrow morning at the store when you come in. xo Willow.' "

"Sounds good."

I pushed send, but then began to worry. "I really hope that she listens to me, and she doesn't show up at David's talk and barrel tasting at Pure tonight."

"What's that about?"

I pulled up the North Fork UnCorked! website on my phone and scrolled to the Friday-night events. "David is giving a talk in the barn at seven o'clock explaining Pure's gravity-fed winemaking process, natural vineyard yeast fermentation, and how wine is barrel aged. Sounds pretty dry and technical."

"Yes, it certainly does." Jackson parked the truck.

I scrolled down. "Hey, Pure is also having a haunted Halloween maze for kids and adults. I forgot about that. It could be fun, right?"

"Sure, but I did want to try and catch the jazz concert in Mitchell Park." Jackson turned the ignition off, and the dogs started barking, wanting to go inside.

I picked up Zeke and helped Qigong to the ground, while Jackson took care of Columbo and Rockford. "We can do both."

When we got to the back door, he said, "Okay, if you really think we need to go to Pure."

"Yes, I think we should." I stared at the screen, waiting for the message to show that Lily had read it. But she hadn't. "We may need to run interference."

I had to hand it to David, when he talked about the technical and creative aspects of winemaking, he was in his element. Pure had drawn a good-size crowd—almost a hundred people—in the winemaking barn Friday evening, considering all the options in Greenport and at various wineries tonight, and David, in a denim shirt, a burgundy-colored tie, black cords, and loafers, held them rapt with his almost-poetic rhapsodizing about how grapes become wine.

Included in the crowd were a bored-looking Ivy, Ramsey Black, Gerald Parker, Leonard Sims, and surprisingly Camille and Carter Crocker, Derek Mortimer, and Carla Olsen. Fortunately, Lily had stayed home. Except for David's family, all our suspects were here. For this reason, Jackson and I stayed in the back to watch out for late arrivals and any trouble that could ensue.

By eight o'clock David had already covered gravity-fed winemaking, and how natural vineyard yeast fermentation worked, and was finishing up with the barrel-aging of wine. He walked over to the barrels that were stacked along the wall.

"Oak is an essential aspect of winemaking—from the type of barrel that is used to the size, age, grain, and treatment of the oak barrel, it all affects the way the finished wine tastes. And we have the Romans to thank for this.

"Before this, way back to the ancient Egyptians, clay amphorae were used to store and transport wine." He took out his phone and pulled up a photo of an ancient clay pot and showed it to the crowd. "But as the Roman Empire marched north into Europe, this process didn't work so well. But then they met the Gauls, who used oak barrels to transport their beer." David's phone rang.

"Excuse me." David flipped a toggle. "Sorry, I should have put that on vibrate."

The crowd laughed.

"Back to the Gauls. Now, not only was the oak tree easy to find in Europe, oak was softer, easier, and faster to bend, and waterproof because of the tighter grain. It also made the wine taste much better, giving it a smoother texture and imparting accents of spices like cloves and cinnamon, and flavors such as vanilla. The longer the wine remained in the barrels, the better it tasted. This fact transformed the way wine was made and enjoyed. Any questions?" David went to put the phone into his pocket, but something stopped him.

"What do you do to give Pure's wine a distinctive flavor?"

David kept staring at the screen.

Finally Simon said, "David?"

"Uh, I can't give away all our secrets." David handed the phone to Scott Peters, his bodyguard, who stood behind him. "But I can tell you that the principles used by the Romans are very much in use today . . . I don't know why someone is doing this. . . ." David stepped back.

"Let's go," Scott said, and took David by the arm and led him toward the door.

chapter fifteen

After Scott and David walked out, Jackson and I began to move through the crowd to the door, and Simon conferred with Ivy. Moments later, she reluctantly stepped in front of the crowd, dressed impeccably in a luxe-looking crème cashmere sweater, pearls, and velvet pants. "Hi, everyone." She smiled. "Not to worry. David, Simon Lewis, and Pure's winemaker Gerald Parker will be happy to answer your questions one-on-one after a short break. In the meantime, Gerald will pour barrel tasting samples, and you can also enjoy our current line of wines." She gestured to a large bar with several current vintages on top, a bartender ready to serve.

Gerald went over to a barrel and picked up a long syringe. "This is a new cabernet sauvignon for next season that I think you'll find very exciting." He extracted or "stole" a few ounces of wine at a time and poured it into a shimmering crystal glass that reflected the lights overhead and handed it to Camille Crocker, who was the first in line.

She thanked him, smiled, and took a sip. She

obviously immediately found it impressive, but she only said, "Nice, Gerald. Thank you."

As Jackson and I got closer to the door, Gerald continued to serve each in line, all the while chatting about the grapes chosen, the special blend, the concentration, the age of the wines, and Pure's criteria for the vintages created. He wasn't as charismatic as David, but he still put on a good show. I could see why the Crockers might want to steal him away.

"Our new wines will be bottled typically twelve to eighteen months from now. Our stock is always limited, and in high demand, so buying futures tonight will ensure you can add our new vintages to your cellar at a reduced price point," Ivy said. "It's an exclusive opportunity to taste tomorrow's wine today. So enjoy." Ivy stepped to the side to confer with Ramsey Black. But Jackson, Simon, and I skipped the tastings and went after David and Scott.

We found them in the main room's bar. David had already downed one beer and was working on another. Jackson gave me a knowing look.

"What the hell is going on?" Simon said.

David didn't say anything, just pushed his cell phone across the bar to us. There, on the screen, was his photo with a big X across his face and the words "Withdraw from the competition or you're DEAD!"

"I'm so sorry, David," I said. "Are you okay?"

"No, I'm not okay. First, I get these threats, then someone tries to poison me, run me down, and lock me in a freezer. I thought things would be different with Scott here, but it keeps happening."

"It's difficult to stop this kind of thing," Scott said. "Unless you want to go off-grid."

"No, no, no." David took another drink. "That's impossible."

I picked up the phone and scanned through his photos. He'd received several with what looked like a vineyard in the background from the person who'd been sending him threatening messages. There was a sign, but only part of it was visible—and the letters *ard*.

"David, have you looked at these photos? It looks like they were taken at a vineyard."

I showed the photos to David. "I know, but I don't recognize it."

I handed the phone to Simon. "Me either."

Since it was North Fork UnCorked! week, too much was at stake for David to go home, so a few minutes later—after drinking another beer—he got himself together and returned to the barn. Simon had forwarded the photo to Detective Koren, but besides that, the only productive and proactive thing to do was to continue our investigation and try to clear Lily and protect David. The best way to do that tonight was to mingle at the party ourselves, try to gather more information, and keep an eye out for trouble.

The barn had been decorated with tiny white lights along the rafters above, cornstalks in the corners, and giant pumpkins on the floor, and the guests milled around the area, with glasses of wine in their hands, to the sounds of jazz.

Clutches of conversation had quickly formed, and one of special note was with Camille and Carter

Crocker and Gerald. Camille now had a big smile on her face and was chatting happily to Gerald.

"So that's why they came," Jackson said. "It's pretty blatant."

"It sure is." Simon sipped a glass of Falling Leaves wine. "And I thought that Hollywood was a tough town. If they do make an offer, I'll have to stop it."

"The way you did with David when they tried to lure him away?" I said.

"Yes." Simon gave me a look. "Who told you that?"

"Carla Olsen. She seems to have the scoop on everything. Including the fact that Leonard Sims tried to partner up with Derek Mortimer of St. Ives to try to buy Vista View Vineyards, now Pure, before you did."

"That's old news," Simon said.

"But something we needed to know," Jackson said.

"I didn't think it was important," Simon said.

"Maybe not Mortimer and Sims, but it definitely shows that the Crockers are hungry for your talent." I looked over at Camille, who had on a faux-leopard-print car coat, jeans, and thigh-high boots, and her manicured hand on Gerald's arm. Carter was in his usual cowboy garb. "Who knows how far she'll go to save her winery?"

Simon narrowed his eyes. "I see what you mean, and I don't like it."

"It's too bad we can't get into Gerald's office again and try and find out."

"Maybe after everyone goes," Simon said, "I can get you in there." He scanned the room, then returned his attention to us. "You two look good, by the way. Best-looking couple in the room, I'd say." I hadn't given my

wardrobe much thought and had just thrown on a corduroy jacket over a beige shirt, and black jeans, while
Jackson had on a gray cotton shirt, jeans, and boots.
Simon, on the other hand, had on a tailored blue-and-
black-check suit, right out of *GQ*.

"Of course that wouldn't be true if Sara were here. I
invited her, but she was busy."

"So you're going for it," Jackson said. "Good man."

"Yeah, I like her."

Jackson's phone rang and he pulled it out. "It's
Shawn Thompson. . . . Shawn, what's going on?" Jackson put his arm around me and whispered, "It's going
to be okay. Shawn is good, Willow."

"Right," Simon said.

"Okay, thanks for the update." Jackson put his
phone back into his pocket. "Bad news. He thinks that
the police are close to charging Lily with Amy's murder."

"Oh, no," I said. "Why?"

"She's got means, motive, and opportunity. Detective Koren says that their investigation has led them to
no one else but her."

"So they're going to arrest her by default? Way to go."

"I hate to say it, but it sounds like Koren," Jackson
said. "He always zeros in on one suspect and that's it."

"Then we've got to show them that they're wrong."

"And quick, too," Simon said. "Shawn says they are
closing in."

"Which means that they'll have the wrong person in
custody, and a killer will still be on the loose." I sucked
in a breath. "This is a nightmare."

"I know it sounds kind of lame, but I've grown to

really like David, a lot. I'd hate it if something happened to him, beyond any effect it might have on the business."

"Simon, it's not lame," I said. "It's good that you care about him. In fact, I think it shows your growth as a human being."

"That's your influence, honey," Jackson said. "She's right, Simon, it's good."

"Gee, thanks, you two," Simon said. "I feel you two are like my moral compass. It's annoying, but true."

"Glad to be of service," I said. "Right, honey?"

"Sure, no problem."

"So there's a lot at stake, all around." Simon looked at Jackson. "Jackson, did you ask her about you know who?"

"Yes."

"Ask me what?"

"We were just wondering if you still think that Lily couldn't have done this."

"Yes. She's mixed up, yes, but I believe that she's innocent. Do you?"

"I told you last night that if it's good enough for you, it's good enough for me," Jackson said.

"Me, too." Simon put his arm around me. "We're good." Suddenly, he spotted someone across the room. "Oh, no. Guess who's here?"

"Lily?" I felt my stomach drop. Why couldn't she just stay away? I mean, I knew why, but still . . . not another scene, not now.

"No, Leonard Sims."

"What are you doing here?" David said, his voice carrying across the room.

We turned to see Leonard Sims, in a cheap-looking suit, at the entrance to the barn. But he hadn't been allowed access because Scott, David's bodyguard, had stopped him.

"We'd better try to defuse this," I said, taking Jackson's hand. "Simon, you keep an eye out for Lily. I don't want her causing a scene like last night."

"Okay, but get rid of him, pronto. We really don't need this right now."

When we reached them, David said, "I want you to leave now. I don't need any more harassment. We're not selling!"

"Leonard, why don't we go outside?" Jackson said.

"But I don't want to go." Sims made a face.

"Too bad." Jackson grabbed his arm and led him out the door.

When we got outside, the night air was cool, and the sky was clear and dotted with stars. Sound carried easily and we could hear kids laughing and screaming from the direction of the haunted Halloween maze. Simon had hired a local special-effects company and high school and college kids to dress up as vampires, ghosts, and zombies. It was supposed to be G-rated, but it sounded more like PG-13.

"What are you doing here, Sims?" I said.

"I came to hear his talk, that's all, and my wife is taking the kids through the maze. What's up with David tonight?"

"Someone has been sending him threatening texts and e-mails, and he received another one in the middle of his talk—which you were late for. Not to mention the attempts on his life over the past week."

"And you think I did it?" Sims looked flummoxed. "Now why would I do that? I want to buy the place back, and its value goes down the tubes if David loses it. It's his talent I'm buying. He's the biggest asset that Pure has. I wouldn't be interested in buying Pure back without him. I'm a businessman, not a killer."

"That may be true," Jackson said. "But I think it's best that you go, and keep your distance from now on. You've stated your interest."

"More than once," I said. "But I'm curious how you'd intend to pay for Pure or any other vineyard like Crocker Cellars when you've had big money problems in the past."

Sims narrowed his eyes. "Who told you that? Probably Carla Olsen, that gossip."

"I can't say."

"I may have had problems before, but I'm more than solvent now, thank you very much. Would you like to check my bank statement?"

"That won't be necessary," Jackson said. "And Simon will be in touch if anything changes here."

Fuming, Sims walked off.

When we went back inside, Simon waved us over.

"He's gone," Jackson said. "Hopefully, he won't bother you again."

"Good. Things are winding down a bit," Simon said. "If you can stick around, I'll try to get you back into Gerald's office."

Jackson checked his watch. "If we can, I'd really like to catch the rest of the jazz concert in Mitchell Park."

"You will. Just stay for a bit longer. I need you."

"Yes, you do." Jackson nodded in the direction of

the door, where Lily, wearing a jean jacket, a polka-dot blouse, and tan cords, had entered and made a beeline for David.

We told Simon that we'd run interference, again, and while he talked to a new distributor for Pure's wines, we went over to talk to David and Lily before things got out of hand. Already, Ivy, who was in a confab with Ramsey Black and Gerald, was shooting daggers in her direction.

"David," Lily said, "I need to talk to you."

"Not now, Lily." He walked across the room to get another glass of wine. Lily started after him, but I stopped her.

"Lily, no." I took her arm. "Didn't you get my text?"

"I'm okay, Willow. I just want to apologize to David for last night."

"Time for some tough love, Willow," Jackson said.

"You're only making things worse for yourself, Lily," I said. "If the police find you here, it will just reinforce their thinking. Simon talked to Shawn, your lawyer, just a few minutes ago, and the police think you tried to kill David because he left you. You have motive, means, and opportunity. You're their primary suspect."

Her face went white, and she sucked in a breath. "I knew it was serious, but they let me go today. I thought . . . I hoped that this was all going to go away. Because I didn't do it, Willow. No way. I'd never hurt him."

I put my arm around her. "We know that, but you need to leave."

"If I could just talk to him . . ."

"Not now," I said firmly. "Jackson, can you walk her out to her car? I'll keep an eye on things here."

"Sure thing," he said. "Be right back."

After they left, I went to find Simon, who was with David and Scott Peters, outside Gerald's office. "Where's Lily?" David said, slightly slurring his words. "I love that girl, you know."

Unfortunately, Carla Olsen and Derek Mortimer were tasting wine at the nearby bar. She wore a purple fleece jacket with jeans and boots, and he had on another conservative three-piece suit. Carla turned around, gave David a disdainful look, and said something to Mortimer, a man she supposedly disliked. He laughed.

"Sure you do, David, but she had to go," Simon said as he took David's wineglass away. "You need to cool it, man."

"I think that's a really good idea," I said. "David, why don't we go into the kitchen and I'll make you some coffee? Anyone else want some?"

"No, thanks, Willow. Some of us are sober," Carla said.

Mortimer touched her arm, said something, and they both laughed. Obviously, it had been difficult for her to hear David express his feelings for Lily. "Besides, I have to get into town. The Blue Crab is featuring my wines in a pairing tonight."

"Fab, darling. I'll go with you," Mortimer said, and turned to David. "Lovely talk, David. Your futures are,

well, rather interesting, but frankly I don't see any con-
tenders like Falling Leaves." The two of them headed
for the door.

"We'll see about that, Mortimer," David said. "You
hack."

Mortimer turned, gave him a smug look, then made
a pointed gesture with his hand and laughed, again. So
much for civility.

"David, coffee?" I said.

"No, thanks, Willow. I just want to get some fresh
air."

He walked out of the barn, stopped under a spot-
light, and lit a cigarette. Scott Peters followed him out
and they started talking.

"He's had one rough night," Simon said.

"He sure has."

Simon glanced inside Gerald's office. "He's going
home if you want to take another look. I'll cover for
you."

We watched as Gerald, Ivy, and Ramsey Black
headed for the door. Most of the guests had left by now
or had gone out to the Halloween maze, so it could be a
good time to snoop.

"But I don't have his computer password," Simon
said. "So we can't check his e-mail."

"I had an idea about that. What if it's something
simple, like 'Amy'?"

"Makes sense. Go for it. I'll tap three times on the
door if you need to get out."

After I checked to see if anyone was watching, I
slipped inside. The lights were off, but the computer
screen glowed blue brightly. First, I checked the files on

the desktop. The four new documents were the lineup for tonight's barrel tasting, the growing plan for next season's vintages, an order for supplies for such things as nutrients and fermentation acids, and a PDF of an elaborate new winepress.

Simon stepped in the room. "Anything new?"

"Not yet. You've got to keep watch."

"Okay." He went back outside and I clicked on Gerald's e-mail. The computer asked me for his password. Holding my breath, I inserted the letters *A-M-Y*. The screen flickered, and the e-mail account opened. Technically, I was hacking his account, but I wasn't looking for proof for the police but a clue to point me to a killer. I was okay with that.

Simon stepped in again. "What about now?"

"I'm in the e-mail account. Pay attention to what's going on out there, not in here, okay?"

"It's boring out here. I want to know what's going on."

"I know. But do it, Simon, please."

"Okay, stop nagging."

He stepped out again, and I quickly scanned the in-box looking for anything that was connected to the Crockers, other wineries, his dissatisfaction with his job at Pure, or Amy Lord. Halfway down, I spotted an e-mail with the subject line "CA Job Offer." I clicked it open and scanned the message, but it was from a vineyard in Napa Valley. Was he really considering moving back to the West Coast? The e-mail was marked read, but when I checked the sent folder, there was no reply. However, in the middle of that group of messages, I did spot a reply to Crocker Cellars.

Gerald Parker To: Camille Crocker
Re: Offer

Hi Camille—It was a pleasure meeting with you
and Carter this week. Thank you for your offer of
employment. I can certainly make time to meet
with you to discuss the details. However, I am still
considering all my options and will not be making a
decision until after Sunday's judging. I hope that this
is acceptable. Best, Gerald.

From: Camille Crocker icrocker@crockercellars.com
Sent: Thursday, October 29, 2015 2:38 PM
To: Gerald Parker
Subject: Offer

Dear Gerald: We would like to hire you for the
position of head winemaker at Crocker Cellars. Our
compensation package, including salary, benefits, and
bonuses, is extremely generous. Please let us know
the level of your interest and when we can set up a
time to meet and discuss the details. Best, Camille

Simon came back in. "Anything?"

"Yes, a vineyard in Napa Valley and Crocker Cellars
are interested in hiring him."

"Crap!"

"But he's not making a decision until after the judging on Sunday."

"Of course not. If we win, he wants to use that to up
his asking price. That bastard. Like I need this right now."

"I know, Simon. But try to remain calm. I want to check one more thing, and I'll be out. Is Jackson back?"

"Not yet."

"Okay, go." Simon went back out again, and I focused on Gerald's in-box. I pressed find and put in the word *Amy*, but I wasn't prepared for what I found. The messages kept scrolling until at final count there were 256. I didn't have time to go through all of them so I went to the first one, which was sent a week ago, last year.

Amy Lord To: Gerald Parker
Re: Today

Not yet. I'll go see him at lunchtime. Please switch
to phone messaging. Ivy seems super-suspicious.
Love, Amy

From: Gerald Parker gparker@pure.com
Sent: Thursday, October 23, 2014 9:32 AM
To: Amy Lord
Subject: Today

MP: :D Did you talk to Ramsey yet? Let me know.
Love, G

Jackson walked in. "Lily is on her way home. You need to finish up in here. There are still people wandering around."

"I know," I said, flummoxed by the messages. "But I just found 256 messages between Gerald and Amy dating back over a year ago."

"So they *were* involved." Jackson read the e-mail.

"Not only that, those initials, MP, are the same ones that were on the inscription on that ring in Ramsey's office drawer."

"Looks like Amy was seeing Ramsey, then became involved with Gerald."

"Right, and here." I pointed to the screen. "Gerald is asking Amy if she broke it off with Ramsey yet, using the MP moniker, and after that he added a smiley face. Maybe as an inside kind of joke." I began to scroll through the other e-mail messages as fast as I could.

"It's obvious she ended it because the engagement ring is still there, in Ramsey's desk."

I nodded. "First, Ivy takes away Amy's love, David, and marries him."

"But that's not enough for Ivy. After Amy breaks up with Ramsey, Ivy wants him, too. I just thought of something. Is it possible that Amy dumped David— not the other way around? That would make her less of a victim since she was making the choices first with David, and then Ramsey. Basically Ivy was taking her leftovers."

"Not from what Grandmother Emily Lord said. She seemed to think that Ivy had manipulated the situation so that she got what she wanted. It's possible she did the same thing with Ramsey. I really think Ivy's the bad guy here."

"She's certainly not very likable."

"No, she isn't." I scrolled down and scanned another e-mail. "The rest of the e-mails seem to be just back and forth about their daily lives and how much Amy and Gerald care for each other. But obviously she didn't want Ivy to know what was going on because she told him to switch to texting on their phones." I logged out of the e-mail account and made sure the desktop was as I'd found it.

"There might be a clause whereby employees can't get involved, so maybe Gerald needed to keep it secret, too."

"Maybe, but Amy was Ivy's sister, one of the owners. I'm thinking she could break the rules if she really wanted to. Now, as for the recent chain of events . . ."

"If Gerald did try to kill David, out of jealousy or whatever, and killed Amy by mistake, it would have been devastating."

"He seemed wrecked, but he's still able to look for new employment," I said. "So it's hard to tell if he's just mourning her death or feeling guilty about it."

"People do handle grief in different ways, you know."

"True, but I tried to talk to him at Salt after the funeral and he wasn't forthcoming. So I don't know how to find out what's going on."

"We could ask Ivy," Jackson said. "Or Ramsey."

"I don't know if we'd get answers from them either."

Jackson pointed at the computer. "By the way, how did you get into the e-mails in the first place? We didn't do that last time we were here."

"I decided to try something simple for the password. A-M-Y."

His eyes opened wide. "Now, that's good thinking, McQuade."

"I thought so." It felt pretty good.

But any self-congratulations stopped when Simon

ran into Gerald's office, panting and out of breath. He stopped in front of the desk and doubled over. "He, he's gone!"

"What do you mean? Who?" Jackson said. "David?"

Simon stood up and nodded as he sucked in breaths. "He's missing, and we have to find him!"

chapter sixteen

"Simon, slow down a bit—what are you talking about?" I said. "We just saw David outside with Scott a few minutes ago."

"Yeah, I just saw him. He was in front of Pure," Jackson said, looking around. "We'd better get out of here." He herded us out of Gerald's office and closed the door. "Okay, tell us what happened."

"David told Scott he was just going around the corner to make a call and he'd be right back," Simon said, bending over again, hyperventilating.

"Probably calling Lily," Jackson said.

"Yes, but when Scott went to look for him a few minutes later, he was gone."

I put my hand on his back. "Simon, breathe, slow down and breathe."

"We've got to find him," Simon said. "He got that message on his phone, and now this."

"Did you look in the main room, the tasting room, the bathrooms, and all the offices, even the B and B?" Jackson said.

Simon stood up and put his hand on his chest. "Checked, or being checked. So far, no David."

"What about the Halloween maze?" I said. "That would be a good place for him to hide."

"Or for someone to stash him," Jackson said. "We'd better have a look."

Jackson, Simon, and I headed across the field to the corn maze. Although the temperature had cooled off considerably—it was now 9:43 on Friday night—and a chilly nip was in the air, the moans of zombies, the cackle of witches, and the screams and excited chatter of visitors affirmed that people were still here and, hopefully, enjoying the event. Now, hopefully, it was where we would find David, before it was too late.

At the entrance to the maze, Dracula greeted us. "Hello, Mr. Lewis, doing a walk-through again?"

"Yes, we're looking for David Farmer. Have you seen him anywhere?"

"I haven't, but I just switched places with Marcy. She's at Creepy Goop Corner in the kids' section if you want to ask her. Do you need a map?"

"No, we'll be fine," Simon said, and led us inside.

"Do you know where you're going?" I said.

"Not sure. I came through in the daytime, when it opened at three o'clock. It was pretty scary even then. I'm not big on these things, but David and Ivy thought it could bring in revenue and raise our profile. So far, so good. The company I hired, East End Events and Escapes, has a good track record with these things.

They set it up and did all the hiring, so it was pretty turnkey."

"I think we need a map, Simon," I said.

"No need." He pointed to the red arrows on the ground. "We just need to follow this."

"What's the difference between the kids' section and the rest?" I said.

"One is for kids, the other is pretty hard-core. But don't worry, we'll protect you, right, Jackson?"

"I'll be fine."

As we turned the first corner, friendly mummies in clean white bandages greeted us, saying, "Welcome to the haunted Halloween maze, boys and girls! Have a ghoulishly good time!"

We moved along quickly, but one mummy kept pace and stayed right behind us until we came to Creepy Goop Corner, a booth painted in colorful Halloween colors, where a pretty witch with a pointy hat and a broom glued to her black shroud cackled and said, "Eat it up, my pretties!" She waved to Simon. "Hi, Mr. Lewis."

Kids who were dressed up as Harry Potter, Ariel, and the Hulk, with blindfolds on, stepped up and put their hands in the first bowl, which was full of cold spaghetti. "Put your hands in and feel gross guts!" The kids did so and screamed in delight.

"Marcy?"

"Just a minute, Mr. Lewis."

"This is cool!" Harry said.

"Ewww!" said Ariel.

"Okay, take your hands out." They did so, and she pulled the bowls out of the way and replaced them with bowls of grapes with oil. "Put your hands in! These are eyeballs from naughty children!"

"Gross!" the Hulk said.

"That feels sick," Harry said.

She pulled the bowls away and put new ones down. "And these are witches' boogers! Eat up!"

Ariel picked up what was a green Jelly Belly and put it down again. "No way!"

But the other two gamely popped the "boogers" into their mouths. "Hey, tastes good!" the Hulk declared.

"Marcy?"

"Finally, you are going to get a kiss from a wolf." In turn, she stroked their cheeks with a sliced dill pickle.

"Yucky!" Ariel said.

Harry Potter said, "Wolf germs!"

The Hulk just wiped his cheek off.

"Marcy, we're kind of in a hurry. Have you seen Mr. Famer anywhere?"

"Yeah, he came through here about fifteen minutes ago. He didn't say much, just walked in."

"Was he alone?"

She nodded. "Okay, kids, take your blindfolds off! Did you have fun?"

"Yesssssssssssssssssssssssssss!" they all yelled.

"Do you want to feel a brain?"

"Yessssssssssssssssssssssssss!"

Marcy pulled out a strawberry-colored brain under a glass bell jar and lifted the top. "Touch it if you dare!"

They all did and all exclaimed, "Gross!"

Simon turned to us. "At least we're on the right path. David's here, and he's alone. Although, where is Peters?"

"David could have given him the slip," Jackson said. "Although I'm surprised Scott let it happen."

We kept walking through the maze, maneuvering past kids, teenagers, and adults dressed in costume, as various friendly monsters, including zombies, mummies, vampires, ghosts, and witches, jumped out and tried to scare us. We moved past an old man who told silly ghost stories, pumpkins with pink wigs on stands, a neon butterfly bush, a face-painting station, blue-and-pink cotton-candy and popcorn stands, and a Gypsy fortune-teller. All along the route, kids and their families stopped to take family fun photos.

That all changed when we entered the area marked SUPER SCARY: TOO INTENSE FOR KIDS, and everything became more menacing, even though I took out a small flashlight from my purse. We knew we were in different territory when it became much darker, smoke started blowing, the red arrows on the ground turned to bloodstains, and a guy in a *Friday the 13th* mask pulled out a chain saw and chased us.

But that was tame compared to the army of bloody scarecrows with pitchforks that were straight out of "the Family of Blood" episodes of *Doctor Who*—Jackson was a fan—and the mad scientist who was operating on a monster's skull, not to mention the disgusting rotting corpses on the ground, with worms crawling all over them, and an elaborate abandoned cemetery with super-creepy zombies in rotting clothes, rising out of their graves to eat their favorite food, brains, or more brain-shaped Jell-O—this time lime flavored. Yuck.

"I'd stop and ask them about David, but they can't hear us," Simon yelled.

"Just keep going. If he's here, we'll find him," Jackson said, taking my hand as we walked across a bridge, low over a black pool of water.

"Jackson, are you scared?" I smiled at him.

"No, not a bit, McQuade. It's just a little loud is all. Are you?"

"Oh, yes, absolutely." My whole life was geared to natural, healthy green living, not noisy death and destruction. "I can't wait to get out of here!"

Simon had already crossed the bridge and yelled back to us, "Hey, move it, you guys. I think I spotted someone who looks like David, and Lily."

"Lily? Oh, no. Where?" I pointed the flashlight in Simon's direction.

"Over here," Simon said. "Throw me the flashlight!"

"No, you'll drop it," I said. "We're coming!" We were a few feet from the end of the bridge when a monster—actually a guy in a wet suit, a lizard mask, and a snorkel—jumped out of the water at us.

Despite knowing that it was fake and meant for entertainment, it startled me. Without thinking I jumped, fell against Jackson, and the two of us tumbled down into the shallow water with a big *splash!* The flashlight skittered to the bottom of the pond.

We dragged ourselves out of the pond and back onto the ground as Simon rushed over. "Are you guys okay?"

Jackson stood first, and the two of them helped me up. Thankfully, nothing felt as if it was broken.

Although tomorrow morning I'd probably be in an Epsom salts bath again. "I'm okay, but the flashlight is a goner. Jackson?"

"Finest kind. Now where did David and Lily go?"

"I can't be sure it was her or him, but I think they exited there." Simon pointed to an opening in the maze. "This is the end of the maze, and we've gone all the way through. Maybe he's back at Pure."

"Okay, so we either make our way across the field without a flashlight or go back through the maze."

"I vote for the field," I said. "I don't want to go back in there, and we think he went out this way."

"Agreed," Jackson said. "Let's go."

Simon pulled out his phone and put the flashlight app on. "Onward."

With only the tiny beam of Simon's flashlight to guide us, it was slow going across the fields and between the rows of vines. Finally, we made it back to the beginning of the maze and went inside Pure.

"Okay, David's car is in the parking lot," Simon said. "Did you see Lily's?"

"No, I didn't," I said. "I hope that she left already and she's not with David."

"So now what do we do?" Simon said.

"We'll have to do one more sweep. Then I think we need to let the police know he's missing," Jackson said. "Simon, why don't you take the offices here—Ivy's, David's, and yours—and the kitchen, check the freezer, to be sure. Willow and I will take the tasting room, the B and B, and go back to the barn, just in case."

"But no one is out there now," Simon said. "They left when we did."

"Let's just do a check, and then we'll reevaluate."

We split up and Jackson and I headed to the tasting room, but David wasn't there. We even checked behind the bar, and in the bathrooms. No David.

"He could have gone on foot to the main road and hitchhiked anywhere," I said. "But why not take his car?"

"I'm not sure that's what happened," Jackson said.

"What do you mean?"

"I have a feeling something is up again, like what happened at Salt and in the barn. First, the warning, then he disappears? Simon thinks he saw David and Lily, but maybe that was just wishful thinking. Let's check the B and B next."

But he wasn't there either. It was still relatively early, just ten thirty, and all the rooms were occupied by guests from out of town. As we walked out of the front door, Jackson said, "If Simon hasn't found him, then the barn is the last place we can look here tonight."

"I'll text him," I said, pulling out my phone.

Moments later Simon replied, No David. Meet you in the barn.

I texted back, K. "No David, he'll meet us." As I shoved the phone back in my pocket, I blew out a breath.

Jackson put his arm around me. "You okay, Willow?"

"No, I think you're right. Something's happened to David."

Jackson opened the barn door and we walked in. The

lights were still on, but no one was there. "Let's look around," Jackson said.

We checked Gerald's office and the bathroom and walked the perimeter, then moved between the racks of wine. "David? David?" I called. No reply. "There just aren't that many places he could be."

Simon ran in. "Is he here?"

"If he is, we haven't found him," Jackson said.

I looked around the room, at the racks, the cases of wine, the barrels where the tasting had been done. Where was he? Then we all heard something. . . .

Tap, tap, tap, tap.

"What's that?" Jackson said.

Tap, tap, tap, tap, tap, tap.

"Where is it coming from?"

Tap, tap, tap, tap, tap, tap.

"I think it's coming from over there." I pointed at a large silver vat in the corner.

"Oh my God," Simon said. "He's in the wine vat!"

I was closest, so I quickly ran over, climbed the stairs to the top of the tank, and threw it open. Inside was David, up to his neck in wine, his hair plastered to his skull, his face white. He was holding his arm. "David! You okay?"

"No, someone knocked me on the head and threw me in here. I think I broke my arm. Get me out!"

Much as I tried, I didn't have the strength to pull him out. I looked down at Jackson and Simon. "Jackson, can we switch places?"

"Come down, and I'll go up."

When I got back to the floor, Jackson started up, and I pulled out my phone. "I'm calling the police and 911."

"Do it," Jackson said. "Okay, David, try to remain calm. I'm going to get you out."

"If you drain the vat, it might make it easier. The batch is ruined anyway."

"Okay, how do I do that?"

"Simon knows. Tell him."

"Simon, David says to drain the vat."

"On it." Simon ran around the vat. "Done. Is the water level going down?"

"It is. It'll be empty in a minute," Jackson said. "David, you ready to try it?"

"Get me out of here," David said.

"Jackson, be careful, remember your back," I said.

"I'm okay." Jackson braced himself against the ladder, then he reached into the tank. "C'mon, David." They tried for a few minutes, but it didn't work.

"I just can't do it with my arm," David said.

"We need a ladder," I said. "Simon?"

"There might be one in the gardening shed, behind the B and B. I'll get it. I've got the flashlight." He ran out.

"He'll be right back, David," I said. "In the meantime, can you remember anything that happened?"

"I don't know. I decided to take a walk and took off. When I got to the maze, I went in, did the tour, and came out. I headed to my car, but then realized I'd left my keys in the barn. So I came in here. It was dark, and I reached for the lights. When I flipped them on, someone hit me, and I went down. Then they threw me in here, and I put my hands out to try and cushion the fall, but I ended up breaking my left arm."

"I wonder what they hit him with," I said. "I could take a look around."

"No, there might be trace evidence, although I doubt it after all the foot traffic in here tonight. Let's just wait. David is our top priority right now."

Moments later, Simon returned with an aluminum ladder, and Scott Peters. "Look who I found."

"Scott, where have you been?" I said. "David's in the wine vat and he's been hurt."

"I don't know. David was out front, and then he took off into the maze. I followed him through, but I lost him. It's pretty crazy in there."

"Funny, we made it through just fine," Simon said, an edge to his voice.

"Forget that for now," Jackson said. "Get me the ladder." Simon carried it over with Scott's help. "I hope it's long enough so he can get out."

"We'll try it and see," Jackson said. Simon and Scott handed him the ladder, and he lifted it up and put it into the tank. "Okay, David, now that the wine is drained out, make sure it's secure on the bottom, and I'll steady it from up here. When it feels stable to you, start climbing."

"I think it's good, Jackson."

Jackson grabbed the top section of the ladder. "Okay, I've got it up here. Start climbing. Just go slow."

"Coming up."

Moments later, David's head appeared, and Jackson grabbed his one good hand and arm. "Now you're going to move over the edge and come down."

Carefully, David maneuvered his way out of the tank and onto the ladder. Jackson climbed back down and spotted David as he did the same. When he got down, he collapsed, but Jackson caught him before he hit the floor. "He's out. Call 911 and tell them to hurry up."

But before I could take out my phone, the paramedics burst through the door with a gurney, followed by Detective Koren and his partner, Detective Coyle.

chapter seventeen

"**Over here,**" **Jackson said, still** holding David up. The paramedics ran over and helped him onto the gurney and then checked his blood pressure and his pulse and examined his left arm. A few minutes later, longtime volunteer Herbie Swanson, wearing an EMT vest and a Yankees baseball cap, said, "I think his left arm is broken, in more than one place, the shoulder and the wrist. We're taking him to the ER."

"I want to go with him," Simon said. "He's my partner and my friend."

"You can go," Detective Koren said. "Ms. McQuade, Mr. Spade, and Mr. Peters, stay put. I want details."

After the paramedics rolled David out, with Simon following, Detective Koren said, "I guess I should be surprised to see you two, since I specifically told you to stay out of this case, but here you are, again."

"Detective, we came for the seminar about wines and for the haunted Halloween maze," I said. "That's why we're here."

"Sure it is." He pulled a pad out of the inside coat pocket of his tailored suit. "Okay, now tell me the truth."

I looked at Jackson, who said, "Simon asked us to look into the threats against David."

"We're looking into the threats," said Detective Coyle, who wore his police jacket over a budget-friendly suit. "And we don't need any help."

I pointed to the vat. "We just found him in there. Obviously you aren't doing a good enough job."

"I suppose your investigating hasn't stopped there," Detective Koren said. "Are you also sticking your nose into Amy Lord's death?"

"The two sides of an investigation often converge," Jackson said. "You know how it works."

"You know why? Because we are the police," Detective Coyle said, sneering. "You are a cop wannabe."

"Koren, after all of this time, can't you keep this guy on a leash?" Jackson said.

Detective Coyle stepped toward him. "That's it. I'm arresting you for, for . . ."

"Shut it, Coyle," Detective Koren said. "Just start with tonight's chain of events, Spade."

Jackson related a sanitized version of what had happened, leaving out Lily's arrival and, of course, the breaking into Gerald's office, again. "When we reached the end of the maze, we hadn't found him, so we headed back here. His car was in the parking lot, so we thought he was still here and we started looking. When we got back here, we heard this tapping coming from the wine vat. It was David, and he told us that someone had knocked him on the back of the head and thrown him in the tank. When he landed, he broke his arm."

Detective Koren turned to Scott Peters. "Scott, what is your role in this?"

"He's playing bodyguard," Detective Coyle said. "That's what I heard."

"Yes. Jackson contacted me and I took the job of bodyguard to David Farmer starting Thursday morning."

"You didn't do such a great job, did you, Peters?" Detective Koren said. "We expect more of our former cops."

Scott shrugged. "I did what I could. Things happen. Farmer took off without my knowledge."

"That may be true," Jackson said. "But I'll be recommending to David that he let you go. I'll find him someone else."

"So be it," Scott said, stoic.

"Do you have anything to add to what Mr. Spade had to say?"

Scott shook his head. "No. I must have been right behind them in the maze, and I also walked back through the field to Pure. I spotted David's car and began looking for him and ran into Simon outside the barn as he was getting a ladder to help David get out of the vat they found him in. That's all I know."

"Okay, you can go," Detective Koren said. "But stay local, for now."

"Right." Scott turned to Jackson. "Sorry it didn't work out."

"Me, too."

"A few more questions, and you two can go as well." Detective Koren made a show of flipping through his notebook as if he was looking for something. But he landed on this: "Was Lily Bryan here tonight?"

I looked at Jackson. "Yes, briefly. But then she went home."

"At what time?"

"I think she got here about nine twenty and left a few minutes later."

"Why didn't she stay longer?"

"I didn't think it was a good idea for her to be here, so I suggested she go home, and she did."

"I walked her to her car and watched her leave," Jackson said.

"Keep going."

"I headed for the entrance and saw David in front of Pure. He was smoking a cigarette and talking to someone on the phone. We didn't talk, though. I just waved to him and came back here. Willow and I were waiting for Simon when he ran in and was in a panic. He told us that David had disappeared."

"How long was it between the time you saw David in front, and when Simon ran in?"

"Probably ten minutes or so."

"Why didn't you go to the car with Mr. Spade and Ms. Bryan, Ms. McQuade?"

"Simon and I were talking, and then he needed to catch someone before they left. So I waited for him, and for Jackson to return, so we could both say good-night to Simon and thank him for the evening," I said. "He is a good friend to both of us."

"We're very interested in your other friend, Lily," Detective Koren said.

"Yes, we know that," I said.

"I shouldn't say this, but as you may have realized, she is looking very good for Amy's death."

"Just because she was here and made the appetizer isn't enough reason to charge her," I said.

"David had also just dumped her," Detective Coyle said. "That's as good a motive as you can get."

"So you're not even looking at anyone else?"

"Okay, I'll humor you, Ms. McQuade," Detective Koren said. "What exactly are we missing?"

"David's brother and father have a very contentious relationship with David. They blame him for leaving the business, and for the foreclosure proceedings on their property. And Carla Olsen, the owner of Sisterhood Wines, was also in a relationship with David, and he just broke it off with her. Maybe she put him in the vat."

"A woman couldn't do that, not all by herself," Detective Coyle said.

"But it's safe to assume that you think Lily put him there," Jackson said. "What's the difference?"

Detective Koren scribbled something in his notebook. "Who else?"

"There is a lot of bad blood in the winemaking community," I said. "Camille and Carter Crocker are second in line to win the *Wine Lovers* magazine contest, and their business is in big trouble. Recently, they lost their winemaker and are trying to hire Gerald Parker, Pure's assistant winemaker. I think it's safe to assume that they are hoping he will bring some of Pure's magic to Crocker Cellars.

"But in the past, they did try to hire David. He said no and went on to create Falling Leaves, the top contender for the prize. It's reasonable to think that Camille and Carter might want to get rid of the competition. Money is a terrific motive to knock someone off. You know that."

"Yes, we know that, Ms. McQuade," Detective Koren said. "Anyone else?"

"I think that Gerald Parker also has a good reason to want David dead," I said. "He was pushed out of the way by David when Simon bought this place. Since Amy's death, he's been actively looking for work elsewhere.

"And finally, there is Ivy Lord. It's obvious that her marriage to David is troubled. We have confirmed rumors that both of them are having affairs, not just David." I left out the part about Ramsey Black because I didn't want it to affect the *Wine Lovers* magazine judging.

Detective Koren put the pad away. "It sounds like despite my warning, you've gone ahead and become very involved in our case."

"It was difficult not to," I said. "Lily is my employee and my friend and so is her uncle, Wallace, and Simon and I are friends as well. I also like David, and he's had a bad go of it lately."

"You should have stopped her, Spade," Detective Koren said.

"Not possible." Jackson smiled at me. "I'm proud of her."

"Isn't that sweet?" Detective Coyle said.

"You're a real head case," Jackson said. "Don't ever change."

"Ignore him," I said.

"Despite your efforts, Ms. McQuade, and Mr. Spade, we are close to coming to a resolution to this case," Detective Koren said. "I'm afraid your friend Lily Bryan is going to face charges."

• • •

Detective Koren released us a few minutes later. "I can't wait to get home," Jackson said as we got into his truck.

I took his hand. "Sorry we didn't make the jazz concert, honey."

He smiled at me. "And miss all of this?" He patted the seat next to him. "Come to me." I scooted over, and we drove to his house, snuggled together.

Qigong, Columbo, Rockford, and Zeke went nuts when we got to his house, barking, running around, wagging their tails, looking for treats. Ordinarily, we didn't leave them alone for more than four hours, max, but this had been a long night. They did have full run of the house, although they usually all got up on the living room couch by the doggie steps and went to sleep in front of the TV, which we left on for a little noise, until we returned.

After we gave them each a few treats, we took them outside into the fenced-in yard to run around. While they did that, Jackson did his nightly check on all his rescues to make sure they all were okay, especially the new arrivals and the ones that had been ill. One of the volunteers had done a walk-through at nine o'clock. Jackson had also installed in the kitchen an alarm, motion sensors, and an intercom to the barn.

Once he was satisfied all was well, and after our dogs had sniffed to their hearts' content and done their business, we went back inside, and Jackson made a fire in the bedroom's fireplace and drew the blinds.

While he did that, I took a hot shower and changed

into my flannel pj's, went into the kitchen, and put an organic gluten-free pizza with a flaxseed crust in the oven. It wasn't vegetarian or vegan, but I wasn't perfect. While it baked, I whipped up green salads with balsamic-vinegar dressing. We'd eaten early, and both of us were ravenous.

Since my muscles still felt sore, I reached into the cabinet over the stove and pulled out a bottle of homeopathic arnica. Interestingly, research has shown that it's the helenalin, an active compound in arnica, that curbs the inflammation that comes when you're injured or overdo it, by stopping the release of NF-κB, an immune system regulator.

I took five tablets of 6X strength—the lower the number, the stronger it is—and would repeat that four times over the next twenty-four hours. I also had arnica cream, which I'd rub on my legs three to five times a day.

That taken care of, I checked the pizza, which was halfway done. While I waited, I washed up a few dishes in Seventh Generation dish soap and straightened up the counter. We spent more than half our time here, but also had hectic lives, so it was important to stay on top of household tasks.

The pizza still needed a few more minutes, so I watered all my plants on and near the windowsill that overlooked the front yard and received the morning sun and exposure from grow lights. I'd planted all the usual herbs in small pots, including basil, chives, cilantro, mint, oregano, parsley, rosemary, sage, tarragon, and thyme, for salads and cooking. Most of these had naturally powerful antioxidants in them. But I'd also added my favorite edibles, including a dwarf avocado tree, whose fruits were full of vitamins A, E, and B_6 and carotenoids; a dwarf mandarin orange tree with fruits with antioxidants, calcium, phosphorous, magnesium, and fiber; and a dwarf lemon tree with fruits chock-full of vitamin C.

In addition, I'd planted superfood garlic greens that I used such as scallions, carrots with vitamins B_6, A, C, and K, and antioxidant-rich mushrooms and tomatoes, not to mention microgreens that are a great source of vitamins A, C, K, and folate. Having fresh herbs and fruits and veggies at hand made whipping up a healthy meal super-easy.

By then, the pizza was done, and I put it, two plates, two microgreen salads with lemon-dill dressing, two Honest peach iced teas, and napkins on a tray and carried it into the bedroom. Jackson toweled himself off from his shower and got in a T-shirt and sweatpants, and both of us climbed on the bed. I put the tray between us, and the dogs settled down at the foot of the bed to go to sleep.

"What do you want to watch?" Jackson said, picking up the remote.

"Something light and funny. I need to wipe away the memories of that gruesome Halloween maze." I put a piece of pizza on one of the plates and handed it to him.

"Thanks." He turned on the TV and flipped through the channels. "That thing was pretty bad, but you handled it like a trouper."

"Thank you, honey."

"Guess what? *Murder, She Wrote* is on, just for you. In fact, it's a marathon."

I took a bite of pizza. "Sounds just about perfect. Love you."

"I love you, too."

Jackson set the alarm for seven o'clock, since the annual Pumpkin Pancake Breakfast at Nature's Way was Saturday morning. He also needed to get up early to help his two morning volunteers, who came at 6:00 a.m., tend to the rescues.

When I arrived at Nature's Way, at seven forty-five, I found Merrily in the kitchen, busily prepping for the breakfast with Lily's help. We'd been doing this event on Halloween morning for the past two years—it had been Merrily's idea—and it always drew a good crowd.

Given that it was North Fork UnCorked! week, we would probably be serving even more this year. The breakfast also inspired new and repeat customers to do some shopping, so it was guaranteed to be a busy morning. Although I was concerned that the police might ruin everything by arresting Lily in the middle of the event.

On my way into the kitchen, I stopped first at the coffeepot. "Rough night, Willow?" Merrily said, smiling. "Where d'ya go, what did you do?"

"Jackson and I went to hear David's talk at Pure about how wines are made, and the barrel tasting afterward. Lily was there, too."

"Yes, but I didn't stay long," Lily said, opening the refrigerator door and blocking my view of her face.

"Lily, are you okay?" I wondered if I should tell her about what had happened to David. Perhaps it could wait.

She closed the door and put a dozen eggs on the counter. "I'm fine. What else do you need, Merrily?"

"Let me think while I whip up the first batch for us." In a bowl, Merrily mixed together milk, pumpkin puree, egg, oil, and vinegar. In a separate bowl she combined flour, brown sugar, baking powder, baking soda, allspice, cinnamon, ginger, and salt, then added it to the first bowl and mixed it all together.

"That smells so good, Merrily," I said. "And I am hungry."

"Good." She smiled. "Oh, I thought of a few things we need from the storeroom, Lily. More brown sugar, and more allspice, cinnamon, and ginger, okay?"

"Sure, I'll get it."

"Thank you." Merrily moved over to the griddle, which was lightly oiled, and scooped one-quarter cup of batter for each pancake onto the surface. "Now we just need to brown on both sides and serve hot with lots of butter, and of course maple syrup."

"Yummy. I can't wait."

"Me either."

I leaned on the counter that faced the stove. "How does Lily seem this morning to you?"

"Like she's very close to breaking down. The thing with David, and the police hassling her, has been a lot to take. Wallace has also been very upset for her. I'm worried about both of them. Have you and Jackson and Simon figured anything out yet?"

"It's a complicated case. And we're still trying to figure out whether it was David's brother or father, or his wife, and/or his wife's lover, or his assistant winemaker, or some disgruntled vineyard owners who might have tried to kill David and killed Amy instead."

Merrily flipped the pancakes over. "That's quite a list."

"Yes, it is, but the police are, unfortunately, closing in on Lily."

"No, really? But I just can't see her doing it."

"Me either," I said. "But it doesn't mean they won't arrest her."

"Well, then, you have to stop them, like you usually do." Merrily flipped the pancake again. "You know, fix it."

"Believe me, we're trying. Once the breakfast is over, I'm back on the case."

By ten o'clock, the Pumpkin Pancake Breakfast was in full swing, with every table full and people lining up to buy staples. It couldn't have been a worse time for Detective Koren and Detective Coyle to walk into Nature's Way. So, of course, that's when they did.

But Lily was back in the storeroom and Wallace saw them first. "What are they doing here?"

Quickly I pulled him to the side. "Wallace, I think they are here to arrest Lily for Amy's murder. But it doesn't mean that Jackson, Simon, and I are going to stop looking for the real killer. We've pulled it out before. So I know it's difficult, but please, please, try to remain calm." I was especially concerned about his reaction since he'd told me a few weeks ago that he'd seen his doctor and he had high blood pressure and a blockage in one of his arteries that would need to be addressed soon.

While Detective Koren and Detective Coyle scanned the room, I headed to the back room to alert Lily, to give her a moment to deal with it on her own. But when I opened the door to the storeroom, she was sitting on a box, crying. Quickly I went into the downstairs bathroom and grabbed a few tissues and gave them to her. "Here, sweetie—what is it?"

"Everything is a mess. David called me last night and told me he loved me but said we needed to spend time apart. I'm so confused, I don't know what to do, or think."

"I hate to do this to you, Lily, but the police are here, and I think they are going to arrest you."

Her eyes opened wide, and her face went white. "No! No!" She started crying again. "But I didn't do it. I wouldn't hurt David! Never!"

I looked out the door and the detectives were heading toward us. "Lily, listen, we don't have much time. They're coming right now. All of us believe that you are innocent, and like I just told your uncle, Jackson, Simon, and I will continue to work on this and find the real killer. We've done it before and we can do it again. Your lawyer, Shawn, is one of the best. I'm asking you to trust us—you just have to keep the faith for a little while longer." I hugged her tightly as the detectives pushed their way in like storm troopers.

"Ms. Bryan?" Detective Koren said. She stepped

away from me and blew her nose. "You are under arrest." Detective Coyle snapped the cuffs on. She sniffled, but didn't cry. He read her the Miranda warning, the one we all knew from TV shows but not in real life. When it was real, it was so ominous and otherworldly and, really, so terrifying.

"Do you understand these rights as I have explained them to you?"

"Yes," she said, her voice trembling.

"Stay strong, Lily, stay strong," I said.

She lifted her head and looked directly at me. In that moment, it was just the two of us. She said, "I will," and I felt the weight of my responsibility to her and her future. Then I watched as the two detectives marched her out of the storeroom, down the aisle, and out of Nature's Way. I sat down on the same box she'd been sitting on and started to cry.

Ten minutes later, Merrily came to find me because, of course, the crowds kept coming. It was one of the most difficult things I'd ever had to do—stay and take care of the business, my business, rather than run out the door and try to find answers to free Lily.

After I alerted Simon, who called Shawn Thompson, her lawyer, and left a message for Jackson, I put my body and brain on autopilot and went through the motions. Although the inquiring glances from customers who had been there for the arrest or heard about it afterward were difficult to ignore. Wallace, too, was on autopilot and walked around like one of those zombies in the Halloween maze. I became worried again about his health, especially his heart.

Finally, at around eleven thirty, things slowed down. But there still was plenty to do. Eventually, the tables emptied and the customers left with their purchases, and we had Nature's Way back to ourselves. I suggested that Merrily brew a pot of chamomile tea and that we all take a break and sit down together to discuss what had happened.

I kept watching the door, but no one came in. Wallace, meanwhile, was busy putting new place settings on the last two tables. But when Merrily brought the tea and shortbread cookies out on a tray, I said, "Wallace, that can wait. Please come and sit down."

He blew out a breath, put down the rest of a setting, came over, and flopped, exhausted, in a chair. Merrily put the tray down, sat, and began to pour tea for all of us.

"I know that we're all upset, so I want to fill you in on what I've done so far. I let Simon know what happened and he has alerted Shawn Thompson, Lily's lawyer, in New York. I'm sure he will be out here today. Simon already told me that he will post the bail for Lily, so, Wallace, that is something that you and your family don't need to worry about."

Wallace nodded. "Thank you, Willow. I'll let her parents know what you've done. They're coming from Boston on the three o'clock ferry. They'll be staying with all of us in Peconic."

"I've left a message for Jackson, too," I said. "And now that things have calmed down a bit, I think the best thing for me to do is to continue my investigation. Is that okay with you two? Or would you like me to call in some of our high school and college help? Maybe Tad?"

Tad Williams had worked in Nature's Way this summer and was efficient, fun, and positive. He attended Juilliard in the city, where he studied voice and opera, so he might be around. I could check.

"Tad would be a big help," Merrily said. "Especially tonight with the Halloween party and the trick-or-treaters. You might not get back here to help us."

"I plan to. But you're right. At this point, I don't know where the day will take me." I pulled out my phone and called Tad. He answered on the first ring.

"Hey, Willow, what's up?"

"Hi, Tad, I know it's late notice and you may have plans, but we could really use your help. Are you home in Greenport?"

"I am, and I'm super-bored. My plans fell through for the day so just tell me when you need me and I'll be there."

"That's really great, Tad, thank you. Can you hold on for a moment?"

"Sure thing."

I turned to Merrily and Wallace. "What time do you need Tad?"

"The sooner, the better," Merrily said.

Wallace didn't respond, just sipped his tea.

"When can you get here, Tad? We could use you today and tomorrow."

"I'm on my way. Thanks for thinking of me."

"Thank you, Tad. I'm going out, but I'll see you later. You'll be a big help to Merrily and Wallace." We said good-bye and ended the call.

"Thanks for the extra help, Willow," Wallace said. "It will make things easier here." But when he took another sip of tea, suddenly he dropped the cup. It landed on the saucer and cracked it in half. Gasping for air, he put his hand to his chest and managed to say, "I think I need to go to the hospital."

I put my hand on his. "Breathe, Wallace, and try to stay calm." On my phone I punched 911 for the second time in twenty-four hours.

chapter eighteen

On the drive over to Eastern Long Island Hospital following the ambulance, I had to remind myself to stay calm. Only with a clear head would I be able to help Wallace, and his niece, Lily. I'd just turned left on the corner from Front Street to Main Street next to the Coronet restaurant when Jackson called me back. Quickly I put the phone in the holder on the dash and pushed the speaker button.

"Hi, honey, are you okay? I'm sorry I didn't pick up. I had an animal come into the rescue, and now I'm on my way to David's, but I can come to you."

"They arrested Lily. We were in the storeroom talking and she was upset over David because she said he called her last night and said he thought they should take a break, and then they came in and arrested her. It was awful. But then it got so much worse because Wallace had a heart attack, at least the paramedics think so."

"Oh, jeez. Is he okay?"

"I don't know. I'm following the ambulance now to ELIH. Can you meet me there?"

"Of course. Turning around right now, and I'll call David and Simon. Maybe you and I can go see David and Ivy afterward. He broke his arm in two places and had another mild concussion and they sent him home. Maybe in a different environment we can finally get some answers to help Lily."

"Wait a minute. Why are you going to David and Ivy's house?"

"Because he just hired me to be his new bodyguard."

"What?"

"He needed someone and he called me, and I couldn't say no. It's just until the competition is over, and then I'll find him someone else if necessary. But I feel like this thing is coming to a head, and hopefully we can nail the real killer by then." Jackson paused for a moment. "It's a good thing we watched those *Murder, She Wrote* episodes last night."

"Ha, ha, Jackson. Very funny."

"Just trying to lighten the mood, hon."

"I know. Actually, she is a good detective, or her writers were. Now we need to be just as good." I turned down the street that led to the hospital.

"Greenport is a lot like Cabot Cove," Jackson said. "The bodies are piling up. We've solved quite a few ourselves."

"And we can do it again." I took a right at the EMERGENCY sign and headed around back to the ER. "You, Simon, and me." I pulled into a spot and parked. "Okay, I'm here. Can you meet me in the ER? How long will you be?"

"Ten minutes, hon, stay strong, I'm coming. Love you."

"I love you, too, and thanks for coming to my rescue. I can take care of myself, but it's also nice to have you there when things go really wrong."

"Back atcha, hon. See you in a few."

Jackson and I didn't sit in the ER waiting room long. Within an hour, the nurse came out and told us that we could go back and see Wallace.

We found Wallace in a bed on the left, hooked up to all kinds of monitors, with oxygen tubes in his nose, and his eyes closed. The doctor who had been writing on Wallace's chart looked up as we entered, motioned us to step outside, and pulled the curtain closed behind us.

"Is he okay? Did he have a heart attack?"

"We're still trying to determine what happened," she said. "But he'll need to stay here for evaluation. I gather from what he told us that he just had a very stressful event at work."

"Yes, that's right," I said. "His niece, Lily, who also works at Nature's Way, my store, has been arrested."

The doctor gave me a curious look. "Arrested?"

"It's all a big misunderstanding, but that's why she isn't here," I said. "I called his wife, Suzy, who was in the city with their daughter, Ella. But they're on the Hampton Jitney right now, and it's due in at two thirty. Suzy's car is at the railroad station where the bus arrives, so she'll come right here. Lily's parents are also on their way from Boston." Although, I thought, their primary focus would be their daughter, who was in jail.

The doctor nodded. "Fine."

"So what happens next?"

"As soon as we have a bed upstairs, Wallace will be transferred up to the ICU, monitored, and evaluated."

"The ICU?" Jackson said. "That must mean that it is serious. Willow said that he's been having some problems. Did the situation escalate because of the news about his niece?"

"We don't know exactly what we're dealing with yet, although he does have a confirmed blockage. And, yes, stress can definitely exacerbate a cardiac condition."

"Is there anything we can do to help?" I said.

"For now, no. He needs to rest. We'll continue to run tests, move him upstairs, and do more tomorrow. Perhaps you can call his wife for an update this evening."

When we stepped out of the ER into the cool autumn air, I took a deep breath and tried to center myself. "This has been a bad day so far. Suddenly, I feel tired and drained. I hope we can turn it around. For Lily's and Wallace's sake."

Jackson took my hand and we walked to our cars. "Of course we can, McQuade. Especially since now that I'll be super-close to David for the next day or so. As for the energy, we can stop for coffee."

"True, and maybe seeing them in their home environment will loosen them up. Or if that doesn't work, with this much at stake, I have no compunction about snooping around. We need answers, and fast."

"I don't blame you, and I can keep them occupied while you snoop from top to bottom."

"Amy lived in a guesthouse there, so I need to check that out, too."

"Absolutely."

"And then I think we need to take a ride to see the Crockers and find out what Camille's planning, beyond Gerald. Did they really try to kill David to get ahead? And are they still trying? Did they put him in that vat?"

"It does seem like a two-person job," Jackson said, taking out his truck keys. "Speaking of which, we really need to talk to David's father and brother, too."

"We can see them on the way back from the Crockers'. We can also check all the vineyard signs to see if one of them matches that sign in those photos that were sent to David."

"Good idea."

"Plus, tonight is Halloween, and all the most prestigious wineries are having pairings with restaurants in town. It's a good way to catch up with the rest of our suspects—Gerald, Derek Mortimer, Carla Olsen, and one Ramsey Black."

Ten minutes later, Jackson took a right on Village Lane in Orient and headed past the post office, the ice cream shop, and the Orient Country Store, past the Oysterponds Historical Society, and took a left onto West Bay Avenue.

David and Ivy's three-story Victorian home was like Nature's Way, but much more elaborate and in the Queen Anne style. Not only was it twice the size, it had an impressive yellow and burnt-sienna exterior and extensive period details, including pink and green gingerbread trim, scalloped shingles, complicated asymmetrical wings and bays, steep, multi-faceted roofs with stained-glass windows, round and octagonal towers, and a large wraparound porch with ornamental spindles and brackets. The expansive lawn led down to a large stone wall, and beyond that the road, a rocky beach, and a dock with rowboats and fishing boats tied up.

Ivy met us at the door, dressed in an expensive-looking black wool wrap over pressed jeans and flats. "Come in, please, David told me you were coming."

"Your house is so beautiful, and what a view," I said, truly impressed.

"Yes, it's inspired by the Boston architect H. H. Richardson, who built the first American Queen Anne house—the Watts Sherman House—in Newport, Rhode Island, in 1874," Ivy said matter-of-factly. "Amy and I spent summers here with our grandparents when we were growing up. Off-season, we were in New York, of course."

"Of course," I said.

"When Grandfather Walter died a few years ago, he left it to me. David and I recently had the exterior repainted and updated the interior as well. I wanted it to be more reflective of David and me and the way we live now." Ivy touched the mahogany banister at the side of the staircase that led to the upper floors. "I think it came out well."

"I'd say so," Jackson said, looking around.

She led us into the front room, which had been completely refurbished and updated from a cramped, dark traditional Victorian interior to a bright white space with navy-blue couches and chairs around a large glass coffee table, floor-to-ceiling bookshelves, a sixty-five-inch HDTV mounted on the wall, an elaborate stereo system, and an enormous picture window that overlooked Orient Harbor, which was choppy on this windy day in late October. A fire blazed in the enormous fireplace, keeping the room toasty and warm.

"What a beautiful room," I said. "It's large, but at the same time very cozy."

"Very nice," Jackson said.

"We like it."

David had made himself comfortable on a couch, his injured arm in an extensive cast on top of a big pillow. Prescription-medicine bottles were on the coffee table, along with a cup of coffee, the remnants of a breakfast bagel, and copies of *Wine Spectator*, *Wine Enthusiast*, and *Decanter* magazines. The TV was on, tuned to HGTV, but David had his eyes closed, with a copy of *Wine & Spirits* magazine tented on his chest.

"Is he sleeping?" Jackson said. "Or just resting?"

"Just resting, I think," Ivy said. "David? Jackson and Willow are here."

David's eyes fluttered open, and he smiled at us. "My rescuers! If it hadn't been for you two and Simon, I'd still be in that vat!"

"How's the arm?" Jackson said as we took seats on the couch opposite his. Ivy left the room.

"Hurts like hell." David reached for a bottle of pills, but tipped it over.

I reached for it and handed it to him. The label said it was oxycodone and acetaminophen, strong stuff. But sometimes, prescription medicines were absolutely necessary, especially for acute pain.

"Thanks, Willow." He opened the bottle and popped a pill in his mouth and followed it with a sip of coffee. "I'm trying to stay awake, but these pills are kicking my ass."

"Just go with it," I said. "You need to respect the injury, and you've got quite a bad one. Did the doctor give you a prognosis?"

"It'll take six to eight weeks to heal, and about the same time in physical therapy to make sure I regain movement in the arm and my hand." He wiggled his fingers at the end of the cast. "At least it's my left hand, and I'm a righty. And now I also have Jackson to protect me. Thanks, buddy, I appreciate it, really. After what happened, I just couldn't trust Scottie anymore."

"No problem," Jackson said. "Scott screwed up. He should have stayed with you. But hopefully we can get this all resolved pretty quickly, and things can get back to normal."

"That would be good." David took another sip of coffee. "Hey, what happened to Lily's uncle? Is he going to be okay?"

"We hope so," I said. "We should know more later."

"I'm worried about Lily. I mean, I told her last night that we should take a break, but she didn't take it well, and now this."

"Actually," I said, "there's more, David, so brace yourself."

"What? What happened? Is she okay?"

"No, she's not. In fact, Lily was arrested this morning at Nature's Way for Amy's murder."

"What? No, no way." David tried to push himself into an upright position.

"Try to remain calm," I said. "You've been through a lot." I went over to him and put another pillow behind him to try to prop him up.

"I know Lily. She wouldn't hurt Amy, or anyone else. Did you call Simon and that lawyer of hers? We've got to get her out on bail. We'll pay for it."

Ivy walked into the room. "Actually, no, David, we won't."

"Stop it, Ivy," David said, angry. "We have to help her. She didn't do this."

"You don't know that, David," Ivy snapped. "Amy might be alive if you hadn't become involved with her."

"I know people," David said. "Lily did not try to kill me and by mistake killed your sister instead."

"You're not exactly objective, David, and we're not helping her. End of story." Ivy turned and left the room.

"She can be such a bitch, and she really stresses me out. I wish I could smoke."

"Smoking is never a good idea, especially if you're wearing a cast. You could get a blood clot." I pulled a bottle of Dr. Bach's Rescue Remedy out of my purse and handed it to David. I always carried a spare, just in case. "Try this instead. It's a combination of five flower essences—cherry plum, clematis, impatiens, rock rose, and star-of-Bethlehem—and it's good for stressful and traumatic circumstances. Just put four drops in a glass of water or in your mouth. Repeat as needed."

He opened the bottle and put the drops in his water glass and sipped it. "Thanks, doc, but I may need a divorce to really solve my problem." He took another sip of the water. "Forget me. What about Lily? How are we going to get her out?"

"Don't worry," I said. "Simon has already said that he'll pay for her bail, and all her legal fees."

"I just don't understand why Ivy is acting this way. I mean, you can tell by looking at Lily that she's innocent. She's not thinking straight."

"They were twins," I said. "It makes sense that she's upset."

"Of course, but to be honest, she and I haven't been getting along for a while now. We're just not connecting on any level, if you know what I mean."

"We get it, David," Jackson said. "I know it's been tough."

"It's the money." David reached for the glass again. "If I'd been able to invest in Pure on my own, this wouldn't be happening. It's like she holds it over my head." He blew out a breath. "Sorry, I guess I needed to get it out."

"That's okay, David," I said. "We understand."

"So what do we do to help Lily?"

Jackson got up and went over to the living-room door and looked out. "If you really want to clear her of these charges, we need some answers. Truth time, David."

"What are you talking about? I've told you the truth."

"Really?" I said. "Like when you said that you

weren't having an affair? And we find out that you're involved with Lily and Carla?"

"You also didn't tell us about your previous relationship with Amy, or that the Crockers tried to hire you away," Jackson said. "If we're going to stop the attempts on your life and help Lily, you need to be straight with us from now on."

"Okay, okay. So what is it that you want to know?"

"Let's start with your relationship with Amy Lord," I said. "You two were engaged at one point?"

"What does that have to do with anything?"

"We're not sure yet," I said. "But is it true?"

"Yes, it's true. I met Amy and Ivy out here and, later, we all ended up going to Boston University. The Lord family lived in the city, but this was their summer home when the girls were growing up, after their parents died."

"Keep going," Jackson said, keeping watch at the door for Ivy.

"Ivy and I were both in the School of Management, and Amy studied painting at the School of Visual Arts there—she was really good. That's one of hers there." David pointed to a portrait above the fireplace of Ivy and Amy as young girls standing in front of cheery sunflowers in the garden, painted in the Impressionist style. Both girls had grins on their faces. "Amy and I were both really into tennis at that time. I was on the men's team and she was on the women's, and we practiced together a lot. That one-on-one time led to us becoming involved and eventually engaged. We set the date for a June wedding, but then . . . things changed."

"What happened?" Jackson said.

"Ivy told me that Amy was pregnant and had decided to get an abortion without telling me. Ivy had proof from the clinic. I broke up with Amy after that."

"And how did you and Ivy get involved?" I said.

"We kept in touch after my breakup with Amy, and I saw her in Boston and out here in the summer. We got together one night at a bar in town, and that was it. We were engaged the following Christmas and married after graduation."

"How did Amy react?"

"She wasn't very happy, but eventually we all got used to it."

"And then she got involved with Ramsey Black," Jackson said.

David nodded. "That's common knowledge, but, yes, they got pretty serious. We all thought that he was going to propose, but then she broke it off."

"Do you know why?"

"No, I don't. I'd moved on with Ivy, and my focus was Pure and creating the next big thing in wine."

"If they had become engaged and married, would that have bothered you?" Jackson said. "Him having your girl and all that?"

David shook his head. "I told you, I'd moved on."

"Would it surprise you to know that we think that Amy broke up with Ramsey because she became involved with Gerald, your winemaker?" I said.

"No. Ivy had her suspicions and tried to stop it. She thought that Gerald was just after our money. But lately, she's been trying to be more friendly to him. I think she feels bad now that Amy's dead."

"Speaking of Ivy," Jackson said, "I know that this is a tough one, but do you think it's possible that Ivy might have tried to kill you over your affair with Lily and other women, like Carla?"

"I doubt it. She's screwing around, too. Our marriage hasn't exactly been the greatest lately. When Simon took over, I poured—no pun intended—myself into my work at Pure. Simon and I were determined to create the next big thing. Ivy spent a lot of time alone and started to look elsewhere."

"Where? Do you know?" Jackson said.

"She's pretty close to Ramsey Black," David said. "They spend a lot of time together."

"Do you think that he could have tried to kill you so he could have her for himself?" I said.

David shrugged. "I don't know. You'd have to talk to him."

"We're planning to, this evening," I said. "Along with vineyard owners who might be carrying a grudge, like the Crockers."

"Oh, them. They tried to hire me away when Simon bought Pure with Ivy, but he topped their offer, by a mile."

"Maybe Camille and Carter might be the ones behind the attempts on your life, and the texts as well," Jackson said. "According to the information we have, they are a close second to Pure for the *Wine Lovers* competition win."

"So? Getting me out of the way won't change that. Falling Leaves will still be the top contender for the win."

"Maybe, but things can change," Jackson said. "You

know how these things go. If you were dead, the judges could change their minds and give it to the Crockers for the wine they've entered and the possibility of what they'll produce in the future."

"Perhaps with Gerald Parker's help," I said. "We've heard that they're trying to lure him away from Pure."

"Bottom line—Gerald is good, but he's not gifted. I don't want to sound immodest, but without me he just won't be able to create a winning wine, either for competition or for the public. He just doesn't have it."

With David's permission I went out to Amy's guesthouse at the back of the property to look around, while Jackson went through the main house checking doors and windows, making sure it was secure.

The guesthouse certainly wasn't as grand as the main house, but it was also in the Queen Anne style with the same pink and green gingerbread trim and scalloped shingles, stained-glass windows, and a modest wraparound porch. As I put the key in the lock, I wondered how it had felt for her to live here while Ivy lived in the main house with her ex-boyfriend and former fiancé.

I stepped inside to find a large open room with a modern kitchen on one end and a living room at the other with windows on three sides, a large L-shaped rose sofa, a wicker coffee table, a colorful throw rug, a TV, bookshelves, and two large plants. Rather than a view of the water, Amy would only have seen the back of her sister's house from the side window, the neighbor's property through the window on the end, and trees through the back window.

I did a quick search around the first floor, starting with the desk near the entrance, but it was empty except for pads of paper, pens, a lip balm, a compact, and various takeout menus from restaurants in town. The laptop or computer that had been here was gone, and just the electrical cord remained plugged into the wall. After that, I checked the cushions of the couch, the kitchen cabinets, and the closet next to the stairs to the second floor, but came up empty. The second floor of the house featured two bedrooms and a large bathroom with a claw-foot tub.

First, I stepped into the room on the right, which had probably been the guest room, since it was much smaller. The bed had been stripped and the closet was empty. I checked the bathroom, then moved on to Amy's bedroom, which featured a queen-size bed with a pink comforter, a sitting area with pink overstuffed chairs, pink area rugs, and a fireplace—and Gerald Parker.

chapter nineteen

"Gerald? What are you doing here?"

"Me? What are *you* doing here?"

"David told me it was okay to come in here and look around. He didn't tell me you would be here, however."

"He doesn't know. I came here through the back, from Skippers Lane."

"Why?"

"I miss Amy." He sat on the edge of the bed. "I just wanted to be near her."

"It's a little creepy, Gerald. You shouldn't be here, not without permission."

"Why did David let you come in here then?"

"Jackson, Simon, and I have been looking into the attempt on David's life and Amy's murder. We've done this before."

"Oh, yeah, I heard something about that."

"So you two were involved. It wasn't something casual?"

He shook his head. "It was serious. We loved each other. We were planning on getting married."

"And everything was good between you two?"

"Except for having to sneak around, most of the time. But toward the end she was upset for me, about not getting credit for Falling Leaves. I did create it, you know, and David stole that formula."

"Are you sure?" From what Carla Olsen and David had said, Gerald just wasn't that talented. It was also why the Crockers had tried to nab David, and not Gerald.

"What kind of a question is that? Of course I'm sure. It was my formulation."

"Let's go back to Amy. Did she end her relationship with Ramsey Black because of you?"

Gerald nodded. "We'd been seeing each other for about two months when she told him it was over. We'd only been going out a little while, but we knew what we had was real."

"Were they serious? Had he asked her to move in, or maybe even proposed?"

Gerald nodded again. "Yes, they'd been seeing each other for over a year."

"I heard a rumor that Ramsey had a special name for her."

"Probably from Carla Olsen, the biggest gossip on the East End?"

I shrugged, but didn't respond.

"He liked to call her My Princess. He even had it engraved on the engagement ring. After he proposed and Amy turned him down, she told me all about it."

"But why didn't anyone know about you two even after she ended it with Ramsey? I mean, Harrison Jones, the winemaker, did, but he was friends with Amy."

"I don't know, we tried to keep it secret at first, because of Ivy. We both knew that she would try to talk Amy out of it because I don't come from money. But I'm no gold digger. It wasn't about that. Not at all."

"But Ivy found out?"

"Yes, David told her. He caught us in my office. Maybe he was jealous because he used to be involved with Amy. I don't know."

"You must have had hard feelings toward David, and not just about that. You were also demoted when Simon and Ivy bought Pure."

"Wait a minute." Gerald got up and came over to me. "If you think that I tried to kill David, you're wrong."

"If you had, and killed Amy instead, it would be a tough thing to live with."

He pointed his index finger at me. "*If* I'd done it, and I'm telling you, *I* did not."

"Okay, you didn't do it. But you are planning on leaving Pure."

"You can't keep anything secret in this community." He clenched his fists. "Now that Amy is gone, yes, I'm exploring my options. Not that it's anyone's business."

"I think you should go, Gerald. You're getting upset."

"Because of you and your stupid questions." He took a step toward me.

I pulled out my phone. "I think I'd better call Jackson. He's just in the main house."

"Your big, bad boyfriend? I'm not scared of him."

"Yes, you are." My finger hovered above the phone. "Now leave."

"Fine." He stomped down the stairs.

Once I heard the front door open and shut, I got busy. He'd kind of freaked me out with his weird behavior over Amy, so I wanted to leave as quickly as possible. First, I went over to the dresser and opened the drawers one by one, but it was just clothes, in her funky bohemian-chic style.

Next, I moved on to the large walk-in closet, but there were only clothes on hangers, and nothing in boxes. I checked the pockets of the jackets and pants, but except for a receipt from the local drugstore for a $40 tube of Bodacious Ruby Red Lip Love, I came up empty again.

Finally, I checked the seat cushions on the chairs, and underneath the bed, but only found several dust bunnies on the hardwood floor. However, I also noticed that the floor sloped from right to left and also seemed uneven in places. Could Amy have hidden something under the floorboards?

To be sure, I walked the floor in a grid pattern. When I got to the bedside rug, I picked it up and examined the floor underneath, but the floorboards were undisturbed. After I'd examined the floor in the rest of the room, I went over to inspect the floor under the rug in front of the fireplace, but again found nothing.

But as I stepped back, for the first time I noticed that the painting above the fireplace was similar in style to the one over the fireplace in the main house. This time, Amy had painted her and Ivy making sand castles on the beach as young girls, also in the Impressionist style. Amy had a red shovel while Ivy held a blue one.

I walked over to the painting and examined the

edges and slowly pulled the right side toward me. The painting popped off the wall, and I moved it to the left. Behind it was a wall safe. Knowing that I probably wouldn't have much luck cracking the code on my own, I called Jackson.

"Hi, hon, what did you find?"

"A wall safe over the fireplace, but I need help from David to open it."

"Okay, I'll put you on speaker. Go ahead, Willow."

"David, I found a wall safe behind the portrait above the fireplace in Amy's cottage. Do you have any idea what the code might be—or be based on? Maybe the twins' birthday or maybe when you guys graduated from BU?"

"Wall safe? I didn't know that she had one. The cops searched the whole cottage and didn't mention it."

"I don't know, but it's here now. Any idea what the combination is?"

"You can try the twins' birthday, but it's probably too obvious—November fifteenth, 1986. So maybe eleven, fifteen, eighty-six? Or eleven, 1986—just the month and year?"

"I'll try them both." I put the phone on the mantel. Neither combination worked. "Try again."

"Maybe when we graduated in 2008? Amy always said that was a very important day in all our lives. I guess it was. Amy and I were supposed to get married and Ivy planned to make her mark in her grandfather's company in New York. We didn't, she did. Then Ivy and I got married and eventually moved back out here full-time when we invested in Pure."

"I think we need two more numbers, though."

"Try adding the day or the month, Willow," Jackson said. "What would that be, David?"

"I believe it was May twenty-second. Five for the month of May won't work so add the twenty-two—maybe twenty-two, 2008?"

"Trying it." When I got to eight, I heard a click. "I think it worked, hold on." Slowly, I pulled the safe's door open. "It looks like a bunch of papers. Let me take a look. Hold on."

As I reached inside the safe, I could hear David wondering aloud what was in it. "What would she put in a safe? . . . Ivy always handled all her finances. . . ."

"Just give me a minute, David." I pulled the contents out. "I'll be right with you."

I pulled out a stack of photographs, $10,000 in $100 bills, a current passport, an old invitation to her wedding to David, and an official-looking document. I put the rest of the stuff in neat piles on top of the fireplace and opened the document first. It was a will—Amy's will—and she'd left her assets, primarily her stake in Pure, to Gerald. Ivy was in second position. This was going to cause a super-big stink. So big that I'd wait until I got back inside to tell David. "You guys, I'll be right in, okay?"

"What did you find, McQuade?"

"I'll be right in."

I closed the safe, twisted the dial, put the picture back in place, placed the contents in my pocketbook, and headed back downstairs. Then I saw Gerald through the window. He was standing outside the cottage and talking to Ivy. What was going on here?

I stepped back into the kitchen so they couldn't see

me, and tried to hear what they were saying. I noticed Ivy's watch on the kitchen counter. Maybe she'd done some cleaning in the cottage and taken off her watch. I wasn't sure how to operate it, but it could be helpful in solving the case if I could access her e-mail and text messages.

Outside, the conversation seemed to be heating up, though I could only catch snatches of it.

"I mean, I'm grateful, but also very confused," Gerald said.

"I know. But I'm sure we can work something out."

"Not if I don't get some of the credit for Falling Leaves before the judging. I mean it, Ivy."

"Gerry, you need to look at the big picture, instead of getting caught up in the minutiae. And now that you and I are good friends, I'm positive that we can make this a win-win situation for everyone. Don't worry."

Ivy said something I couldn't hear, but it sounded as if they were walking away from the cottage. I snuck a look out the window and saw them by the other corner of the house.

It sounded as if Gerald and Ivy might know about Amy's will. She'd died on Sunday, and it was almost a week later, so her lawyer might already have contacted him about being a beneficiary, and Ivy as well. I glanced out the window again—Ivy and Gerald were still talking. The best course of action was to tuck away thoughts about the will for the time being and focus on the watch instead. After a few moments, I managed to get into the texts and the e-mails, but I didn't have much time to look around.

I went for the e-mails first, since there wasn't

much correspondence between Ivy and Ramsey on the laptop in her office. Luckily once again, Ivy hadn't used a pass code for her e-mail account. Plenty of correspondence was on the watch, but it was going to be super-difficult in this time frame to find e-mails that might be incriminating. Quickly, I ran through them and spotted one where she complained about the possibility of Gerald's leaving Pure. I kept scanning, looking at the subject lines, but nothing popped out at me.

I switched to the text messages and zeroed in on the ones to and from Ramsey. But the conversation thread between the two of them had repeatedly been erased and didn't make much sense from one section to the next. However, she had written Ramsey a text an hour earlier that said:

A has gone and done it.
There will be no way to get rid of G now.
I

You don't know that.
You may be able to work with him
to take control of Pure. Turn
lemons into lemonade.
xo RB

True. We are SO much smarter than him.
We could use him and he wouldn't even know. . . .
Or I could contest it and keep him tied up in court
for years. Maybe it's not the end of the world. I

There you go! See you tonight. xo RB

"What are you doing in here?" Ivy said as she came in the door. "And what are you doing with my watch?"

Quickly, I switched to the main menu, turned the watch off, and put it back on the counter. "Oh, I thought this might be yours. I was just admiring it. Simon has one, too, and I was thinking about getting one. Is it expensive?"

She gave me a look as if she didn't believe me, grabbed the watch, and switched it on. "No, not at all." She glanced at the screen and put it back on her wrist. "Who told you that it was okay to come in here?"

"David did. Jackson, Simon, and I are looking into the attempts on David's life and Amy's death. He told me I could come back here and look at Amy's house."

"Did he, really? Well, I think the police have things in hand. In fact, I heard that your precious assistant, Lily, was arrested this morning."

"That may be. But we believe, and David does, too, that she is innocent."

"As I said before, David is not exactly objective about her."

"Listen, she was having an affair with your husband. No one would expect you to have warm and fuzzy feelings about her or even maybe to give her the benefit of the doubt. But we think someone else did this." I headed for the door. "Now, if you'll excuse me, I have work to do."

Back in the living room, I found Simon, Jackson, and David discussing the events of the past week over cups of coffee. Simon sat at the end of the couch that David was lying on, while Jackson sat opposite them.

"Hi, hon, how did it go?" Jackson pointed to his cup. "Fresh coffee for those brain cells."

"Have a cup, Willow." David motioned to the carafe on the coffee table. "It's cruelty-free kopi luwak. That means it's from the droppings of free-range civet cats, not caged ones, who eat only the ripest coffee cherries. You should appreciate that."

Simon pointed to his cup. "It's the most expensive cup of coffee in the world. A single cup runs from thirty-five to eighty bucks, and a one-pound bag of beans costs from one hundred to six hundred dollars. I always keep it on hand. Ivy turned us on to it."

"On second thought," Jackson said, putting his cup down. "You may want to skip it. Even though it's cruelty-free."

"Thanks, but I'm good," I said. "Any news about Lily, Simon?"

"Shawn is at the jail, but since Detective Koren won't drop the charges, he's working on getting her out on bail, which I told him I'll be paying for."

"Thanks, Simon," David said. "Ivy is being very unreasonable."

"I guess that's understandable," Simon said. "You did say you were in love with her, man."

"Yeah, yeah, I know." David adjusted his arm on the pillow. "So, Willow, did you find anything out there?"

"Yes, Gerald Parker."

"What the hell?"

"What was he doing out there?" Jackson said.

"It was kind of creepy. He said he missed Amy. I guess he feels closer to her out there."

"That is weird," Simon said. "Was he looking for anything?"

"Not that I could tell. But I found a few things in the safe." I sat down next to Jackson, pulled the contents of the safe out of my bag, and showed them the photos, the cash, the passport, and the old wedding invitation.

David leaned over and picked up the wedding invitation and examined it. "I can't believe she kept this." He put it down and picked up the sheaf of photos. "These are all from when the girls were little." He held up the photos of the girls posing in the garden and on the beach that she'd used for the paintings that were now in the living room and the guesthouse. "I remember when she picked these out. She used these photos for her final painting project at BU. I remember she got an A."

"Unfortunately, there's more." I pulled the will out. "I found Amy's will and . . . it's strange."

"How so?" Jackson pushed his coffee cup away.

"Because Amy left everything to Gerald."

David's eyes went wide. "What in the hell are you talking about?"

Simon shook his head. "This can't be happening. Amy owned a quarter of Pure—a gift from Ivy, actually; she did it for tax purposes—but now we're going to have to contend with this joker?"

"Gerald told me that they were very much in love," I said. "So I guess it makes sense."

"No, it doesn't," David said. "Not at all."

"Listen to this," Jackson said. "There's a clause that says that if either Ivy or Gerald predeceased the other, the survivor would get the bulk of the estate. So if Gerald gets knocked off, Ivy gets his share."

"Now wait a minute. That's crazy," David said. "My wife is not a killer."

"Okay, David, but you didn't know about the will?" Simon got up and started pacing around the room.

"No, does it sound like I knew? I wonder . . ."

"What, David?" Simon said. "What are you thinking?"

"I'm thinking it's possible that Amy did this less out of love for her new boyfriend, Gerald, than to get back at Ivy and me. You know, for what happened after college."

"You mean the fact that Ivy stole you away from Amy?"

"I wouldn't put it that way," David said. "We had our problems."

"I talked to Grandmother Lord after the funeral and she seemed to think that whatever Ivy wants, Ivy gets."

"That's ridiculous. I'm not someone who can be manipulated that easily. I did what I wanted to do, and that was marry Ivy."

"Are you sure?" Simon said, and leaned over the couch to look David in the eye.

"That's enough." David turned away from him. "Stop it. All of you."

"It's possible that Ivy and Gerald could align against us and take control," Simon said. "Damn!"

"No, Ivy would never do that."

"Really? I overheard Ivy talking to Gerald outside Amy's cottage. I got the feeling that she knows about the will and was trying to make some kind of deal," I said. "Maybe the estate lawyer or even Gerald told her."

"But she didn't tell you, David," Jackson said. "That's gotta make you think."

"I want to be alone, now." David grabbed the chenille throw and put it over his legs. "If you don't mind."

"Okay, buddy," Simon said. "We'll leave you alone."

When we got out into the hall, Simon said, "What a freakin' mess. If Ivy goes with Gerald, and I have no problem seeing her do it, we'll have a real problem at Pure. Even if we do win tomorrow."

"Don't panic," Jackson said. "Not yet. Willow always comes through in the end."

"True, but first, I'm going to have an expert look at the will. Just to see if there are any loopholes in it that might help us maintain control."

"I don't know," Jackson said. "It's her will. You can't change it."

"I just want someone on our side to see it." Simon pulled out his phone. "I'll get my lawyer working on it. Not Shawn, another lawyer in the firm, Rick Connelly. He specializes in wills, trusts, probate, and estate law, and he's just as good. He handles all my financial and estate planning. He'll know what to do."

"You'll need to do it on the way," I said. "Gerald is on the move, and I think we need to follow him." I pointed at Gerald, whom I'd spotted through the back door, heading across the field and north to Skippers Lane.

"You two go," Jackson said. "I'll stay here and keep an eye on David, and Ivy."

I gave him a quick kiss. "We'll report back. Stay safe."

"You, too."

We took Simon's car and quickly headed back down West Bay Avenue to Village Lane and headed north toward Main Road. As we approached Skippers Lane, Gerald pulled out in front of us, driving a beat-up blue Dodge truck.

"Don't get too close," I said. "He'll spot us."

"Are you kidding? All he's thinking about are dollar signs thanks to Amy's crazy will. This could really be a big problem."

"It could also be a big motive. Maybe he killed her to get the share."

Gerald got to the end of Village Lane and took a left onto Main Road.

Simon waited a beat, then turned, too. "So we follow him and hope he'll lead us to some answers?"

"This is what's been presented to us, so, yes, we follow him," I said. "If that doesn't pan out, we also need to check the vineyard signs to see if someone from one of the vineyards has been sending David those nasty texts and e-mails."

"Plus, tonight is the biggest night for wine tastings at all the restaurants, including Salt. Everyone will be out and about."

"Yes, and I'm counting on that. If we don't find answers this afternoon, we have a good chance of nailing something down tonight."

Gerald Parker headed to Crocker Cellars in Mattituck, most likely to discuss the job offer they'd made, although in his e-mail to Camille he'd said he wouldn't make a decision until after the competition results. Perhaps Amy's will had changed his mind.

chapter twenty

Simon waited until Gerald had pulled in, parked, and headed inside before turning into the parking lot. But as we did, a silver BMW pulled out, and the driver, Nora Evans, the editor of *Wine Lovers* magazine, rolled her window down, took off her designer sunglasses, and gave Simon a dazzling smile.

"Simon, darling. What are you doing up here? This isn't your neck of the woods. You should be back at Pure making more of that fabulous wine. You haven't sold it all yet, have you? I hope not. I want to put in my order, after the judging, of course."

Simon, ever the charmer, smiled back. "Nora, for you, anything! It's great to see you. This is my friend Willow McQuade. She owns Nature's Way in Greenport."

"Oh, that charming health food store on Front Street. I've been meaning to check it out."

"Please do," I said. "I'd love to show you around, anytime, really."

"Just so you know, it won't affect my judging." She smiled even more broadly, then put a finger in front of her lips. "But just between us, Pure is the favorite to win."

Simon practically jumped out of his seat. "Really? I mean, I knew we had a good chance, but I wouldn't presume to know what . . ."

"No false modesty, Simon. Falling Leaves is a winner. No doubt about it."

"So what are you doing here," Simon said, "if you've already made up your mind?"

"I said you were a favorite, not that it was in the bag. Crocker Cellars has a nice vintage, too. But I am sharing my findings on Facebook, Instagram, Snapchat, and Twitter." Nora put on her blinker. "Gotta run. See you at Southwold Hall tomorrow night!" She zoomed out of the driveway, hit the road, tires squealing, and took off in a dirt-filled cloud.

"Damn!" Simon said. "I thought she was saying we had it."

"Simon, you know she can't do that. But she's obviously impressed."

"That doesn't mean we won." He made a face, gunned the engine, and parked next to the walkway that led to the entrance. He shut off the engine and picked up his phone. "I'm going to check her postings on social media. Maybe that will give me a better idea of what she's thinking."

"Don't forget why we're here." I pointed to the Crocker Cellars window, where we could see Camille talking to Gerald. "We're following him to try and figure out who is trying to kill David and who killed Amy."

"Blah, blah, blah. You go spy. I'll stay here and keep watch."

I gave him an incredulous look. "While you have your head in your phone."

"I can do both."

"Simon, this is important. We need answers."

He pointed at his phone. "This is important, too. We got a like from Nora on Facebook and she says we're the one to beat."

"Good for you." I opened the car door. "I'll be right back."

Instead of taking the walkway, I stayed to the left of the door, so that Camille and Gerald wouldn't spot me. Fortunately, the door was partially open, so I could hear pretty well.

"So you can see what I mean," Gerald said. "Things have changed for me. I think I'm better off staying put."

"Maybe we could do something together," Camille said. "Combine forces."

"I don't know. I wouldn't even be here but you kept e-mailing me even though I said that I wanted to wait to make a decision until after the judging results tomorrow night, and then I found out about Amy's will."

"I understand, but we really want you as part of our team. I certainly didn't mean to be intrusive."

"For now, I need time to think," Gerald said. "I'll be in touch if things change."

"Are you sure?"

Before they could wrap up their conversation, I scurried back to the car and got in. Simon still had his head in his phone. "Camille wants to join forces with Gerald, but I don't think he's going for it."

"That's nice. Nora put a photo of the tasting at Pure

that features a bottle of Falling Leaves on Facebook, too, and she tweeted that Falling Leaves is a winner and that David is a genius. I checked, and she hasn't given the other vineyards or their vintages the same positive buzz."

"Congratulations. I'm going to wait for him to leave and go in to talk to her, so I think we should move the car toward the end of the lot."

"Okay." Simon stashed the phone in the glove compartment. He put the car in gear, backed up, and drove to the other end of the lot and slipped in next to a black Mercedes. He turned the ignition off, reached for the phone, and continued his search.

So while he kept his eye on social media, I kept an eye on the door to the Crockers' tasting room. About five minutes later, Gerald came out, got in his truck, and left. "I'm going in," I said.

"Sounds good," Simon said, still searching on his phone for mentions of Pure or Falling Leaves or the competition.

But when I got to the door, it didn't look as if Camille was still inside. "Hello? Anyone here?"

Moments later, Camille walked out from the back, holding two bottles of red wine. "Willow, what are you doing back here?"

"I need to ask you a few more questions."

"Are you still working on your little investigation?" She put the wines on the counter and picked up a corkscrew.

"It's not a little investigation. Someone has been trying to kill David Farmer and has killed Amy Lord."

She pulled out a cork and poured a glass of wine.

"Would you like to taste it?" She put the glass to her lips. "It's our entry in the competition and it's excellent." She gave me a sly smile, as if she had a secret.

"No, thanks. I'm here because I'm wondering why you tried to hire David away when Simon bought Pure with Ivy and why you're trying to poach Gerald now."

"That, *chérie*, is none of your business."

"It is if you are hurting my friends, and Simon Lewis is one of my best friends, and if it's connected to this murder."

"But before, you were lovers, no? How do you make that transition, is what I'd like to know."

"It wasn't all that easy, but don't try to change the subject. Why are you trying to nab Pure's talent? Can't you make it on your own?"

"Business is business." She downed the rest of the glass. "Now I need to get back to work."

"Camille, what I really want to know is this. Would you go as far as trying to kill David to get what you want? Was Amy Lord just collateral damage?"

Just then, Carter Crocker, in full cowboy mode, came out from the back. "Kill David?" He put his hands on his hips and frowned. "What are you talking about?"

"I'm trying to solve Amy's murder and stop the threats to David's life. Someone threw him in a wine vat last night and he broke his arm in two places. You two were there last night."

"Now wait a minute," Carter said. "You are out of line, lady."

"No, I don't think so. I'm trying to get to the truth."

"Then I have no idea why you're here," Carter

said. "We don't have time for this. We have a tasting tonight."

"You'd better go," Camille said. "I really thought you were better than this, Willow."

"I feel the same way about you, Camille."

Simon managed to take his eyes off his phone and got back on the road, and we headed to Greenport. I told him about the conversation with Camille while I snapped photos of the vineyard signs. I'd taken one of Crocker Cellars and Derek Mortimer's St. Ives Estate Vineyards and a dozen others on both the North Road and Route 25. The Farmer vineyard would be coming up next.

"My talk with Camille really didn't accomplish anything," I said. "Except to make me pretty sure that she and her husband could be behind this. I don't know how we were ever friends."

"You bonded when she came to take that tour of the medicinal garden this summer, but you haven't spent much time with her, between your book and the store and Jackson, and hanging with me, of course. You're not friends. How much do you really know about her?"

"I guess you're right. . . . Hey, slow down. I want to take a photo of the Farmer vineyard sign. Can you pull over?"

Once he stopped the car, I got out and went up to the sign, which was battered, faded, and worn and had a CLOSED placard tacked to the bottom. The vineyard had also seen better days—the house and the barn looked run-down, and no cars or trucks were in the driveway, but several wrecked vehicles had been pushed out into the field. Winning the $200,000 would give them a new lease on life, and a fighting chance to stay open. Stepping back, I took a few shots from both sides.

Before I left, and since no one was home, I circled the house and the barn, checking for poison hemlock. I found it behind the barn on the edge of the vineyard. I snapped a photo of it, too, and headed back to the car.

Simon wasn't surfing sites, though; he was on the phone. "So how much is it?" He listened for a bit. "Fine, fine. Just let Rick know. He'll take care of it."

I mouthed, *Shawn?*

Simon nodded. "Okay, we'll look for her release in the morning. Thank you, Shawn." Simon put the phone down. "Lily can post bail. The judge asked for two hundred and fifty thousand dollars, so we just need to come up with ten percent or twenty-five K, and as you heard, I'm taking care of it."

"Thank you, Simon. I really appreciate it. You're a good friend."

"I know." He laughed. "No, really, it's okay. Glad to do it. Where to next?"

I needed to get back to Nature's Way since tonight was Halloween and we usually had a good-size crowd of kids and their families for trick or treat. The kids got organic candy, and the adults got free samples of organic products we carried, so it was fun all around, not to mention the hot cocoa and cookies that Merrily provided.

That Tad Williams had agreed to come in was great, but they would need my help as well. So we headed back to Greenport, stopping to take a photo of Carla Olsen's Sisterhood Wines sign on the North Road before switching back to Route 25.

But when we got to the Mill Creek Bridge, on the way into Greenport, it became obvious that something had gone terribly wrong there. Cop cars blocked the way, along with an ambulance, and a policeman put his hand up for us to stop.

"What's going on here?"

"Pull down there," I said, "so we can get out and take a look."

Simon waved to the cop, quickly took a right, and turned down the road that ran past the seafood restaurants that were directly on the water. We got out and walked back to the bridge. That's when we saw Gerald's truck bobbing in the gray-blue water.

Fortunately, Gerald had survived and was being hoisted onto a rowboat that would head to shore. When he arrived there, the medics rushed to him with blankets and helped him into the ambulance. After they checked his vital signs, the ambulance took off for ELIH. Traffic had backed up, with drivers taking the same route we had, but circling back to Route 25 and taking a different way to Greenport village.

"David is a talented winemaker and there have now been four attempts on his life," I said. "What are the odds that someone tried to bump Gerald off for the same reason?"

"Excellent point," Simon said. "Who could we ask?"

I spotted a patrolman I knew, Matthew Hart, and waved to him. Tall and lanky, Matt had been born and raised on the East End and had dated my friend Allie, the masseuse, last year. After two months they had broken up when she couldn't deal with his straitlaced ways and he couldn't deal with her go-with-the-flow attitude. "Hey, Willow, you shouldn't be here. Detective Koren will be here any minute. And you two do not mix."

"I know, Matt. But what happened to Gerald Parker? Is he going to be okay?"

Matt ran his hand through his hair. "From what we can tell, someone ran him off the road at a very high rate of speed. He's going to be okay, we think, but whoever did it took off. So we've got a lot of work to do." Car doors slammed shut and Matt turned around. "He's here. You'd better go. I'll see ya."

We took his advice and headed back to Simon's car and took the long way back to Nature's Way.

By eight o'clock Saturday night, Nature's Way was buzzing with activity, like the rest of the town, since, yes, it was Halloween, but it was also the last night before the judges' choice for the winner of the *Wine Lovers* magazine competition would be revealed. The Nature's Way exterior looked fun and festive, and inside all the tables were full of kids and their families enjoying hot chocolate and organic cookies, along with the treats of organic sweets and free samples of organic soap, moisturizer, toothpaste, shampoo, and conditioner. Some of the adults even took the opportunity to pick up wants and needs from the shelves. Tad was a lifesaver, and between him, Merrily, and me, we managed to take care of everybody and everything in a timely manner.

Jackson arrived around eight thirty with Qigong, Rockford, Columbo, and Zeke, happy and frisky as ever, and I went over to the door to greet them all. "Hi, hon." I gave Jackson a kiss and petted the dogs. "How did you get away? Who's watching David?"

"I managed to get in touch with Tony, the cop we used to guard the garden last year, and he's watching him. I knew that you wanted to do some investigating tonight, especially about Gerald's accident, and I didn't want you to go alone."

"Thank you, I do." I'd already updated Jackson over the phone about the trip to Crocker Cellars, seeing Nora Evans, my confrontation with Camille and Carter, and Gerald's accident. Jackson told me that Ivy had left right after Simon and I had gone to follow Gerald, and we both wondered if either she or perhaps Camille and/or Carter Crocker were responsible for Gerald's accident.

I went back over to the counter and picked up the packet of photos I'd taken and had developed and the brochure of North Fork UnCorked! activities and handed both to Jackson, along with a small bone for each dog, which they eagerly gobbled up. "I thought you could look at these in my office while I change and take a look at what's on for tonight. We need to decide where to focus our energy. I'll be right back."

By the time I'd changed from my Nature's Way uniform into a gray wool sweater and gray jeans and boots—which matched Jackson's outfit of a gray zip-up fleece and black jeans—and returned to the office, the dogs were asleep on the couch and Jackson had a plan.

"I think we should go to Harry's Half Shell first because the Farmer wines are featured in a pairing and they'll be there, then move on to the Oyster Bar because Gerald is doing a tasting for Pure, if he's up to it. Have you checked on him?"

"Yes, he's been released, and I checked on Wallace, too, of course, and he's stable and feeling better."

"That's good news at least."

"Sure is. Where else?"

"After that, we go to Whitman's, for the Crocker Cellars tasting, and end up at Salt and check in with Simon, David, and Ivy. Of course, if we spot anyone doing something interesting as we walk around, we can check that out, too."

I picked up the photos. "Did you spot anything interesting here?"

He shook his head as he zipped up his fleece. "I didn't see any sign that matched the one in the photo that was sent to David."

Harry's Half Shell on Front Street, located a block before Main Street, had a big crowd inside, most of them with North Fork UnCorked! bracelets, so Jackson and I had to wait our turn to get to the tasting at the oversize mahogany bar.

The restaurant had no real seafood feel, but the food here rated four stars in the foodie guidebooks. At the bar, a smiling and clean-shaven Kurt Famer, dressed in a suit and tie, poured wine into glasses and passed them around. A menu in a laminated frame on top of the bar itemized the dishes that featured Farmer wines.

Jackson pointed to my bracelet. I'd bought one for each of us more to support the cause than to sample wines. "You want to taste the wine?"

"No, I want to stay sharp. There's just too much at stake."

"Look who's here," Jackson said, after surveying the crowd. "Nora Evans, and she's talking to Walter Farmer."

Nora and Walter sat at the end of the bar drinking wine and chatting amicably. "If we move in closer, we may be able to hear what they're saying," Jackson said, taking my hand and moving toward them. When we got next to them, Jackson picked up a glass of wine and handed it to me. "Cheers, McQuade."

"Thanks, honey."

Walter, also dressed in a suit, and Nora, who wore an autumn-orange-colored wool dress, a brown scarf around her throat, and thigh-high boots, continued to talk, but it was about his business and the *Wine Lovers* magazine contest. "I'm glad that you like the vintage," Walter said. "Kurt worked really hard to get it right."

"You must miss working with David, though," Nora

said. "He's quite talented and, I'm sure you know, the front-runner in our little competition."

"Yes, and I taught him everything he knows. I think you're better off with the chicken rather than the egg. Don't you, ma'am?"

She giggled and took a sip of wine. "You do have a point, Mr. Farmer."

"Please call me Walter." He waved Kurt over. "This is the genius behind the wine. Kurt, meet Ms. Evans. She likes your wine."

"Thanks very much," Kurt said, and noticing us, he turned so that his back blocked our view of them.

We moved down the bar a bit and reassessed. "Not much there," Jackson said.

"No, nothing unexpected."

"Hey," Kurt said as he came over to us, "what are you two doing here? You're the enemy."

"I'm sorry you feel that way, Kurt," I said. "We're just checking out the various vintages around town."

"Sure you are. I think you'd better leave."

"Counterproposal—why don't you step outside?" Jackson said. "We've got a few questions and then we'll go."

Kurt thought it over for a moment, then grabbed another glass of wine and followed us out. He closed the door behind us. "So what do you want?"

"Given your history with your brother, David," I said. "We were wondering just how far you might go to win the competition tomorrow night."

"What do you mean?"

"We mean that since you attacked David at his sister-in-law Amy's wake, we're wondering if you're behind the repeated attempts on his life," Jackson said. "So far he's been almost poisoned, almost crushed, and almost frozen, and last night someone threw him into a wine vat and he broke his arm in two places."

"No way. He's my brother. We may not get along, but I wouldn't do that."

"He's also been receiving threatening texts and e-mails telling him to withdraw from the competition. Know anything about that?"

"No." But as Kurt said it, he averted his eyes.

"And we're supposed to take your word for it?"

"I don't care what you do." Kurt reached for the door handle. "I wouldn't hurt my brother."

chapter twenty-one

We took the crosswalk to Main Street and walked toward the Oyster Bar, which was wedged between an insurance office and a clothing store. The place had started out as a gelato shop but had changed hands several times until its most recent incarnation, thanks to the owner of an apparel company in New York.

"So what did you think? Was Kurt telling the truth?" I said. "Did you notice how he wouldn't look at us when he said he wouldn't hurt David?"

"Yes, but it's not an admission of guilt. In fact, there's no benefit for him to admit anything. He'd have to be caught in a lie."

"How do we do that?"

"I don't know."

"Nora Evans and Walter Farmer seemed pretty cozy," I said. "It's a good thing that Simon wasn't with us."

"That's for sure."

We walked up to the Oyster Bar, a nondescript redbrick storefront with a neon sign and a poster in the window advertising pairings of Pure wine with signature dishes, and the wine tasting for Pure with Gerald Parker.

Inside, I spotted Gerald at the bar that ran the length of the place, talking to Derek Mortimer of St. Ives Estate Vineyards and pouring him a glass of wine. Once he was finished and Mortimer stepped away, we went over to him. The Oyster Bar wasn't nearly as crowded as Harry's Half Shell because it didn't have the same reputation for fine seafood.

"Are you okay, Gerald?" I said. "Simon and I were on Route Twenty-Five this afternoon and we saw your truck in the water."

"I really don't have time to talk right now. I'm super-busy. Get you something?"

"No, thanks," I said. "Did you get a look at who was in the car?"

He turned away to serve a new customer. Suddenly, I felt a tap on my shoulder, and I turned to find Derek Mortimer. He wore his usual three-piece suit and held an unlit cigar. "I can fill you in."

"I didn't see you at the bridge," I said.

"I saw the whole thing. I just didn't stick around afterward because I had a meeting to go to."

"So what happened?"

"When we passed the Seafood Barge, Gerald was two cars in front of me, and he wasn't going very fast. But then when we got to the straightaway, this black Jeep Grand Cherokee zoomed past me and the car in front of me and just managed to squeeze in behind Gerald's truck. As they approached the bridge, he or she, I guess, hit the gas hard, but Gerald spotted him and sped up. But the Jeep caught up to him and rammed his bumper, really hard. The truck skidded off the road, flew into the air, and ended up in the water. It's a miracle that he's here tonight."

"Any idea who was in the Jeep?" Jackson said.

"No," Mortimer said. "Tinted windows." The door to the Oyster Bar opened and he waved to someone he knew. "I need to say hello to someone, please excuse me."

"That's quite a story," I said. "I wonder who was driving the Jeep?"

"I don't know, but there's no one else of interest here, and I just saw Ramsey Black walk by outside. Shall we follow him?"

"Definitely."

We followed Ramsey Black to Whitman's, a quaint new boutique hotel in Sterling Square, four blocks north of the harbor. The menu and accommodations had quickly won raves, and that Crocker Cellars was the featured vintner here tonight indicated the winery's dominance in the market—besides Pure. We waited a few minutes after Ramsey went in before we followed.

When we did enter, the place was packed, and the bar was crowded with customers wanting a taste from Camille and Carter of Crocker Cellars' entry in the *Wine Lovers* magazine contest, while others waited for tables to sample the wine pairings with various dishes.

The interior had the appeal of an English pub, with table groupings around a fireplace that blazed in the low light of the dining room. Bookshelves filled with the nineteenth-century poet Walt Whitman's literary works lined the walls along with illustrations and photos of him, and his sister's house on South Street in Greenport, where he often visited, along with other memorabilia.

Because it was so dark, though, it was difficult to see who exactly was here, including Ramsey, who seemed to have vanished. But then I spotted him heading back to the bar from Carla Olsen's table in the dining room. She sat at a table with a woman I didn't recognize.

We walked over toward him. "Evening, Jackson, Willow," he said. "How are you two this evening?"

"We're fine, Ramsey," Jackson said.

An awkward silence ensued, after which Ramsey said, "I heard about the arrest of your employee, Willow. It's difficult to imagine someone that young and pretty doing something like this."

"We don't think she did," I said.

"From what I can gather, she did have motive."

"She wasn't the only one," Jackson said.

"You, for example," I said. "We've heard rumors that you are involved with Ivy Lord. It's not beyond the realm of possibility that you might want her husband, David, out of the way."

Ramsey waved the suggestion away. "That's preposterous, on both counts. Ivy and I are just good friends."

"But you were involved with her sister, Amy, right?" Jackson said. "Until she broke it off?"

"I don't see what that has to do with anything."

"If you and Ivy are such good friends, you must know about Amy's will and the fact that she left her estate to Gerald Parker," Jackson said. "I imagine that Ivy isn't very happy about that."

"I don't know anything about that. Now, if you'll excuse me, I need to circulate."

"In a minute," Jackson said. "Where were you this afternoon around four o'clock?"

"Not that it's any of your business, but I was at a wine tasting with Ivy at Harrison Jones's vineyard, Wave Crest. I met Nora Evans there, along with the other judges. Why?"

"Because Gerald Parker had an accident around that time on the Mill Creek Bridge. Someone rammed the back of his truck and he ended up in Peconic Bay."

"Fortunately, he's okay," I said. "So he'll still inherit. If he hadn't, a clause in the will stipulates that his share of the Pure vineyard would go to Ivy."

"I did no such thing, and I'm sure that Ivy didn't either. Now, I need to go." Ramsey pushed past us into the crowd.

"I think we're done here," Jackson said. "Let's go check in with Simon and David at Salt."

But as we turned to go, Carter Crocker blocked our way. "I have a bone to pick with you, Willow. You upset my wife this afternoon, and at a very inopportune time. This tasting tonight is very important to us, but it was all I could do just to get her to come."

"I didn't mean to upset Camille," I said.

"Well, you did, and I don't like it much."

"I don't like it either, but I had reason to believe that you were trying to lure Gerald Parker away from Pure, which would have been a problem for my friend Simon Lewis and, more important, may have something to do with Amy Lord's murder."

"Come again?"

"From what we've been told, Crocker Cellars is a close second to Pure in the *Wine Lovers* competition,"

Jackson said. "I guess we're wondering how far you might go to win. Maybe trying to hire Gerald away was just the tip of the iceberg. Maybe you two took a run at David Farmer at the party on Sunday and killed Amy Lord instead. Maybe you didn't stop there and you two are behind the attempts on his life over the past week."

"And since Gerald didn't jump at the chance to work for you, it's also possible that either you or your wife ran him off the road earlier today, just to get rid of the competition."

"Both of you are out of your minds," Carter said. "And if you repeat any of this to anyone else, I'll be calling my lawyer and suing you for slander."

After the confrontations with Ramsey Black and Carter Crocker, breathing in the crisp fall air was a welcome relief. We decided to go to Salt and check in and go home. Tomorrow would be a busy day, with Lily's release, a weekend crowd at Nature's Way, and a slate of activities at Pure, not to mention the ball at Southwold Hall, where the winner of the *Wine Lovers* magazine competition would be announced.

Salt, like Harry's Half Shell and Whitman's, was packed with people, dining and queuing up to the bar to sample Falling Leaves and other Pure vintages. Simon sat at the end of the bar with Harrison Jones of Wave Crest Vineyard, which was opportune, since I wanted to check Ramsey Black's alibi for the time of Gerald's accident this afternoon.

"Hey, you two," Simon said, waving us over. He

had on a smart-looking teal-blue suit with a brown tie, while Harrison was dressed casually in jeans, a T-shirt, and a checkered blazer.

Harrison stood and kissed me on the cheek and shook Jackson's hand. "Good to see you again. Twice in one week, lucky me."

"We just saw Ramsey Black at the Whitman Inn," I said. "He told us that he was at your place this afternoon for a tasting with Nora Evans. What time was that?"

"Three thirty, why?"

"We're still trying to figure out who is making the attempts on David's life and who killed Amy Lord. My assistant, Lily Bryan, has been arrested, so we need answers."

"I understand. He was there from three thirty to five o'clock and I didn't see him leave in between. Does that help?"

I looked at Jackson. "We're not sure."

"Is David here with Tony?" Jackson said, looking around.

"Came and went," Simon said. "His arm was really bothering him, so he and Ivy made an appearance around eight o'clock and went home an hour later. He did say to tell you that Tony is working out great, but he'd like you to be at Pure tomorrow since there will be a lot going on. We've got a concert on the lawn, arcade games, a bouncy castle, and a Halloween costume contest for the kids, not to mention all the people coming in for tours and tastings."

"I'll be there," Jackson said. "With all that activity, it's the perfect smoke screen if someone is planning another attempt on David's life."

• • •

Since it was getting late, we decided that we'd stay at
Nature's Way for the night and headed back to the store.
After Jackson checked in with his volunteer and made
sure that all the animals were doing well, we headed
upstairs with the dogs, and my cats, Ginger and Ginkgo.

Jackson changed into sweats and got in bed, while I
changed into a T-shirt and pajama pants and went into
the bathroom to wash my face. When I came out, Jackson had a pad of paper and was writing notes. The dogs
were at the foot of the bed, already sleeping, while the
cats, curious sorts that they are, sat on the windowsills.
"What are you doing, hon?"

"Jotting down the people we think may be involved
and possible means, motive, and opportunity. This is
what I've got so far." He showed me the first page.

Suspect	Means	Motive	Opportunity
Lily Bryan	Poison (OH)	Anger at David over breakup	Food Prep

"Why do you have Lily listed? We know that she
didn't do it."

"Just to be thorough, keep reading."

Camille C.	Poison (OH)	Win competition, be #1 vineyard	At party
Carter C.	Poison (OH)	Be #1, save wife's dream	At party
Ivy Lord	Poison (OH)	Control of Pure, Relationship with RB	At party
Ramsey B.	Poison (OH)	Relationship with Ivy, Control of Pure	At party

Gerald P.	Poison (OH)	Take over as Pure's head winemaker	At party
Kurt F.	Poison (OH)	Revenge for leaving family business	At party
Walter F.	Poison (OH)	Same motive as Kurt	At party
Carla O.	Poison (OH)	Revenge for breakup	At party
Derek M.	Poison (OH)	Destroy Pure's dominance	At party

"Did I forget anyone?"

"I don't think so, but what does OH mean?"

"'On hand,' meaning they had poison-hemlock plants on their property or had access to it."

"One other thing: Camille and Carter Crocker, Ivy Lord and Ramsey Black, and Kurt and Walter Farmer could have worked together or acted alone."

"True," Jackson said. "Oh, wait. Should we include Leonard Sims on the list?"

"Probably, since he wanted Pure back, but I don't think that Derek Mortimer should be on here. His vineyard is way back in the pack, and he doesn't have much of a motive." I handed the pad back to Jackson.

He scribbled out Mortimer's name and info, flipped the page, and added Sims's.

Suspect	Means	Motive	Opportunity
~~Derek M.~~	~~Poison (OH)~~	~~Destroy Pure's dominance~~	~~At party~~
Leonard Sims	Poison (OH)	Get Pure back?	At party

"Okay, Mortimer is out, and Sims is in." Jackson handed me the pad. "So who did it, Miss Fletcher?"

"Ha, ha." I gave him a smile, got into bed with the pad, and snuggled up next to him. We examined the names and each person's motive, means, and opportunity together. "We also need to keep in mind that we don't know if the person or persons sending the nasty texts and e-mails and whoever attacked David are the same people."

"It's also possible that there are three possibilities: whoever tried to kill Amy, whoever is attacking David since her death, and whoever is sending the messages."

"I just don't see how we are going to figure this out. And we have to, for Lily's sake."

"Yes, but going for the jugular with Kurt Farmer, Ramsey Black, and Carter Crocker didn't yield much. Maybe we should have taken a more subtle approach."

"We don't have time to be subtle. We need answers."

"What we need," Jackson said. "Is a break. Once that happens, the rest should fall into place."

"Maybe we need to just clear our minds for now and go to sleep." I leaned over and gave him a kiss. "We might get answers while we're dreaming. I've had that happen before."

Jackson dropped the pad on the floor, put the pen on the nightstand, and pulled me close. "I've got a much better idea."

It seemed as if a good night's sleep and fun between the sheets had been good for both of us. We woke up early Sunday morning feeling clearheaded and ready for action. After we showered and got dressed in jeans, T-shirts, sweatshirts, and boots, we headed downstairs with the dogs for breakfast and to plan our day. We were due at Pure at noon, but since Tad was on deck again, I had the freedom this morning to try to find answers.

Happily, Merrily had the fixings for more pumpkin pancakes, so after Tad served us, Jackson and I sat down at the table near the window and enjoyed them— and gave tiny tidbits to the dogs as well. We were just finishing up when my cell phone buzzed. "It's Simon. I'll put it on speaker since no one is here."

"Hi, guys, just wanted to tell you that Lily has been released from jail."

"That's good news," I said, and it might give us a bit of breathing room to solve her case. "Where is she going?"

Jackson picked up our plates and took them into the kitchen. I mouthed, *Thanks*, and pointed to my cup. He nodded.

"Obviously, she can't leave the state and go to her parents' house in Boston, so they'll be at Wallace's house with his wife. They're headed to the hospital now, and then they'll go back there."

Jackson came back with the coffee server and poured us both fresh cups of coffee. But when he sat down, he also had the packet of photos that I'd taken of the vineyard signs yesterday and began to go through them again.

"Okay, thanks, Simon," I said. "I'll check in with Wallace and Lily in a few minutes. How is David today?" Jackson continued to go through the photos. I mouthed, *What are you doing?*

"Looking for a break."

"What?"

"No, go ahead, Simon." I picked up the photos
Jackson had discarded of Crocker Cellars and St. Ives
Estate Vineyards. He shook his head.

"David's arm is really bothering him, so I suggested
he take a pain pill and go back to bed. We're not opening until noon, so he has time. He won't be up to staying the whole time anyway, especially with the judging
tonight, but he wants to show his face."

"We'll be there at noon," I said, to keep an eye on
David and everyone else.

"What are you doing this morning? I know that
you're not just sitting there. Or are you busy at the
store?"

"I think I found something," Jackson said.

"Simon, hold on for a minute." I turned to Jackson.
"What is it?"

He turned a photo of Farmer's Vineyard to show me
the sign. "I think I see something, but I need to magnify it."

"Simon, I'll call you back." I ended the call, asked
Merrily and Tad to look for something that could magnify parts of a photo, and went into my office. I came
up empty, but when I came back out, Merrily, smiling,
stood next to the counter, holding up Wallace's glasses.
"Will these help? He told me that they magnify things
one hundred and sixty percent. He uses them to read
labels when he's stocking items."

"They sure will, thanks." I handed them to Jackson.

He smoothed the photo out on the table, then used
the glasses to zero in on the barn behind the sign. "You
see that?"

"I'm not sure."

"Look closer." He pointed to a large white sign with grapes leaning on the wall, inside the open barn door. "If I'm not mistaken, that's the sign that was in the background of the photo that was sent to David."

"And if they did that," I said. "Maybe they tried to kill David, too."

chapter twenty-two

We jumped into Jackson's truck and took off for Farmer's Vineyard. We alerted Simon, but waited to call the police to be sure our hunch was correct. We arrived there ten minutes later, but again no one seemed to be home. Jackson parked on the street and we surveyed the property—for some reason, the barn door was now closed.

"These two could be dangerous," Jackson said. "So I want you to follow my lead." He reached into the glove compartment and pulled out a small handgun and put it in a case on his belt. "Even though it looks like they're not home, they could be here. So we'll use the neighbors' property to the left and cut over when we get to the front of the barn. You'll stay put and I'll go across to the door and check for the sign." He grabbed his binoculars from the glove compartment, closed it, and looked at me. "In fact, you should really stay in the truck."

"Forget it, I'm coming." I held up my camera. "For proof. Let's go." We got out of the truck, closed the doors quietly, and headed for the property of the neighbors—who luckily weren't home either—while keeping an eye on the Farmers' property.

When we drew even with the front of the barn, we stepped over the property line and went over to the building. Jackson took out his binoculars and peered around the corner at the house. "I really don't think anyone is home. I'm going to check it out. You stay put."

"But I want to see. And take photos."

Jackson blew out a breath. "I told you this would get dangerous at some point, but you didn't listen."

"I couldn't turn my back on Simon and David and Lily and Wallace."

"I know, I know. At least let me get the door open and take a look first. Then I'll wave you in, okay?"

I nodded. "Okay."

He used his binoculars to check out the house and grounds again before slowly stepping toward the barn door. I craned my head around the building and watched him as he reached the door, opened it, and went inside. He came back out, nodded, and took his gun out. He looked around again, then waved me in.

The inside of the barn was dusty, dirty, and dank and filled with old farm equipment and a riding lawn mower. But the one thing it had in its favor was the brand-new Farmer's Vineyard sign, leaning against the wall, featuring a bunch of grapes on a white background.

"Kurt or Walter must have taken the photos they

sent to David, with this new sign in the background, and then realized their mistake too late," I said as I snapped photos of the sign.

"But they didn't hide it well enough," Jackson said.

"Is this enough to prove that they tried to kill David and killed Amy instead?"

"No, just harassment for now." Jackson went to the door. "We need to get out of here and call the police."

I snapped a few more photos, and we returned to the truck the way we'd come, with Jackson serving as lookout. When we got back inside and Jackson had pulled away from the vineyard, he said, "I wish there was a way to get these to the cops without them tracing it to us. Because they'll definitely give us a hard time about breaking into the barn. And if for some reason we're wrong, the Farmers could have us arrested for trespassing."

"We could send them to Simon and he could forward them, maybe say that he got them anonymously."

"Detective Koren won't believe that for one second. Check the police department website—maybe they have a place for tips and information."

I found the website for the police and checked it for a way to send photos. "There's nothing here. But we could print the photos out and fax them over with a note. What do you think?"

"I like it."

We returned to Nature's Way, where I used Photoshop on the office computer to enlarge the section of the photo that featured the new sign hidden in the barn as seen from the road and printed it out, along with two up-close photos of the sign in the barn, and attached all of them to single pieces of copy paper with a glue stick. Next, I printed out a note outlining our theory of why the new sign had been hidden.

After that, Jackson drove me to a busy drugstore two towns away, so I could fax all four pages to the police station. That done, we headed back to Jackson's house in East Marion with the dogs, so he could check on his animals and we could grab lunch before we headed over to Pure.

We arrived at Pure at noon on Sunday to find the parking lot jam-packed, kids jumping in a pink bouncy castle, and people dancing on the front lawn to the band playing a variety of songs. It felt strange to realize that it had only been a week since Amy's murder because so much had transpired since then.

We found a crowd inside, people who already had glasses of wine and others who were in line to get to the tasting room or the bar. We found Simon working quietly in his office, while David slept on the couch, his cast propped up on two pillows, and Tony kept watch at the door. He waved us in, but Simon got up and came over to us and we went back downstairs. "It's better that he sleeps," Simon said. "We need him in good shape for the judging at Southwold Hall tonight."

"If David is sleeping and you're with us, who's handling the tasting and the activities outside?" I said.

"Simple. Ivy is in the tasting room, Gerald's giving tours of the barn, and East End Events hired the band, got the bouncy castle delivered, and the rest. You just have to delegate, that's all."

"I see." Jackson smiled. "Now why didn't I think of that?"

We walked over to the bar. "I'm so nervous about tonight that I can barely stand it. I need a drink." Simon waved over the bartender and asked for a vodka and soda with a lime wedge, then looked at us. We both shook our heads no.

"Good job with that photo, Jackson," Simon said, picking up his glass and walking over to the windows that overlooked the lawn. "That's pretty amazing. But I'll bet that Detective Koren won't like the fact that you were on the property."

"We found a way around that," Jackson said.

The crowd clapped as the band ended a song. Simon said, "Did you know that they've done research at Heriot-Watt University that shows that certain types of music improved the taste of wine up to sixty percent? Want to enjoy cabernet sauvignon, then tune in to powerful and heavy music like the Rolling Stones and the Who. Prefer chardonnay? Play zingy and refreshing sounds like Blondie and Tina Turner. Merlot? Try Otis Redding and Lionel Richie."

"It sounds fascinating," Jackson said. "I guess if you're all set here, we could go outside and check things out."

But he spoke too soon because Tony came hustling down the stairs. "Simon? David got another text. He wants you to come up."

We followed Simon up the stairs to his office. David, his face drawn and pale, was now sitting up on the couch and staring at his phone. "They did it again." He turned the phone to show us an image of a skull and the words *Pull out of the* Wine Lovers *contest or you die!*

"I can't take much more of this. You gotta do something!"

Jackson and I looked at each other, then I said, "David, we found out who is doing this to you—the texts and the e-mails, at least."

"We know this is tough to hear," Jackson said. "But we think it's either Kurt or your father."

"What are you talking about?"

"Jackson examined the photo I'd taken of the Farmer's Vineyard sign and spotted something being stored in the barn. When we checked it out, we found a new sign that had been stashed there, the same one that was in the background of the photo you were sent Friday night and didn't recognize. We think they put the old sign back up, and the new one in the barn, once they realized what they'd done, so it couldn't be traced.

"We sent the evidence to the police," Jackson said. "So they're going to want to talk to your father and brother."

"But they're here," David said. "I spotted them outside a few minutes ago. I don't know, though. Are they the ones who've been attacking me this week? Did they kill Amy?"

"We're not sure about anything but the texts and e-mails," Jackson said. "That doesn't mean that they have or haven't done anything else to harm you."

"That little punk." David tried to push himself up from the couch. "I'll kill him!"

• • •

After we searched the grounds, the crowds, the offices, the bathrooms, and the tasting room, we went out back to the barn. When we walked inside, small groups of people were wandering around, checking out the equipment and the bottled wines. And Kurt and Walter were hunched over a wine barrel, extracting samples with a syringe and putting them into glass containers. They were so engrossed in what they were doing that they didn't hear David walk up behind them.

"Is that enough?" Kurt said.

"This is not right," Walter said. "It isn't fair to your brother."

"We need an edge. Suck it up, Dad."

"I can't believe you two," David said.

Startled, Kurt turned back to look at him, and as he did, the syringe dribbled "futures" wine all over the floor, while his father dropped the glass container on the floor, shattering it.

"This is really low, even for you, Kurt."

"I can explain."

"Oh, yeah? Can you explain this?" David showed them the skull and warning. "What were you doing, trying to throw me off my game?" He pointed to his arm. "Did you do this, too?"

"No, man," Kurt said. "It was just the messages, and Dad had nothing to do with it."

"There he is," Detective Koren said as he entered the room with Detective Coyle and two patrolmen. "Kurt Farmer. You're under arrest."

"You called the cops on me?" Kurt frowned at his brother. "That's low, man."

"No, what you've done is low, despicable, really."

"It is," I said.

"How did you know he was here?" Jackson said.

"We tracked the messages to his phone and his phone to this location. It's called police work, Spade," Detective Koren said.

"Plus we got a tip with photos by fax," Detective Coyle said, looking pleased with himself.

"Shut up, Coyle," Detective Koren said, putting the cuffs on Kurt. "Let's go."

Named for owner Charles Attwater's ancestral home in Southwold, Suffolk, UK, Southwold Hall had been constructed between 1849 and 1855 on a bluff over Long Island Sound. Attwater made his fortune as a shipbuilder, whaling-fleet owner, and bank owner. The hall was the family residence, and several generations of the family lived there until the 1990s, when it fell into disrepair. In 2000, the Southwold Hall Foundation was formed to refurbish, preserve, and maintain the home for the community. Now a noted historical landmark, it was used for cultural events and educational programs, along with weddings and other celebrations.

The hall was impressive, built in the Italianate style using stone cut from the glacial deposits on the land, which are unusual for sandy eastern Long Island. The exterior resembled the rocks found on our local Sound beaches, gray, white, brown, and beige, with bright white wood trim, and an expansive gray stone walkway and lavish plantings that led to the door. As we pulled in Sunday night, a little before seven o'clock, and drove around back to park, every window on the top and bottom floors was ablaze.

We could have walked, but since I had chosen a strapless royal-blue evening gown with a sweetheart bodice and beaded silver lace in a flower pattern, paired with gunmetal strappy high-heeled sandals, matching clutch, opera-length gloves, and sparkly cobalt rhinestone earrings, it really wasn't an option.

Jackson wore a vintage gray pinstripe suit, complete with vest, pressed white shirt, black tie, pocket square, and wing-tip shoes. When it came to dressing up, I always preferred to go vintage, and Jackson had grown to like it a lot, too.

"I have to say, you are really working that dress, hon," Jackson said as we reached the walkway. "It really hugs your curves, especially in the hips. But really, Willow, you look beautiful. You always do."

"Thank you, kind sir, and you look fab, too. Love the suit. We match."

He took my hand. "We certainly do." He reached inside his jacket and pulled out a box. "And I have something else for you."

"What? But we haven't talked about this lately."

"This isn't that. But we both know that it's coming." Jackson handed me the box. "Open it."

Inside I found a cool retro cocktail ring. "It's perfect for my outfit."

"I know, that's why I picked it up. It's green prehnite

and sterling silver." He slipped it on. "Think of it as a placeholder."

"I love it." I kissed him. "And I love you."

"I love you, too." He took my hand and gestured to the entrance. "Shall we go in?"

"Yes, let's go to the ball."

Jackson opened the door and we stepped into the foyer, which had been painted a lemon yellow, with white trim, and had refinished hardwood floors, three large mirrors on the wall, an elaborate gold chandelier, a Steinway piano, and carpeted stairs that led to the second floor.

We joined the line to enter the ballroom, and when we reached the double doors, an attendant took our tickets and gave us programs. The tickets weren't cheap—$150 per—but we wanted to support Simon and also thought it would be a fun event. Of course, this was months ago, before the events of the past week.

The spacious three-thousand-square-foot ballroom had also been restored to its original grandeur, with a travertine floor, embellished European plasterwork, and a hand-painted ceiling, with four crystal chandeliers, two mahogany bars, two fireplaces, and banquette seating near the entrance.

For the event, the organizers had added a stage for the jazz band and the *Wine Lovers* magazine judging, and four wine-tasting stations featuring all the vintages in contention for the prize. In the crowd I spotted the Crockers, Ramsey Black, Derek Mortimer, Harrison Jones, Carla Olsen, Gerald Parker, and Leonard Sims.

David and Simon entered with Tony a few minutes

later and headed over to join us. David and Simon looked like twins in well-tailored black suits, except for David's cast—and that he hadn't bothered to shave—while Tony had made an effort by donning black pants, a green shirt, and a black blazer. But no tie.

"Hi, you two," Simon said. "You look great. Love the coordination with the shades of gray."

I held out my hand to show them the ring. "Look what Jackson just gave me. Isn't it pretty?"

Simon grinned. "Willow, Jackson, is this what I think it is?"

"Think of it as an appetizer," Jackson said. "Main course to come."

"Okay, got it. Cool."

"So are you two excited?" I said. "Pretty soon, you'll know what Nora decided."

"Excited, nervous, anxious—the trifecta," Simon said.

"My stomach is in knots," David said. "We worked really hard on that vintage. I hope it pays off."

"Let's talk about something else," Simon said. "They won't announce it for another two hours."

"Any word from Shawn about Lily?"

"Yes, Shawn told me that Lily is home at the Bryans' as of five o'clock. He's back in New York, but before he left, he heard some news from another lawyer about Kurt Farmer. Seems he's sticking with his story. He admits to sending the messages but not the attacks. He said he was just trying to scare David into dropping out and coming back to the family business. It was like you said: once he realized that the new sign was in the photos he'd sent, he hid it in the barn. Walter didn't know anything about it. They're keeping him overnight and then they'll have a bail hearing."

"They do have poison hemlock on the property," I said. "I saw it."

"That must be new," David said. "We never had it before."

"It's behind the barn."

"Even though that's true," Simon said. "He's not budging."

"I just can't believe that he would do this to me," David said. "I mean, don't get me wrong, I'm relieved that the messages have stopped, it was completely unnerving, but I'm also really angry at my brother for what he did."

"Sometimes people want to win so badly that they lose sight of everything else," Jackson said.

"Like whoever is behind the attacks on you and whoever killed Amy," I said.

"I know, but I want to thank you for figuring this out. Sorry about before at the house. I know that you two are only trying to help."

"No problem," Jackson said.

"And we're still working on the rest of it," I said. "We haven't given up."

"Thanks, but for tonight, I just want to forget about all of that and try to enjoy ourselves. I need a drink."

"With painkillers?" I said. "You need to be careful."

"Don't worry, I will be. Tony, let's go." David went over to one of the tasting bars with Tony.

"Where's Ivy?" I said.

"Out in the foyer, talking to one of the judges," Simon said. "Ms. Sara Fletcher, PhD, is here. She just stopped in the ladies' room. Wait, there she is." He smiled and waved her over. "Sara's really great, isn't she?"

"Yes, she is, and she knows her poison plants, too."

"Good going, Simon," Jackson said. "Sara could be really great for you."

"I think so, too. We've been talking on the phone since we met, and I really like her. She's unpretentious, easygoing, supersmart, and really funny, and not at all affected by my TV career and who I know or my money, not to mention that she's a knockout."

"Can't ask for much more than that," Jackson said.

Sara walked up to us, smiled, and said, "Hi, you two, it's so good to see you both again." She looked absolutely terrific in a black velvet V-neck gown, which worked perfectly with her shoulder-length blond hair and her distinctive glasses.

"You, too, Sara," I said.

"Glad you could come," Jackson said.

"You look beautiful, Sara," Simon said. "That dress is amazing on you."

She gave him a dazzling smile. "Thanks, Simon. You look great, too. I like that suit."

"Uh-oh," Simon said. "Here's trouble."

Ivy, in a vibrant red sleeveless, formfitting, most-likely-designer gown marched over to us, an angry look on her face. When she reached us, she said, "We've got trouble."

"Nice dress, Ivy," Simon said.

"Focus, Simon. I just talked to one of the judges, and she said that some of them are leaning toward Crocker Cellars for the win."

Simon sucked in a breath. "This can't be happening. Is it final? That's their decision, really?"

"No, Simon," Ivy said, frustrated. "There are five judges. I know Ramsey is for us, and I think two others. But I'm worried about Nora and the judge from the New York Wine Council."

"So it's three for us, and two against. We're still good. Stop freaking out, Ivy."

"I don't like loose ends."

"When we saw Nora yesterday, at Crocker Cellars, she seemed to be saying that you had it," I said. "But still, she visited Crockers and Wave Crest, and last night we saw her talking to Kurt Farmer in Harry's Half Shell. She has to make the rounds and make nice, but it doesn't mean that she's going to vote for them."

"I guess that's true," Ivy said. "Where's David?"

"Over there," Simon said. "At the bar."

She stomped off.

"Nice lady," Sara said.

"That's no lady, that's my partner."

We were here to enjoy ourselves, so after Ivy went over to speak to her husband, David, and Simon took Sara with them to talk to the judges to try to get the scoop, Jackson and I danced to a few numbers by the band, beginning with "All of Me," one of our favorites. Aunt Claire had taught me how to dance with a partner when I was a teenager, and I'd taught Jackson, so we drew the attention of the crowd as we danced and even received applause at the end of the songs. Afterward, we went to the wine bar, where I had a glass of cabernet sauvignon and Jackson had a seltzer.

At the other end of the bar, Gerald Parker chatted with Derek Mortimer and Carla Olsen. The Crockers headed over to the bar, too, but upon seeing me, Camille turned and went to a tasting station at the opposite end of the room. Derek and Carla wandered off, too, and Ramsey and Ivy went up to the bar. "Let's see if they found out anything about the judging," I said. "And should we ask them about Amy's murder?"

Jackson shook his head. "No, not tonight. Let's keep it casual, except for the competition."

"Simon is anything but. Look at him," I said. "He's talking to Nora Evans and he's pouring on the charm." We watched as Simon did his thing, smiling, touching, chatting, and in general trying to convince Nora to vote for Pure.

I walked up to Ramsey and Ivy, as Jackson followed. "Ivy, are you feeling better about the judging now? I really think that you will win."

"I don't know, and you certainly don't know," Ivy snapped.

"And I can't talk about it," Ramsey said, grabbing two glasses of wine and leading Ivy away.

"I really don't like either of them," I said. "I've tried, or maybe I haven't, but I just can't do it."

"I know what you mean." The band began playing again. "Let's dance." Jackson put his hand out.

We stayed on the dance floor for "Bewitched, Bothered and Bewildered" and "Come Fly with Me," before retreating to the banquette seating by the entrance. A few moments later, Simon and Sara came over to us. "How did it go?"

"I don't know. And I think I'm over it. I just want to know."

Jackson looked at his watch. "Won't be long now."

"Can you believe this?" David said as he joined us. "Ivy said we're in danger of not winning."

"I think she's overreacting," Simon said. "She does that, you know."

"True, but she's even worse tonight, and she's driving me crazy. I think it's Amy's will and the fact that she left her share in Pure to Gerald. It's all she can talk about."

"I've already contacted my estate lawyer," Simon said. "In the meantime, she talked to Ramsey, so maybe he calmed her down."

"I'm sure he can," David said sharply. "What time is it?"

"Almost nine o'clock," Jackson said.

Jackson and I moved toward the stage and danced while the band played "I Only Have Eyes for You" and "Mack the Knife." When they were done, the lead singer announced that the winners of the *Wine Lovers* magazine competition would be announced next. The crowd clapped.

After the band left, two Southwold Hall employees carried a dais onto the stage, placed it in the middle, and set up a microphone, while the rest of the crowd gathered. A few minutes later, the judges climbed the stairs to the stage, conferred for a moment, and stood behind Nora Evans as she went to the microphone.

"Hi, everyone, thanks for joining us at historic

Southwold Hall this evening. I think I speak for all the judges when I say that we have really enjoyed visiting the East End during North Fork UnCorked! week. Meeting all the local vintners and vineyard owners has been nothing less than inspiring. Getting to know you, and observe your process, has only made our decision tonight harder as we've found your community vibrant, talented, and welcoming, and a credit to winemaking here and around the world. You should be very proud."

The crowd clapped. I leaned over and squeezed Simon's arm. "Win or lose, I'm proud of you, Simon."

"Yeah, you done good," Jackson said.

"Thanks, you guys."

"We'll start with the third-place winner. This vineyard will be featured in *Wine Lovers* magazine at some point during 2016 and will receive this award." Nora held up a bronze sculpture of a wineglass with a placard on the base. She turned to confer with Ramsey Black. She said something, and he nodded.

She turned back around. "We think that this vineyard shows real promise and is doing really interesting things with their vintages. The third-place winner is Carla Olsen, of Sisterhood Wines, and her very special Riesling wine—Drunken Vines."

The crowd erupted into cheers, and applause followed Carla up to the stage. She looked surprised and happy as Evans handed her the trophy. "This is a big surprise," Carla said. "There are so many talented vintners here, and I'm proud to be in your company. Thank you."

"Thank you, Carla, and congratulations." Nora

checked her notes. "The second-place vineyard hasn't been around for very long, but it has already made its mark, winning local and regional competitions. We feel they hold great promise for the future. The winner will also be featured in the pages of our magazine and will receive the second-place award."

"This is it," Simon said, taking Sara's hand. "This could be us or we could win."

"Breathe," I said. "It will be okay."

"The second-place winner is . . . Crocker Cellars and their Bordeaux Red Rose."

The crowd clapped, but it was more subdued. Obviously, the Crockers weren't as popular with them as Carla was.

"We did it—did we do it?" Simon said.

"Hold on. You're almost there," I said.

Camille and Carter Crocker stepped onto the stage and went over to the microphone. Unlike Carla, they were not happy, and Carter's statement reflected it. "Thank you, judges, for this award. We worked hard to make a vintage that was worth recognition. Although this isn't what we were hoping for, we are grateful nonetheless. Thank you."

The Crockers headed off the stage, and Evans stepped back to the microphone. Jackson and I and Simon and Sara took one another's hands. Simon gave a thumbs-up to David, who stood to our right with Ivy and Tony.

"Now, the moment we've all been waiting for." Evans smiled. "This vineyard has been the leader in innovation on the East End, in the region, and nationwide. We think this is the case because the winemaker here views winemaking as art and science, and this imbues each vintage with something almost intangible, truly special, and excitingly unique."

She picked up the award. "The winner of the *Wine Lovers* magazine competition will receive a four-page photo spread in the spring 2016 issue of our publication, and the two-hundred-thousand-dollar prize."

The drummer of the band got back in place and did a drumroll. "The winner is . . . Pure vineyard and their pinot noir Falling Leaves! Come on up, David and Ivy Lord and Simon Lewis!"

chapter twenty-three

Simon jumped into the air and pumped his fist. "We did it!" He hugged Sara, then hugged me and Jackson. "Thanks, guys. Let's do this!" David gave Simon a high five with his good hand and kissed Ivy. The three of them headed up to the stage.

Nora Evans handed the trophy to David and shook all their hands. "Great job—really a top-notch vintage! Very impressive all around. We're excited to see what you craft next year, aren't we, folks?"

The crowd clapped loudly, and a few people whistled.

"Wow, wow, wow," David said. "Thank you, *Wine Lovers* magazine. We are very grateful for the award and everything it means. We do try to combine art and science at Pure, and this honor will only encourage us to push the boundaries of winemaking, not only for our vineyard but to raise the bar for the industry.

"I'd like to also thank my wife, Ivy Lord, and our partner, Simon Lewis, and Gerald Parker." David looked at Jackson and me. "And two good friends, Willow McQuade and Jackson Spade, for watching my back. It's been a rough week, losing Ivy's sister, Amy, and we all miss her. So this is for Amy. Thanks, everyone!"

Ivy, smiling, stepped up to the mike. "Thank you so much. This award is all because of my husband, David, and his brilliance, and out-of-the-box thinking." She kissed David.

"Thank you!" Simon said into the mike. "It's been a long and winding road for me from Hollywood producer and screenwriter to vintner, but I've enjoyed every minute of it. I want to thank Willow McQuade for introducing me to this, the beautiful East End of Long Island, and her support, along with Jackson Spade." Simon waved to us, and the crowd turned to look. He held up the award. "And I promise you that you'll see this prize money invested in our new and even more exciting 'futures'!"

The crowd laughed, but Gerald, who was on the other side of the stage, turned and walked out.

An hour later, after photos were taken of all the winners and the winning vintages, Simon, Ivy, David, and Gerald were all still being inundated by local, regional, and national press. Meanwhile, the rest of the crowd, including Jackson and me, enjoyed themselves on the dance floor and were chatting to one another. All were in a celebratory mood and, for the evening, focused on the present moment and enjoying the event.

But then I saw Lily enter, dressed in a champagne-colored one-shoulder gown, with a slit down the side that hugged her body, bronze evening sandals, opera-length gloves, and her hair up in a French twist.

"Lily's here," I said as I danced with Jackson to "P.S. I Love You."

"That's not good." He turned to look at her. "We'd better go talk to her, make sure she doesn't make a scene again or, even better, leaves. It's more than likely a condition of her bail that she stay away from David."

We left the dance floor and walked over to her at the tasting bar closest to the door. "Lily, what are you doing here? You need to lie low. By the way, you look amazing."

"You do," Jackson said. "But this is a bad idea. It could revoke your bail. Didn't the judge tell you to stay away from David?"

"I guess, but I won't make a scene, don't worry." She picked up a glass of chablis. "It's just that I had planned to come and I really needed to get out. Did Pure win?"

I nodded. "Yes, and everyone is very happy about it. Please don't spoil it by trying to confront David and getting upset all over again."

"You have my promise. But I do see a few of my friends that I'd like to say hi to. Is that okay? I promise that I won't stay long."

"Sure," I said. "Just chill, no drama."

"You got it."

As she walked over to a group of her friends, David spotted her and said something to Simon. "I'll bet that Simon is giving David the same lecture we just did to Lily."

Jackson blew out a sigh. "I have a hard time believing that this will end well."

• • •

Half an hour later, Jackson and I were back on the dance floor, dancing to "Puttin' On the Ritz," when Simon, in a panic, came over to us. "Have you seen David? The *New York Times* Long Island reporter wants to interview us and I can't find him."

"Lily?"

"Probably, I can't find her either."

"We'll help you look," I said.

"I'll check the foyer and search upstairs," Jackson said. "Why don't you two look around down here? I'll be right back."

We separated and looked for David, and possibly Lily, at opposite ends of the ballroom, including behind the stage, in the bathrooms, and in the cloakroom. We met back in the middle between two tasting stations, next to the doors that led to the back lawn.

"Where's Jackson?" I said. "Should we check upstairs or outside?"

"He's probably still looking around." Simon took off his jacket. "Put this on, and we'll check the backyard."

Outside, spotlights illuminated the back stone terrace and the steps to the rolling green lawn. Beyond that, the only light came from the moon. "Do you have your flashlight?" Simon said.

I pointed to my purse. "In this thing, no. But we could use our phones."

"No can do, my battery just died. It was all those interviews. Some of the reporters had more questions on their way home."

"Mine is fully charged, and I didn't use it tonight at all."

"How do you live without it out at all times?"

"I get by." I reached inside to grab my phone, but the edge of the rubber case had become hooked on my wallet's zipper. Gently, I pulled it off and separated the two. As I did, I noticed a receipt sticking out of the wallet.

"Flashlight, please?"

I closed the purse and handed my phone to Simon, and he turned the flashlight on.

"Hey, look over there!" Simon said. "Someone is on the edge of the cliff. It looks like they're fighting or something. Is that Ivy? I think it is."

"Is she with David?"

"Can't tell, but it looks like a guy, and Amy . . . no, I meant to say Ivy. You know, even when she was alive, if it wasn't for the way they were dressed—you know, Ivy in her designer labels and Amy in her bohemian chic—I couldn't tell them apart. It must be crazy being twins."

His words stopped me in my tracks. I opened my purse, took out my wallet, and pulled out the receipt. I remembered it now. "Can I have the flashlight, please?" I trained the light on the piece of paper. "Why didn't I spot this before?"

"Spot what?" Simon said. "Wait a minute, she pushed him! I can't tell if he went over the cliff or not."

He started running, so I shoved the receipt back in my purse and followed him, but stumbled and fell in my high heels to the dew-damp ground, right on top of a grouping of poison-hemlock plants.

"You okay?"

As Simon helped me up, I pointed to the ground. "There's poison hemlock here, too."

"Forget that, I think she pushed that guy off the cliff!" The moon was so bright that Simon put the flashlight in his pocket and we ran across the path of light to the edge of the cliff. But when we got there, the woman was gone.

"Look! He's down there!" Simon pointed down at the beach.

Lying on the beach was a man's body, but it was difficult to tell if it was David or not. I pointed to the stairs. "We can take those down to the beach."

"Shouldn't we wait for backup?"

"The man could be dying, Simon! Let's go!"

"I'll do it on the way!"

I took off my heels and his jacket and left the items on the cliff face, and we headed down the wooden steps that led to the rocky beach. Any kid who grew up out here, including me, knew that there were 101 steps from the top to the bottom, and it certainly seemed like a long way down tonight. The steps were in need of repair, and more than once I almost put my foot right through, and the railing was rickety and unstable.

As we got closer to the beach, Simon tried repeatedly to call Jackson and 911, but he couldn't get a signal. "I have no bars," he kept screaming. "Is it too much to ask for one freakin' stinkin' bar!"

A few minutes later we reached the beach and made our way across the large stones and between the boulders to the cliff's edge, where the body had fallen.

But it wasn't David Farmer, it was Gerald Parker.

"Gerald? Gerald! It's Simon and Willow," Simon said. "Are you okay?"

Gerald opened his eyes and choked out, "No . . . just wanted to talk. Make it fair." He closed his eyes again.

"Gerald, who did this to you?" I said, but his eyes remained closed. He had a bloody gash over his left eye, and bruises all over his face. His pants were ripped at the knees, and his right arm stuck out at an odd angle and was probably broken.

"Gerald! Answer her," Simon yelled.

Gerald opened his eyes and stared into the inky blackness of the sky. "Two of them." His eyes closed, and he opened his hand. On his palm were two leaves from one of the poison-hemlock plants on the lawn. Suddenly, the night seemed so still, except for the waves lapping at the shore.

"Oh my God, he's dead, isn't he?"

"Simon, we need to get out of here." I stood up. "I think I know what's going on."

"Now you figure it out? You couldn't have done so a little earlier?"

"Stuff it. Get going, and try to get the police and Jackson again."

We climbed back up at double time while Simon repeatedly tried to reach someone and became more and more panicked as we neared the top of the steps. "I still can't get a freakin' bar! What is it with this place? I thought that sound signals or something travel better over water. I can't believe this. We should never have come out here alone. We should have waited for Jackson. Oh my God, I realize that we could be next!"

"Keep trying. And try not to freak out."

"I can't stay calm at a time like this! Damnit! It won't go through. Hey, what were you saying about figuring it out? Who did this?"

Finally, we reached the top and stepped onto the ground. As we did, I said, "It all fits now, I think it's—"

But before I could finish, someone stepped out of the shadows, pointing a gun at us. "Surprise, you two. It's me, Amy." She had a fiendish look in her eyes, as if the mask she'd been wearing for the past week had slipped, and the bottom of her red formfitting dress now had grass and dirt stains on the hem.

"Amy?" Simon said. "Amy's dead. Amy? Oh my God! What is happening?"

"Actually, I'm very much alive." Amy smiled. She'd put back on the red lipstick that she'd always worn in life. In the moonlight, her skin washed of color, she looked almost ghoulish.

"It's Amy, all right," I said. "And I think I can prove it. But I need to open my purse."

"Do you have a gun?"

"No, of course not."

"You should in your line of work. It can be dangerous." She smiled even wider. "Go ahead, open it."

I opened it, pulled out the wallet, and took out the receipt. "I found this in Amy's coat in the guesthouse closet. It's a receipt for a very particular shade of lipstick. The only shade that Amy likes to wear—Ivy, on the other hand, goes for pink and coral hues."

"I don't get it." Simon shook his head. "Lipstick? What?"

"This receipt is dated Thursday, four days after

Amy died. She wouldn't have much use for lipstick in the afterlife."

"Very good, Willow. I picked it up this week. You see, I'd run out of Bodacious Ruby Red Lip Love, and it is *my* signature hue. And I like to wear it when I'm by myself at night in my guesthouse."

"That's why you didn't get rid of any of your clothes, too."

"I might need them."

"I don't get it. If you're Amy, then why did you kill Gerald?"

"Usually, I am very organized, but it slipped my mind that I'd left my share of Pure to Gerald. Things happened so fast on Sunday that I had to improvise. Gerald inheriting part of Pure just didn't work for me, so I eliminated that glitch. Now, Amy's money will go to me as Ivy. It keeps it all in the family." She took out her cell phone and checked something.

"What happened to your watch?"

"That was my sister Ivy's, it's not something I need or want. So I got rid of it." She put the phone in her pocket. "You're very clever to have figured it out, Willow, but it's too bad that you won't live to tell anyone."

It was after midnight, early Monday morning, when Amy Lord took our cell phones and threw them into the Sound, pointed her gun at us, and told us to walk directly to the parking lot on the east side of Southwold Hall. Simon seemed to be barely holding it together and kept throwing me panicky looks, but thanks to daily meditation, even though I was very cold, my mind was clear, and I quickly formulated a plan.

Beginning with the steps at the cliffside, heading toward the parking lot, I decided to create a trail for Jackson and others to follow. Thanks to the cloud cover that obscured the moon, it was now pitch-black outside, and Amy Lord would have limited visibility. I was free to act.

First, acting as if I were brushing my hair out of my face, I carefully reached up and pulled my right earring off and dropped it to the ground. When I had walked another few feet, I repeated my actions with the left earring. The next time, I dropped the ring that Jackson had just given me, and when I was out of jewelry, I tugged at the beads that were attached to the silver lace on my dress and dropped them, too.

Amy directed us to her late sister's Mercedes and handed Simon the keys. "Simon, you drive. Willow, sit in the passenger seat. I'll be in the back and I'll have the gun on both of you. So no surprises."

We got inside the car. Amy got in the back. As Simon fastened his seat belt, he gave me a look of pure desperation. Turning my head so that Amy couldn't see, I mouthed, *It's going to be okay.*

He blew out a breath and put the key in the ignition. "Where are we going?"

"Back to Pure. I have to make a deposit, and a withdrawal."

"What?" Simon said. "What does that mean?"

"Go! And no talking!"

When we arrived at Pure, Amy said, "Go around and pull up next to the B and B so no one sees the car."

Simon did as he was told and drove across the grass path next to the vines in front of Pure, around the bed-and-breakfast, and parked the car. I couldn't decide whether we should try to jump her or wait it out and hope that Jackson and the police arrived soon.

"I know what you're thinking, and don't try it," Amy said. "Now, get out of the car slowly, and remember that I have a gun pointed at your backs." We got out of the car and waited for her instructions. "Go to the barn, and open the door." When we got inside, she pointed to the far side of the barn. "Walk down there."

"You're not going to shoot us, are you?" Simon said. "Don't shoot us!"

"No, I'm not going to shoot you, but I am going to put you in a place where you can't escape. You see that handle on the floor? Simon, grab it and pull."

He opened the compartment and looked in. "What is this?"

"That's the crawl space. Get in."

"I'm not going in there," Simon said. "It's dark and creepy."

"Okay, so you want me to shoot you instead? Fine."

"No, no! Don't shoot! I'll go!" He climbed down the ladder.

"Now, you."

"Amy, this is nuts, you can't get away with this."

"I think I can. I have plenty of cash since I withdrew most of Ivy and David's money, I have a current passport, and if they ever do find you, I'll be in a nice warm climate."

"Did you plan to kill Gerald tonight?"

"No, things got out of hand, and people saw me go outside with him. So when they find his body they'll put it together—even these dumb cops. So that's why I have to leave. For good. Now get in there."

chapter twenty-four

Stuffy, dusty, and dirty, the crawl space ran the length and width of the barn, but with only about three feet from the ground to the beams that bolstered the wine cellar's floor. Cobwebs covered the walls, the corners, the beams, the window frames, and discarded objects, including an old hot-water heater, a broken lawn chair, a cracked BBQ, and a tarp. But at least the light near the stairs worked.

"This place is filthy," Simon said. "This is really going to set off all my allergies, big-time, plus I'm all hunched over because I can't stand up in here, so there goes my back."

"Simon, you're alive, that's what's important. So give it a rest and start thinking of ways to get out."

"How are we going to do that? She locked the door, and those windows are too small."

"If we could find some kind of tool, we could dig around one of the windows to make the opening larger and crawl out. Let's take a look around and see what we can find." The two of us began to scuttle around the space, trying to avoid hitting our heads on the beams above.

"Okay," Simon said, "I really wish she hadn't taken your phone."

"Tell me about it." As I stepped forward, I kicked something with my foot that made a metallic sound as it hit the wall.

"What's that?"

"I think it's a hammer." I went over and picked it up. "Yup."

"Hey, I found a screwdriver."

"Good, I'll work on the left side of the window, you work on the right."

Half an hour later, we hadn't made much progress, and we were both cold, tired, and thirsty.

"Now what?" Simon said. "We just hope that someone finds us, and if not, we die down here? I hate that plan."

"Me, too." I used the hammer to shatter the window, and glass shards landed on the grass outside. "Start yelling. If anyone is around besides Amy, maybe they'll hear us."

"Help! Help! We're stuck in the crawl space!"

"Yeah, help us! We're in the barn—under the barn in the crawl space. Help!"

A few minutes later, the handle on the door to the crawl space turned, and the door opened. "You called?"

"Jackson!" I ran up the stairs, and he enveloped me in a warm hug. "I'm so glad that you're here!"

"Me, too, McQuade, me, too. I was worried about you. But then I heard you two yelling, and here I am."

Simon climbed out and collapsed on the floor. "Thank goodness you came. We were trying to dig ourselves out and it wasn't going well."

"Not at all. But how did you know that we were here?"

"Well, when you two didn't come back inside, I went outside to look for you using a flashlight from one of the guys who works at the hall. I did a grid pattern, and on the first pass, I saw your earring by the cliff—and spotted Gerald's body on the beach—then I spotted the other one, and then the ring, and the beads from your dress and followed them to an empty space in the parking lot."

"But how did you know that we were here?" I said.

"After I found the empty parking space near the last few beads you dropped on the asphalt, I went into the security center at Southwold Hall and asked them to run the surveillance video. One of the cameras had a good view of you and Simon and Ivy behind you with a gun, walking into the parking lot and getting into her Mercedes. So I called the police and told them about Gerald and what Ivy had done, and came here since I thought this is where she might take you, parked halfway down the road so she wouldn't hear me, and walked the rest of the way. If you weren't here, Ivy's house would have been my next stop."

"But it isn't Ivy, it's Amy," I said.

"What are you talking about?"

"Somehow Amy switched identities with Ivy. But I'm not sure how."

"What are you talking about? Please, please explain."

"In my wallet tonight, I found the receipt from

Amy's guest cottage for this specific type of lipstick that only she wore."

"Lipstick? I don't get it."

"The date on the receipt for Amy's special lipstick?"

"Yes . . ."

"Was Thursday, four days after her death. So unless Amy needed lipstick, specifically Bodacious Ruby Red Lip Love, in the afterlife, there is no reason to buy it."

"Unless Amy was very much alive."

"Exactly. And when I told Ivy my theory, she confirmed that it was true. Ivy *is* really Amy Lord."

"Wow," Jackson said. "Amazing. You're good."

"She is," Simon said.

"So where is Amy now?" Jackson said. "There's still a Mercedes parked next to the B and B."

"She said she had to make a deposit and a withdrawal. I think that we were the deposit."

"Me, too," Simon said. "For sure."

"So what's the withdrawal?"

"That's a very good question," Jackson said.

chapter twenty-five

Jackson, Simon, and I left the barn and began looking for Amy Lord. First, we checked the bed-and-breakfast, and not finding her there, we went into the main building at Pure. But the tasting room was empty, with only the lights above the art on the walls for illumination.

"Where to next?" I said.

"Wait a minute," Jackson said. "Did you hear that?"

"What?" I said.

"Listen, it sounds like someone is moving around in Ivy's office."

We moved quietly toward the door in the tasting room that led to the office and listened again. "I think she's in there," Jackson said, taking out his gun. "Is she armed?"

"Yes, she has a gun."

"Where are the police?" Jackson said. "I called them when I left Southwold Hall."

"If we wait, she might get away," I said. "And Lily might go to prison for a crime she didn't commit."

"It wouldn't even be for the right person, because Amy is alive and Ivy is dead," Simon said.

"I know. We need to act, we can't wait," Jackson said. "I'm going to see if the other door to the office is open and I can see what she's doing."

He took off and went around the corner to Ivy's office. We couldn't hear him moving around: hopefully neither could she. Moments later, he returned and waved us over to the doorway. "She's trying to get into the office safe."

"I guess that's what she meant about making a withdrawal," I said. "But she told us she already had money."

"If you're going to live your life on the run," Jackson said. "You always need more money."

"But why did she wait until now to get it?" Simon said.

"Because she wasn't planning on going," I said. "Until she had that confrontation with Gerald and killed him, she was good. The police had arrested Lily. She could stay as long as she liked."

"So what's the plan?" Simon said.

"The safe is over the couch on the right wall facing the desk," Jackson said. "She's standing on the couch and trying different combinations. I spotted the gun on the desk."

"At least she's not holding it," I said.

"Yes, but she could grab it."

"What are you going to do?" Simon said.

"I've got the element of surprise on my side, at least. I'll go in the door from the main room and pull my gun on her, but she may try for the gun or make a run for it, so you two need to stay away from this door."

I nodded. "Where should we be stationed?"

"Get behind the tasting bar, and stay low. If you hear shots, run out the back."

"Be careful," I said.

"I will," Jackson said. "Stay alert."

He left the room, and Simon and I got behind the mahogany tasting-room bar, where I found a full-size flashlight that worked. Moments later, we heard Jackson say, "Amy, put your hands up. It's over." Then we heard the sound of glass shattering, a gunshot, and someone running. Seconds later, Amy burst through the tasting-room door, headed for the barn.

"Jackson? Jackson!"

"I'm okay." He ran through the tasting-room door. "She threw the painting that was over the safe at me, and I shot at her leg but missed. I just wanted to stop her, but now we've got to catch her. She's got the cash from the safe, and she's on the run."

"Does she have the gun?"

"Unfortunately, yes."

We ran out of the tasting room following the beam of the flashlight I'd found inside, and down the pathway in time to see Amy running toward the B and B.

"Amy, stop!" Jackson fired a warning shot over her head, but she kept running. When she got to the B and B, she turned the corner.

"She's going for the car!" Simon said.

When we reached the corner, Jackson said, "You two, stay back!"

He stuck his head around the corner of the building, and Amy fired a shot, then revved the engine. "I'm going to try and blow out the tires to stop her." Jackson stepped out and fired. *Bam!* "I got the rear tire! She's out of the car and running for the back fields!"

Simon and I ran up to Jackson and watched as Amy ran away from the car carrying a satchel. We ran after her as she headed across the field, past row after row of vines, toward the Halloween corn maze.

By now the cloud cover had passed, and the full moon illuminated the land, casting a wide beam of light across the vineyard, but as we approached the corn maze, the clouds returned, plunging us into darkness. Sunday had been the last night of the festivities here, but all the decorations were still in place, if not the friendly Dracula who'd greeted us on Friday night.

"How do you want to do this?" I said.

"Slowly, and I'll go first since I have the gun," Jackson said. "You two stay behind me. Hopefully, the police will get here soon, so if we flush her out, they can catch her as she runs to her car. There's really no place else for her to go."

I pointed the beam of the flashlight onto the red arrows spray-painted on the ground. "Let's go."

With Simon and I walking behind Jackson, we made our way past Marcy's Creepy Goop Corner, but no mummies greeted us this time. Neither did we see the costumed Harry Potter, Ariel from *The Little Mermaid*, or the Hulk touching gross guts, the eyeballs of naughty children, and a strawberry-colored brain, and eating witches' boogers or being kissed by a wolf. Or the zombies, mummies, vampires, and ghosts who had jumped out to scare us.

Slowly, we rounded another corner and found the central station for the kids with the neon butterfly bush, the face-painting station, and pumpkins with pink wigs.

Jackson stopped and whispered, "Did you hear that?"

"What?" I said, looking around.

"I thought I heard someone behind us."

"That can't be Amy," Simon said. We took a few more steps in silence, and he stopped. "Wait a minute, you hear that?" He pointed ahead. "I think I heard somebody up there."

"Keep going slowly," Jackson said. "We're moving into the Super Scary area. She could be hiding there."

We continued along, following the bloodstains that now led the way. No *Friday the 13th* actor was chasing us with a chain saw tonight, but this was far more intense—an armed killer could be waiting in the shadows.

We walked past the place where the army of bloody scarecrows with pitchforks had been and came to the area where the mad scientist had been operating on a monster's skull, and the fake corpse was still on the table. Suddenly, a shot rang out.

"Get down, everyone!" Jackson said. A shot zinged past his shoulder and exited through the wall of the corn maze. Jackson grabbed my arm and Simon's and pulled us to the right, and around the corner. *Zing!* Another shot rang out and flew through the corn maze.

"You're making me mad." Amy's voice sounded disembodied and otherworldly. "And you're going to pay for it."

"She must be on the PA," Jackson said. A cloud of black smoke started blowing through the maze.

"Now she's trying to disorient us. It sounds like she's to the left." Jackson pointed to his right. "We need to keep moving. If we can get out of the maze and circle around, we can trap her from behind."

"You're not going to get away," Amy taunted. We started to run, as fast as we could, with Jackson in the lead, then me, then Simon. We passed the elaborate abandoned cemetery without the zombies and—*zing!* Another shot rang out.

Jackson pushed us out of the way and fired back. "She's getting closer, keep running, as fast as you can!"

We turned the corner and kept running, through the darkness and the smoke, and another shot rang out. "Unfortunately, I think she's got a semiautomatic," Jackson said. "Which means that she's not going to run out of ammo anytime soon." He fired back at her. "Our only hope is to get out of here. Double-time it!"

We made the next corner and took the turn, but then Jackson tripped over another corpse in the middle of the path, and Simon and I ended up in a scrum on top of him. Another shot rang out, and then another, and we heard a woman scream. We stopped and listened to the silence.

The PA crackled, and Amy said, "I have some friends of yours, and mine. Stop and stay where you are if you want them to stay alive."

Moments later, out of the smoke appeared David; Tony, who held his hand; and Lily, who favored her shoulder—and Amy with her semiautomatic pistol pointed at their backs. In her other hand she carried the satchel full of money from Ivy's safe.

"What did you do to them?" I said. "Lily, Tony, are you all right?"

"She shot the gun out of my hand and winged Lily in the shoulder. But we're okay."

Amy gestured to Jackson. "Drop the gun, or your girlfriend gets it."

Jackson looked at me, then put his gun on the ground. "You need to give yourself up. We've called the police. They're on their way."

"I don't think so. You see, I called them and told them that it was a false alarm. That you all had been found and everyone was okay."

"They're cops," Jackson said. "And I told them that you kidnapped Willow and Simon. They're coming."

"Okay, you got me. I called them and told them I was holding you two hostage at my house in Orient." She looked at her watch. "They should be there right about now."

"And when they don't find you, they'll come here," Jackson said. "They're not stupid."

"I think they are. But I'll be long gone before that."

Lily moved her shoulder and let out a groan.

"I really wish you hadn't come here, Lily. What are you doing here?" I said.

"We couldn't find you at Southwold Hall, so I checked in with Max Becker, a cop friend of mine, now retired, who's the head of security," Tony said. "He told us about Jackson viewing the surveillance tapes and what he'd found. We both figured you'd be here. The cops are AWOL, so I called them and we headed over."

"We searched the grounds and got to the barn,"

David said. "And then we heard someone on the PA that sounded like Ivy, saying she was mad or something. We didn't understand what was going on, but we figured you were in the maze, so we headed in, and Ivy came at us with a gun. I think she's lost her mind."

"Her name is Amy," I said. "Not Ivy."

"Amy? Amy's dead," David said. "Now you've lost it."

"It's true, David," Simon said. "Ivy is dead. This is Amy."

David's eyes opened wide. "What in the hell are you talking about?"

Quickly I explained again how I'd figured out that Ivy was actually Amy.

"That's totally crazy," David said. "I know my wife."

Amy pointed the gun at David. "Clearly you don't."

"What is happening? I don't understand."

Amy smiled. "I killed my sister, Ivy, with the poison hemlock that I found last week during my walk through the fields. I garnished four of the scallop appetizers with it, and brought them to Ivy on my plate. I told her I'd saved them for her because that appetizer was almost completely gone. I knew she'd eat them without question, because she loves scallops."

"And then we were talking and she offered me two of hers, because she knows I love them, too," David said.

Amy nodded. "Yes, I didn't cound on that. And then you offered one to me. Hilarious." She smirked.

"But then I got that call from Nora," David said.

"Yes, and you left your scallop appetizer on the table. If you hadn't, you'd be dead by now, too."

"But if you're Amy—you ate it," David said. "I saw you."

She shook her head. "No, I didn't. I knew it was poisoned, duh. It only looked like I did."

"So when the poison killed Ivy, it's because it had been on the appetizer she ate," Jackson said. "That's why they found it in her stomach."

"Correct, but I threw out the remains of the poison hemlock on both of your plates so it could never be tested or traced to me. Not that anyone would have figured it out."

"And after Ivy was dead, before you screamed at the party and we all ran in, you switched places with her—you became her," I said. "But why? How? David told me that Ivy had a distinctive birthmark on her leg—how did you fake that?"

"Fooling all of you was easy. When we were kids, we'd often dress up as each other and fool people. We had different tastes even then. I loved pink and she loved purple. But as we got older, we kept doing it, even in college at parties and events if we were bored. As for the birthmark, I just didn't sleep with David right away and went up the island to a shop and had a tattoo artist fake one. David never questioned it."

"Wait a minute, what do you mean about switching identities when you were at college?" David said, aghast. "Was I engaged to you or Ivy when we were at BU?"

"That was all me." Amy stepped closer and leveled the gun at David's chest. "I loved you so much. The day we got engaged was the happiest day of my life. But, of course, my big sister, Ivy, ruined that."

"What? How?"

"I know that Ivy sent you a letter before graduation telling you that I had been pregnant with a baby boy and ended it without telling you. She even went so far as to create a phony lab report from the clinic. And you believed her and broke off our engagement. But it was all a lie. I was never pregnant."

"But that document looked so real, and when I talked to Ivy, she seemed so sure, like she was telling the truth."

"She wasn't." Amy poked the gun at David's chest. "And because you wouldn't let me explain, no matter how many times I tried, I never had the chance to tell you the truth. The fact that you ended up engaged to Ivy—which is what she wanted, and we all know that she gets what she wants—destroyed my life. And when last week I found the letter that she'd sent to you, I decided you both needed to pay."

Suddenly, I realized something. "You're the one who sent that message to Ivy on her watch the day of the party about her being a bitch and paying for something she did."

"Very good, Willow," Amy said.

"Wait a minute," David said. "You found the letter? I don't remember keeping it."

"Ivy did. Just to remind herself how smart she really was. But that was a mistake, because I found it in an old trunk in the attic at the Orient house when I was up there looking for a photo of my grandmother Emily to frame and put in the guesthouse. Ivy had managed to squirrel them all away and left none for me. Typical."

"But you didn't want a photo of your grandfather, too?" I said, stalling for time. Where were the police?

She gave me an angry look. "Of course not. Ivy was always Grandfather's special little girl, the smart and talented one, the logical one, the one with a head for business. He always loved her the most, and I was pushed aside and ignored or, when I was noticed, pushed around. In college, for example, I wanted to go to BU's management school so after graduation I could work in Grandfather's hedge-fund firm in the city, like Ivy, but he insisted I enroll in fine arts instead because he and Ivy said I didn't have a head for business. Eventually, I gave up and became who they said I was—the bohemian flake, always second best, Ivy's little sister, the one she had to take care of because I couldn't take care of myself. I did turn out to be a hell of an artist, though."

"It sounds like you have a lot of resentment," I said. "Which is understandable. You never got the chance to live your own life. But not the killing, Amy. Not that."

"I had to take control, finally. You can understand that, right? It's very normal to want to be in charge of your own life, and I'd been denied that for too long."

"Normal? I don't think so," Simon said.

"But wouldn't it have been easier to take action and stay as yourself, as Amy, and not switch identities?" Jackson said. "If you want to find yourself, becoming your sister probably isn't the best way to go about it."

"You're wrong. As Ivy, I became David's wife, which gave me status in the community because of his meteoric rise in the wine business, not to mention that it made me the sole heir to the family fortune, head of the family trust, and hopefully the recipient of the prize money. It finally put me in a position of power, for once in my life. Really, once I thought about it, it only made good financial sense. It should have been my plan from the beginning, but I had to improvise when you just wouldn't die."

David went white. "Oh my God . . . no, I can't believe it! That it's really you—Amy!" He thought for a moment. "But that means . . . oh, dear God, no!"

"Yes, your dear Ivy is the one who is dead. Boohoo."

"I thought you were acting strangely, but never . . . never this."

"Honey, I was under a tremendous amount of pressure." Amy smiled slyly. "I was living a lie."

"And Ramsey? What was that about?"

"Ivy had been having an affair with him so I had to keep up the pretense. It wasn't difficult since we used to be involved before I met Gerald, and he was a valuable source of information, especially when Gerald was thinking of leaving Pure, after I ended it with him a week ago Sunday, before the party. The same day that David broke it off with you, Lily." Amy pointed the gun at her. "Anyway, it was all just getting too complicated. And if I'm honest, I'd started to fall in love with David again. At first, it was a charade, but as time went on, I wanted a marriage, the one I'd always deserved with David, so I ended it with Gerald."

"And then you killed him," I said.

"Things happened so fast on Sunday that I forgot that I stuck it to Ivy in my will by giving my share in Pure to Gerald. I had to improvise. But it all worked out."

"Not for him," Jackson said. "And who attacked David in the barn and the freezer? Who put him in that wine vat?"

"Ramsey and I both believe that it was the Crockers," Amy said. "After David's accident in the wine vat, I realized that I'd seen them before each 'accident' he'd had—at the barn when he was almost crushed, and in the freezer. We talked about it, and put two and two together. It was them. I think they really, really wanted to win and thought that getting David out of the way would affect the judges' decision, or at least remove a talented rival winemaker." Amy sneered. "I think they're going to have to revoke that award."

"That makes sense," Simon said. "Even though you're crazy, lady."

"Maybe." She smiled. "But I'm having a hell of a lot of fun." She poked Lily with the gun. "Let's go, little girl. I need to get out of here. All of you start walking that way." Amy pointed to the north end of the maze.

We walked up the maze and around the corner with Simon and me in front, followed by David, Lily, Tony, and Jackson. Amy, of course, brought up the rear and urged us along. Several times I turned around to check to see what Jackson was doing and noticed him motioning to Tony. We were almost to the end of the maze when we came to the bridge over the pool of dark water. I felt that if Jackson was going to try something, it would be here. It reminded me of Gerald's accident scenario on the Mill Creek Bridge. To try to help distract Amy so they could make a move, I turned, looked at Jackson, and said, "Amy, one more question?"

"You are tiresome, Willow."

"Do you know who rammed into Gerald's truck with their car and pushed it"—I turned to look again at Jackson—"off the *bridge*?" This time he nodded, motioned to Tony, and secretly grabbed a post that was propped up next to the corn maze wall.

"I have to take credit for that one, too," Amy said. "Because of the will, I just had to get rid of him. So I stole a car out of our neighbors' driveway in Orient and went looking for him. I was even following you and Simon for a while on Saturday."

"What kind of car did you use?" I tried to get Simon's attention.

"Now what good will these questions do—really?"

"I'm just curious." Simon looked at me and I mouthed, *Get ready!*

"It was a black Jeep Grand Cherokee from the Cavendishs' garage on Skippers Lane. It's common knowledge that they always leave the keys in the ignition."

Simon, David, Lily, and I had now crossed the bridge, but Jackson and Tony waited, blocking Amy's way. "What are you doing? Move!"

"Now!" Jackson yelled, and he swung the post at Amy's head and connected.

She screamed, dropped the gun on the ground, and sank to her knees. "I should have killed you when I had the chance. You and your girlfriend." Amy reached around for the gun, but Tony got to it first.

She managed to get to her feet and lunged for Jackson, but he stepped aside, and she went over the railing and fell into the shallow black pool, hitting her head on a large rock. Jackson waded in and checked her pulse. "She's alive. Simon, help me drag her out. Tony, keep a bead on her."

"We'll take it from here," Detective Koren said as he came through the opening in the maze at the north end, with two patrolmen and Detective Coyle.

"Glad to see you, finally," Jackson said.

"We got your message, and a call from Ivy Lord, too, which directed us to the house in Orient. But when we got there, she wasn't there, so we doubled back to Pure. We heard the shots and double-timed it across the field." Koren turned to Tony. "I'll take the gun." Koren took it and handed it to one of the patrolmen. "Now, is anybody hurt?"

"Minor injuries, but overall, I think we're okay," Jackson said. He and Simon got Amy to her feet. Her red dress clung limply to her body, but the red lip-stick had stayed on, and her pale face shimmered in the moonlight now that the clouds had cleared again. "Amy hit her head, and she shot Lily and Tony."

"Amy Lord? What?"

"Detective Koren," I said, "this is actually Amy Lord, and she killed her sister, Ivy, and Gerald Parker."

"We found his body on the beach behind Southwold Hall," Detective Koren said to Jackson. "Thanks for the call. You sent the Farmer fax as well, didn't you?"

"No comment." Jackson smiled at me.

"Well, I have to admit it was helpful," Detective Koren said. "Now, will someone please tell me what in the hell is going on here?"

We didn't get back to Jackson's house in East Marion until after five o'clock on Monday morning. The story was, to say the least, complicated, with lots of moving parts, and four perpetrators. Kurt Farmer had accommodations in the jail for the menacing messages he'd sent, and Amy for killing Ivy Lord and Gerald Parker. Amy did her best to be uncooperative, and once she called her family's lawyer, one of the most prominent practitioners in the United States, she didn't say another word.

The police picked up Camille and Carter Crocker as well for a possible connection to attempts on David's life, and by the time their lawyer got there, it was a full house with Kurt Farmer, Amy Lord, the Crockers, and their legal teams.

Meanwhile, the coroner had been dispatched to Southwold Hall's beach to recover Gerald Parker's body, and forensic teams had been sent to Pure, to Ivy's office, the tasting room, and the crawl space in the barn, along with the Mercedes that was stuck with a flat behind the bed-and-breakfast, not to mention the Cavendishes' Jeep in their garage in Orient.

When Jackson and I pulled into the driveway next to his house, the dogs went nuts, barking, howling, and barking some more. Jackson had asked one of his volunteers to check on them at nine o'clock, and again at midnight, but they were still pretty darn happy to see us. After we gave them a few treats, we took them outside into the corral so they could sniff and do their business.

The air outside smelled fresh and sweet—of grass, trees, plants, and the damp ground—and as the sun began to rise, it felt exhilarating to be alive, especially after last night.

"I'm still wide-awake," Jackson said, putting his arm around me. "Want to take them for a walk in the fields before we go to bed?"

"That sounds really nice. Being out in nature sounds like the best possible remedy for what just happened. But I'll need a sweatshirt and my Crocs. It's a bit chilly, and it will be tough to walk in these sandals."

After he came back outside, with a sweatshirt and yellow Crocs for me, and leashes for the dogs, we followed a well-worn path across the fields and through the tree line and to the edge of the Sound. The cliffs here were much less foreboding, and it was easy to follow a path that led from the top of the bluff to the beach below.

When we got to the water's edge, as Qigong, Columbo, Rockford, and Zeke sniffed the seaweed and sand in between the stones, Jackson reached into his suit pocket and pulled out the ring he'd given me the night before. "I thought you'd want this back."

"I definitely do." I put it back on my left middle finger.

But then he dropped to one knee and looked at me, and I felt my heart flutter with excitement. "Remember what I said to Simon? That the ring was an appetizer and that the main course was coming?"

I nodded.

He pulled a small box out of his inside jacket pocket. "I just can't wait any longer to make this permanent."

"Because of what happened last night?"

"Yes. But mostly because I really love you and want to share the rest of my life with you."

"I feel the same way, Jackson."

He cleared his throat and smiled at me. "Willow McQuade, will you do me the honor of becoming my wife?"

"Yes! Yes! Of course, I'll marry you."

He pulled me into an embrace, and as the cool water from the Sound lapped at our feet, we kissed.

epilogue

Jackson and I decided to go with tradition and get married on the third Saturday in June. Mostly because I wanted to have the ceremony in Aunt Claire's medicinal herb garden when it was at its most beautiful with the flowers in bloom, with a lovely rose bower over our heads.

We'd started planning for our special day way back in November, and after we'd decided to have the wedding in the garden, we chose to have our reception on the outside deck at Salt, Simon's restaurant, with a view of Peconic Bay and Shelter Island. After all, it was our favorite seafood restaurant on the East End. Besides, as Simon told us repeatedly, it was the only logical choice because he wanted to host it, and it was on him.

There was Amy's trial and the fact that she planned to plead insanity. According to Simon, who'd heard it from an insider, the rumor was that Amy's defense lawyer intended to argue that Amy wasn't able to determine right from wrong because of the mental and emotional abuse she'd endured as a child. She'd been under the total control of her sister, Ivy, and her grandfather, Walter, all her life and it had turned her into a sociopath with no regard for people's feelings. Trying to kill David, and killing Ivy and Gerald Parker, was her way of seeking love and trying to be in control of her life for the first time as an adult.

I wouldn't buy it either.

Camille and Carter Crocker were charged with the three attempts on David's life and both sent to prison, while Kurt Farmer spent only two months in jail with a year's probation and counseling. It helped that David had put in a good word for him with the judge. David had also joined AA and was now sober and doing well.

Wallace Bryan, my manager at Nature's Way, had recovered and, thanks to a vegan diet, made incredible strides in improving his heart health. And the best news of all? All the murder charges against Lily were dropped, and she was now in love with Lucas, twenty-five, who worked part-time at Salt as a waitperson and was studying art history as a graduate student at New York University. Lily was also Salt's new sous-chef.

Speaking of happy couples, Simon and Sara were still going strong. They divided their time between the East End and Pure, and his producing duties on a new drama series about a family winery in Napa Valley— *Bitter Grapes*. He liked to say it was like *Dallas*, only with wine.

Meanwhile, back on the East End I was busy running Nature's Way, although I left most of the managerial duties to Wallace and Merrily so I could focus on the medicinal herb garden, teaching classes, writing books, and assisting Jackson at the animal sanctuary. Tad Williams was home from college and suggested we hire his friends Ron and Tabatha, so we were staffed for the summer season. My major focus was preparing for the wedding, and that included finding a vintage wedding dress and formal attire for Jackson. After looking locally, in New York, and online, I'd found the perfect dress and an outfit for Jackson.

Right now I was up in my bedroom at Nature's Way getting ready, while Ginger and Ginkgo, Allie, my maid of honor and masseuse at Nature's Way, and Hector, my dear friend and my acupuncturist, lounged on the bed. Allie looked fab in a vintage sky-blue sleeveless cocktail-length dress with tiny lemon-rose appliqués on the skirt, a tapered neckline and bodice, a pleated waist, and a tulle underskirt, while Hector looked downright dashing in a custom black tux, purple suspenders, and a black cravat.

Jackson, my husband-to-be, was with Simon, his best man, and the dogs, getting ready at our house in East Marion. We hadn't spent the night together, just to keep it interesting.

Still in a robe, I put the finishing touches on my hair—I'd decided to wear it down with a rhinestone comb on one side—and stepped back in the bedroom. "It's time."

"Goody, goody, goody!" Allie said, and went over to the garment bag on the back of the door. "Do you want to take it out or me?"

"I'll do it." I unzipped the bag and pulled out the prettiest dress I'd ever seen.

• • •

Nick Holmes, my late aunt Claire's longtime love, walked me down the path in the medicinal herb garden past blooming lavender, sage, daisies, and clematis— to the sound of a string quartet playing the "Wedding March"—to the patio and Jackson standing under- neath the pink-rose bower.

Standing next to Jackson, Simon, dressed in a light blue linen suit with a navy bow tie and waistcoat, gave me a big grin and held the leashes of Qigong, Columbo, Rockford, and Zeke, who'd all been groomed for the occasion and wore navy bow ties, too.

Jackson was my lover, best friend, and soon-to- be-husband, and Simon, my ex-boyfriend from L.A., had turned out to be my closest friend. It's funny how things can change. Life is full of sweet surprises.

"You look absolutely beautiful," Jackson said. "That dress is perfect." I loved the dress, too. I'd chosen a vintage ivory floral-appliqué gown, with a sheer tulle panel at the neckline and a ball-skirt silhouette, and a removable charmeuse sash, and an ivory veil. My ivory sandals were accented with tiny roses.

Jackson wore a vintage navy-blue linen suit, with a pink rose on his lapel, a waistcoat with pocket watch— a wedding gift from Simon—navy suspenders, and a slender blue tie, with a silver tie clip, and chocolate- brown brogues. "You look incredibly handsome. That suit is perfect."

As the minister took us through our vows, I could feel Aunt Claire's radiating presence and the love ema- nating from our family and friends who flanked us on

either side: my mom and my sister, Natasha; Jackson's
father, Bill; his brother Dan and his wife, Lori; Allie
and Hector; Lily and Lucas; Merrily and Wallace; Tad
and Ron—now a couple; Tabatha; Tony and his wife,
Kathy; Harrison Jones and Julie; Simon's girlfriend,
Sara Fletcher; the volunteers from Jackson's rescue
farm; the head of the North Fork Animal Welfare
League, and of S.A.V.E.S.; and all our other friends
from the community. We'd kept it simple, as we only
wanted people that we truly treasured to share this day
with us.

The ceremony whizzed by, and soon the minister
said, "Do you, Willow McQuade, take this man to be
your husband and best friend from this day forward,
for better or worse, for richer or poorer, in sickness
and in health, to love and cherish and help each other
evolve to your best selves, until death parts you?"

"I do." I meant it with all my heart.

"Do you, Jackson Spade, take this woman to be your
wife and best friend from this day forward, for better or
worse, for richer or poorer, in sickness and in health, to
love and cherish and help each other evolve to your best
selves, until death parts you?"

"You bet I do." Jackson smiled from ear to ear. "Just
try and get rid of me." Our friends and family laughed
and cheered.

"Now, do you two have anything you'd like to say to
each other?"

"Yes," I said. "Jackson, before I met you, I never
really believed that I could find someone who could
be my best friend and my lover, make me feel safe and
protected yet encourage me to grow and become the

very best version of myself. I feel truly blessed to have found you. I love you, and I like you."

Jackson smiled and squeezed my hands. "Willow, before I met you, life seemed pretty random to me, and it was very challenging, especially after I got hurt on the job. But that injury led me to Nature's Way looking for help for my back, and I found your terrific aunt Claire and then, you."

"When you came into my life, you made everything so clear. I knew that I wanted to be with you, and that together we could take on the world and try to make it better. I love you from the bottom of my heart, and I really like you, too. Wherever you are, I am home."

"That was truly lovely," the minister said. "The rings, please."

Simon leaned over and handed Jackson my ring, and I put out my left hand.

"Jackson, please repeat after me," she said. "With this ring, I thee wed."

"With this ring, I thee wed." Jackson slipped the ring on.

Allie handed me Jackson's wedding band.

"Willow, please repeat after me. With this ring, I thee wed."

Jackson held out his left hand, and I slipped the ring on as I said, "With this ring, I thee wed."

The minister smiled. "As an officiant from the great state of New York, I now pronounce you husband and wife! You may kiss the bride!"

Jackson took me in his arms and kissed me, and our friends and family clapped and cheered us on.

Simon slapped Jackson on the back and said, "I couldn't ask for a better man to marry my best friend."

"Thanks, Simon. You're next."

"I'm good with that." He smiled at Sara.

Then, just for a moment, the world telescoped down to just Jackson and me.

"I love you, Jackson."

"I love you, Willow."

Qigong barked, and the rest of the dogs joined in.

"One big happy family," I said, laughing.

"You bet." Jackson took my hands in his. "It's me and you, McQuade, together forever."

From out of the trees, a beautiful bluebird flew to the rose bower. It looked down at us from above and started to sing.

acknowledgments

Special thanks go to Natasha Simons and copyeditor Steve Boldt for making my book the absolute best it can be, and the rest of the team at Pocket Books, especially the art department for the wonderful and vibrant cover that captured the essence of my story. I'd also like to thank my agent, Ann Collette, for her wise advice and publishing savvy. As always, my gratitude goes to my teachers in holistic health, starting with my mom, Marian Fiedler, along with Brigitte Mars, A.H.G.; Jacob Teitelbaum, MD; Suzy Cohen, rPh; and Deborah Wiancek, ND. I'd also like to thank all the readers who are so enthusiastic about my books, and the cozy blogs and websites, librarians, reviewers, and booksellers that have helped to promote the series. If there were a real Nature's Way Market & Café, I'd have you all over for vegan cupcakes!

resources

A. Edible Plants
B. Animal Rescue
C. Vegan Living
D. Long Island Wineries

A. Edible Plants

It's easier than you think to develop a new appreciation for edible plants and use them as ingredients in your breakfast, lunch, and dinner. Edible plants are chock-full of important nutrients that impart strength and vitality. All are gluten-free and sugar-free. From yard, forest, field, or garden to your table with no loss of freshness. Imagine savoring a salad, or a fresh green drink, from plants that have been foraged and collected only five minutes before consuming!

Before you forage, it's absolutely essential to learn how to identify the most poisonous plants. Not only do some plants have poisonous look-alikes, but certain parts of some plants are poisonous. For example, blue elderberries are yummy, but the leaves are toxic.

To avoid any problems, choose and use a good

guidebook. You'll find recommendations at the end of this section, or even better, take an herb walk with an herbalist to learn more about edible plants you'd like to grow, forage for, enjoy, and use in natural remedies.

Remember: Safety first!

Here are a few of my favorite edible plants, some of which you've learned about in this book.

Dandelion (*Taraxacum* spp.): Although most everyone recognizes dandelion, not everyone realizes that nearly every part of the plant is edible. The leaves, which are most palatable in spring before the plant flowers, are high in iron, beta-carotene, and potassium. Dandelions are also mildly diuretic. I like to sauté well-scrubbed dandelion roots in a little toasted sesame oil and tamari. Herbalists have long prescribed dandelion-root tea to relieve acne and eczema as well as to enhance liver function.

Chickweed (*Stellaria media*): Delicate and delicious, chickweed is high in vitamin C. Its leaves, flowers, and stems are great when included in salads, soups, and stir-fries. Store up to two weeks in a plastic bag in the refrigerator. Herbalists make the tops into a tea to soothe bladder and bronchial irritation and ulcers; they also put them in salves to relieve skin disorders ranging from diaper rash to psoriasis.

Lamb's-quarters (*Chenopodium album*): The leaves of lamb's-quarters have long been used as a nourishing food during times of war and famine. They may be eaten raw or cooked and are rich in iron, calcium, beta-carotene, and vitamin C. To make a tea from the leaves, pour one cup of boiling water over two heaping teaspoons of fresh leaves (or one heaping teaspoon dried). Steep, covered, for ten minutes. When cool, the tea may also be used to moisten a compress to relieve headache or sunburn.

Malva (*Malva neglecta*) is a member of the Malvaceae (mallow) family. The word *malva* is Latin meaning "soft," and *neglecta* means "neglected." Malva leaves are soothing and anti-inflammatory and can be eaten raw along with the seeds. Malva leaves have served as a traditional medicine in a tea for sore throats and ulcers. Malva can also be used in a simple poultice for treating skin rashes, burns, and insect bites. The leaves are rich in beta-carotene and have been included in teas and syrups for coughs and irritated lungs.

Nettles (*Urtica dioica*) are a member of the Urtica-ceae (nettle) family. *Urtica* is from the Latin meaning "to burn," and the plant is probably best known for the stinging hairs that can cause pain when touched. Taking nettles in capsule, tea, or tincture form before the hay-fever season can help minimize its symp-toms. That's because nettles stabilize mast-cell walls, stopping mucus production and inflammation and reducing irritating histamine release. Nettles are also high in beta-carotene and vitamin C, which helps to strengthen mucous membranes. *Cure caution:* Use gloves and scissors when collecting nettles, and only the young plants should be consumed as nettles become irritating to the kidneys when they start flowering.

Purslane (*Portulaca oleracea, P. sativa*) is a member of the Portulacaceae (purslane) family. The genus name *Portulaca* is from the Latin *porto* and *laca* meaning "milk carrier," in reference to the plant's juicy liquid. High in the essential fatty acid omega-3, purslane is also rich in beta-carotene and vitamin C. Not only does it make a good salad herb but it is wonderful in raw soups such as gazpacho or used in place of okra in recipes. As a poultice, it is used to treat bee stings, boils, burns, and hemorrhoids.

Violet: Found in shady areas, with heart-shaped leaves, brilliant purple flowers, and a lovely aroma, the violet (*Viola odorata*) is a member of the Violaceae (violet) family. While violet leaves are edible year-round, the flowers are in their prime in the spring. I like to use raw violet blossoms on the dishes I serve to add an element of whimsy. The leaves and flowers are both high in vitamin C and are a valuable remedy for coughs, fevers, and lung complaints such as bronchitis.

How You Can Use Edible Plants
1. Salads. Except for nettles, which must be pureed, all the above greens, when young (before flowering), may be included in a salad.
2. Blend clean chopped greens (except nettles) into some soaked nuts to make a pâté. Season with lemon, garlic, salt, and chopped onion to make a dip.
3. Use greens as you would spinach in making raw lasagna.
4. Puree young greens to make a raw pesto or soup.
5. Enjoy fresh wild-greens drinks!

Edible Plant Recipes

Note: When trying a new food for the first time, it's good to have only a moderate amount, just to test how it affects you.

Green Smoothie
1 cup of apple juice
1 ripe banana, peeled
1 cup of wild greens such as malva, violet, lamb's-quarters

Blend for 2 to 3 minutes, strain, and pour into large glass. Enjoy this nutrient-packed drink.

Dandelion-Green Quiche

Crust
⅓ cup of coconut oil
2 tablespoons of organic milk
¾ cup of brown-rice flour
¾ cup of cornmeal
1 tablespoon sage
½ teaspoon salt
¼ teaspoon pepper

Mix ⅓ cup of coconut oil and 2 tablespoons of organic milk together. Combine the dry ingredients, then add to the liquid mixture and blend. Pour into a 10-inch pie pan. Bake 15 minutes in a preheated 425° F. oven.

Filling
1 medium onion, chopped
1 tablespoon of canola or sunflower oil
1 cup of grated organic cheddar cheese

2½ cups washed and chopped dandelion greens
2 organic eggs
2 ounces of organic cottage cheese
Salt and pepper to taste

Chop a medium onion, then lightly sauté it in oil. When translucent, place into the crust. Combine the grated cheese and the dandelion greens and place into the crust. In a blender, combine 2 eggs, 2 ounces of cottage cheese, and salt and pepper for 60 seconds. Pour over the greens, cheddar cheese, and onions in the pie shell. Bake at 350° F. for 35 minutes. Let stand a few minutes before serving.

Recommended Reading

Eating on the Wild Side: The Missing Link to Optimum Health. Jo Robinson. Reprint edition. Little, Brown: May 2014.

Wild Edibles: A Practical Guide to Foraging, with Easy Identification of 60 Edible Plants and 67 Recipes. Sergei Boutenko. North Atlantic Books: 2013.

Backyard Foraging: 65 Familiar Plants You Didn't Know You Could Eat. Ellen Zachos. Storey Books: 2013.

The Wild Wisdom of Weeds: 13 Essential Plants for Human Survival. Katrina Blair. Chelsea Green Publishing: 2014.

Nature's Garden: A Guide to Identifying, Harvesting, and Preparing Wild Edible Plants. Samuel Thayer. Forager's Harvest Press: 2010.

B. Animal Rescue

Each year, millions of animals who need a forever home end up in rescue groups and shelters, including kill shelters, across the country. But you can make a difference. Adopt your next dog or cat; don't buy one, especially not from a pet store that is supplied by a puppy mill. Many rescues offer transport from one location to another, so don't let distance stand in the way of your new best friend. The fees are more than reasonable and usually include a full vet check, medical treatment, and spaying or neutering.

You may be able to tell that I love dachshunds just as Willow McQuade and Jackson Spade do! I grew up with a dachshund named Snipsi and love them madly. In 2015, my elderly dachshund Holmes died, and I dedicate this book to him.

Today, both of my dachshunds, Wallander, six, and Murdoch, six months, came from a wonderful organization called All American Dachshund Rescue (www .allamericandachshundrescue.org). If you are interested in a particular breed, you can find any dog you'd like to adopt. Just put the breed of dog you are interested in in your search engine and include the word *rescue*. Or look for a breed rescue in your area. Mutts make wonderful pets, too, and so do cats and many other animals.

Remember that when you adopt a rescue, you are saving two lives, that of the pet you adopt and that of the new animal you make a space for to be rescued and given a better tomorrow.

For More Information

The Humane Society of the United States
www.humanesociety.org

The American Society for the Prevention of Cruelty
to Animals (ASPCA)
www.aspca.org

North Shore Animal League America
www.animalleague.org

Best Friends Animal Society
www.bestfriends.org

All Breed Rescue, Vermont
www.allbreedrescue.vt.com

C. Vegan Living

Learn more about what you can do to help animals,
Mother Earth, and yourself by choosing to go vegan here:

The Farm Sanctuary
www.farmsanctuary.org

Humane Society International
www.hsi.org

Leaping Bunny Program
www.leapingbunny.org

Mercy for Animals
www.mercyforanimals.org

One Green Planet
www.onegreenplanet.org

PETA
www.peta.com

peta2
www.peta2.com

The Vegan Society
www.vegansociety.com

Vegan Outreach
www.veganoutreach.org

VegNews Magazine
www.vegnews.com

Vegan Beauty Review
www.veganbeautyreview.com

D. Long Island Wineries

For more information about Long Island wineries, visit www.liwines.com.